MER

Mobile Library
Llyfrgell Symudol
☎ 02920 871 333

6 / 6 / 13		
2 3 NOV 2015	ME 1 4 JAN 2019	
HB62 , A	Llc 2 8 MAY 2019	
HB16	Cf 1 8 AUG 2019	
HB02	0 9 OCT 2019	
HB15	DB - 9 DEC 2019	
HB79	1 7 APR 2020	
HB49	3 1 JAN 2022	
HB26	7 FEB 2022	
HB36	Llz	
HB06		

This book must be returned or renewed on or before the
latest date above, otherwise a fine will be charged.
Rhaid dychwelyd neu adnewyddu y llyfr hwn erbyn y dyddiad
diweddaraf uchod, neu bydd dirwy i'w thalu.

19Sg/54   NOC   LAB01

Emily Hendrickson lives in Reno, Nevada, with her husband. In addition to her many Regency romances, she has also written a Regency reference book.

THE ROGUISH MISS PENN

Lovely Katherine Penn longs to have her play performed. However in the stuffy environs of Cambridge playwrights are considered rogues, but she's quite proper . . . isn't she? Her talented group of actors welcomes the patronage of Philip, Lord Ramsey, yet unaccustomed feelings stir within Katherine when near this handsome gentleman. Viscount Ramsey offers his own theatre for the theatrical group's practice, pleased to have Katherine nearby. He assists with her play's production during Sturbridge Fair, but suddenly danger haunts her every step. Katherine's life is in jeopardy. Philip does all he can to protect her. But can he save her for himself?

EMILY HENDRICKSON

THE ROGUISH MISS PENN

Complete and Unabridged

ULVERSCROFT
Leicester

First published in Great Britain in 2008 by
Robert Hale Limited
London

First Large Print Edition
published 2009
by arrangement with
Robert Hale Limited
London

British Library CIP Data

Hendrickson, Emily.
    The roguish Miss Penn
    1. Theater- -England- -Fiction.
    2. Romantic suspense novels.
    3. Large type books.
    I. Title
    813.5'4–dc22

    ISBN 978–1–84782–704–3

Published by
F. A. Thorpe (Publishing)
Anstey, Leicestershire

Set by Words & Graphics Ltd.
Anstey, Leicestershire
Printed and bound in Great Britain by
T. J. International Ltd., Padstow, Cornwall

This book is printed on acid-free paper

1

'I shall find a way to get what I want, somehow, in some manner. To call me a rogue and a vagabond is truly the outside of enough.'

Katherine Penn argued her case with the family donkey as it pulled her little cart across the Silver Street bridge. The River Cam flowed lethargically south toward Sheep's Green, where she suspected her brother was taking time from his studies to indulge in a welcome swim. If only the Cambridge city fathers would do something about the shortage of water within the central portion of the town. Katherine detested the necessity for her meager sponge baths and envied her brother, Teddy, his splash in the river.

She sighed with longing at the thought of a truly magnificent bath, one that might cover every bit of her body. It seemed wicked, and sinfully wasteful of water, but utterly delicious. Glancing at her companion, who perched rather precariously on the wooden seat at her side, she said, 'I wager you would adore a good swim as well, my friend. I promise you shall have a wonderful paddle when we get to Fairfax Hall. Near the Gothic

Tower is an excellent pond, just right for you. If only I dared to jump in as well.'

Her companion gave a muted honk, then nudged his mistress with an affectionate touch of his orange beak. Gabriel was a magnificent goose, mostly white with patches of dark gray. Dull orange ringed his intelligent eyes, and they peered ahead with what seemed to be anticipation.

'For the present I shall ignore my problem and gather some flowers to press. I have near run out of them,' Katherine confided to her pet. 'There ought to be no difficulty, what with his lordship being away. No word has reached town of his presence, and heaven knows Mely would have spread the news immediately once she heard. We shall be safe.' Amelia Bonner, or Mely, was the daughter of the greatest gossip in the county, and if she didn't know a thing, it had not happened.

Katherine urged the donkey to take the turn at the next corner, heading north to the entrance leading to Fairfax Hall. Once there, she intended to veer off toward the Gothic Tower, a charming bit of a folly done under the supervision of Capability Brown some years past. It suited her mood precisely. She had just completed writing a play, a satire on the current rage of the theater, the gothic melodrama.

'And to think they can carouse from dinner to dawn and no one points out their want of behavior,' she reverted to her original complaint. 'Some fine example those old men set for the undergraduates. Hmpf.' Katherine did not include her father, who was the Regius Professor of Divinity at Trinity College. He was known to indulge upon special occasions, but never to excess. Since her mother died, he had spent more and more of his time at the college, making a rare appearance at home when he recalled his two children and their possible needs.

'Scandalous,' Katherine declared to Gabriel at her side, thinking of the university officials and their continued opposition to theatrical productions. 'As though those precious students might be corrupted by a mere play when they have everything from cockfighting to bearbaiting at their disposal.' She firmed her lips with anger. No theater was permitted in town, and no plays performed for the general public except for the three weeks during Sturbridge Fair.

The goose bobbed his head up and down as though he quite understood the impossible ways of the fellows, professors, and other officials of the university.

The cart wobbled as it bumped along a rutted lane toward the Gothic Tower. Once within walking distance, Katherine persuaded the donkey to halt beneath the shade of a spreading oak. She tied the reins to a branch, then scooped the protesting goose beneath her arm and set off toward the pond.

After letting Gabriel down at the water's edge, she began to collect perfect specimens of the flowers that grew in such abundance. How lovely of Mr Brown to set this area aside as a tranquil reserve. Gabriel honked his apparent agreement from the pond, where he blissfully swam about with no competitors for the tasty treats he enjoyed.

Katherine had a respectable number of flowers neatly positioned between the heavy papers of her portable press when she was startled nearly out of her wits by a male voice, deep and resonant.

'Good day, miss. I trust you found all the flowers you desire?' She could not fail to catch the trace of sarcasm in his voice.

Katherine stood up so quickly she nearly lost her balance. Heart pounding and mouth suddenly dry, she relaxed a trifle when she discovered a non-threatening gentleman watching her. At least he did not have a stick in his hand, nor did he frown at her like an irate landowner. A tall, slender man possessing an excellent form and rather nice gray eyes, he sent her heart thumping for reasons other than fear. Dark-brown hair tumbled over his brow in heedless disorder, negligent but engaging.

'Yes,' she said frankly, doing her best to ignore her peculiar heartbeats. 'This place has the nicest flower-gathering spot for miles around; the cattle cannot munch them for dinner and few ducks or geese seem to be around.' Then she observed a large tan dog gamboling about the edge of the pond. Gabriel serenely paddled to the center of the water, keeping a careful eye on the dog. 'Usually.'

'You come here often, then?' He ignored the dog, who was yapping at the goose, concentrating his attention on Katherine, to her increasing discomfort.

'As often as weather permits and I can get away. There always seems so much to be done, you see.' She darted a cautious glance at Gabriel. He kept a prudent distance from the dog. Katherine had no real fears for the large goose, for he was quite able to defend himself in a contest.

'Weather?' The man glanced up at the clouds that had gathered overhead since Katherine left Cambridge to jaunt out to the countryside.

'Oh, dear.' She looked at the sky, noting how dark the clouds had become. 'I'd best be going. I fear I get preoccupied when gathering blooms.' She placed her neat collection of pressed flowers on a rock, then marched off to the pond to collect her feathered friend. 'Gabriel, we must head for home now. Come.' She snapped her fingers and succeeded only in bringing the tan dog to her side. She glanced down to note its curious eyes and sighed with disgust. Turning to the stranger, for whom, oddly enough, she felt not a shred of fear, she requested, 'Please call your dog so that I might get my pet from the pond. Gabriel is not precisely afraid of the dog, but does prefer to keep a good distance.'

'Hector,' commanded the man.

The animal ignored his master's summons. Rather, the dog jumped up on Katherine, grinning at her. Normally this would not create a crisis, but she stood on the slippery bank of the pond. His weight was all it took to throw her off balance and into the water.

'Oh,' she cried, her arms waving frantically, as over she went. The cold water engulfed her with a sudden shock. Had she actually wished she might have a bath in this frigid liquid? She bobbed to the surface of the shallow pond, then waded to the rim with great difficulty. Pond weed and long grasses combined with her gown to tangle about her legs, making each step an effort.

Then she noticed the man. The wretch tried not to laugh, with little success. He was standing not far away, his shoulders shaking with mirth at her predicament. At his heels the dog peered around those elegantly long legs encased in nankeen pantaloons and polished boots to cast a worried look at Katherine.

She gave the man — no gentleman could behave thus — a derisive glare, then tried to pull herself up the bank. Between her clinging, sodden skirt, the slippery grass, and the distance from the pond bottom to the bank, she was lost.

'You might at least give me a hand,' she muttered through clenched teeth while grasping at the slippery grass. Her earlier opinion of the man was abruptly revised. He was not kindly in the least.

'If you promise not to pull me in with you, I might.' The teasing note in his voice failed to favorably impress the young woman in need of help.

'You think me such a rudesby as that? I assure you that I, at least, possess some manners.' Her lofty tone of address was somewhat marred by her bedraggled appearance. Mercifully she had no mirror at hand to see the effect of her plunge. Several strands of pond weed clung to her once-pretty yellow muslin, while one green string hung down from her hair to add a bizarre touch to her untidy coiffure.

Cautiously the man offered his hand. It was well-shaped, strong, and more than able to provide her with purchase on the pond edge. Katherine welcomed his warm touch, not to mention leaving the cold water.

When she at last stood a short distance from the pond, she called to her goose, hoping that for once he would not take a notion to become the haughty creature he sometimes fancied himself. 'Come, Gabriel,' she called. She shivered as a breeze whipped about her, raising duck bumps on her tender skin.

'Here, you are taking a chill,' the stranger said, suddenly aware of her condition. His gaze traveled over her slender form draped in wet muslin. 'Best ignore the bird for the moment. Come into the house and I shall see that you get dry.'

Katherine shot him a startled look, wondering where he lived. Glancing behind her, she recalled the cozy house behind the church that stood on the property. She turned in that direction, only to find his hand staying her.

'This way, please.'

He was leading her to the great house.

8

Katherine stopped in her tracks, a feeling of dread slipping over her. 'Who are you?'

He ignored her question. 'I assure you that my sister is in residence with me, so all will be proper. Actually, you might be a welcome diversion. I fear she is still in a melancholy following the death of her husband two years ago. The sight of you with pond weed draped about you could cheer her immensely.'

'Thanks, ever so much,' Katherine muttered in a soft aside. Then she repeated her question, her suspicions having grown considerably since the first asking.

When he still failed to reply, she voiced her own conclusion. 'I suspect you are Lord Ramsey. And I very much fear I am trespassing on your property.'

They were over halfway up the broad path to the house. Lord Ramsey had picked up Katherine's pressed flowers. He now glanced at the awkward parcel the press made, then at Katherine. 'If you do no worse than pick a few wildflowers and allow your pet goose a swim, I daresay there is no problem. I do not mind in the least. Come, now, before you catch your death of a cold, or worse.'

Realizing he was being most sensible, for she felt truly quivery, Katherine obediently followed along, a rising excitement at actually going inside the imposing hall beginning to take hold of her. She had seen the place from a distance a great many times. Never had she thought to view the interior.

They hurried up broad steps to the terrace. He guided her to a French door that led into a small saloon. Just outside the door Katherine paused to wring out some of the water from her gown, hoping Lord Ramsey would be gentleman enough to look the other way. When she glanced up, he was staring off toward the tower. A smile lurked about his lips that made her wonder a trifle.

He held open the door, ushering her inside as though she was a proper guest. As it closed behind them, a gentle rain began to fall. Katherine glanced outside with dismay. How was she to get home in her little cart without another soaking?

'Philip, what have you done?' A woman who looked to be somewhere in her thirties crossed the room to stand at Katherine's side, giving her a look of sympathy mixed with a tinge of amusement. She was of medium height with dark-brown hair much like Lord Ramsey's. Katherine thought that, for her age, the lady looked rather attractive.

'I found her near the Gothic Tower and she is mine. I lay claim to all the strays that wander on to the land, you know.' He grinned, and Katherine did a sudden reversal

10

in her opinion of him once again. He had an entrancing smile. And those gray eyes sparkled with devastating effect, even if he spoke airy nonsense.

He reached out to touch Katherine's pert nose, coming away with a speck of green on the tip of his fingers. 'I believe nothing short of another bath, this time a proper one, will do the trick. The pond weed has gone to seed and you are covered with green spots. Looks like a rare case of the green measles,' he said solemnly, that twinkle peeping out once again in those rather nice eyes.

The woman chuckled. 'Allow me to introduce myself. I am Gisela Cheney, Lord Ramsey's sister. You seem to have a severe effect on his memory and manners.'

Katherine shot a cool look at her savior. Then she turned to face Gisela again, adding, 'I am Katherine Penn. My father is a professor at Trinity College.'

'You are creating puddles on the floor,' Lord Ramsey inserted — a bit nastily, Katherine thought. 'We had best hustle you up the stairs before Mrs Stedman has an attack of spasms.'

Contrite, for she well knew the effect of water upon wood, Katherine followed the others across the saloon into what appeared to be a breakfast room, through another door, and up a flight of stairs.

'This once was an open courtyard until my father decided to turn it into a plunge bath,' Lord Ramsey announced. 'You may elect to take a shower bath if you prefer, although I suspect that nothing short of a total immersion will do the trick properly. I shall leave you to my sister's tender mercies.' Turning to his sister, he added, 'I trust you can find something for her to wear.'

'Leave her to me,' Gisela replied, her amusement still clear in her voice.

Katherine thought she heard him murmur something to the effect he would much prefer to do the job himself, but that had to be nonsense. A gentleman such as Lord Ramsey would never say something like that.

The plunge bath was a delightful little room with a lofty ceiling.

Katherine cautiously walked down the curved staircase until she reached a narrow stone shelf.

'I shall leave you to your ablutions. Here are several towels for when you come out. If you will place your gown near the steps, the maid can tend to it later.' Gisela gave Katherine a warm smile, then added, 'Do enjoy yourself.'

By the time the door closed behind Mrs Cheney, Katherine had discarded her ruined half-boots and dipped a toe into blissfully warm water. From what she knew about plunge baths, they were infrequently used and the water only changed periodically. But this water was still warm, so someone had filled it recently.

She hastily peeled off her wet garments, then ran down the remaining steps into the bath to submerge herself. What a difference from the pond! The warm, silken water caressed her body in a sensuous flow as it rippled about her. She dived beneath the surface to cleanse her hair of the green seeds, then lazily splashed about from one end to the other of the immense tiled bath. One could grow to adore this sort of thing quite easily, she decided. Perhaps she might even learn to swim.

She could well understand why the boys from the university loved to jump into the Cam from Sheep's Green or Coe Fen. Her brother confessed they swam in the nude, a situation accepted by one and all, and a scene assiduously avoided by proper young ladies.

She left the bath with great reluctance. How heavenly to loll about in warm water in such privacy. If she possessed such a delight, she would spend time in it every day. Lord Ramsey probably used this bath, she reflected. The image of a naked male flashed before her. Katherine shook her head to rid it of such an improper vision. One might find it impossible to ignore the Greek statues viewed occasionally, but a true lady did not consider their likeness to a living male.

Wrapped in the luxury of a Turkish towel of a size such as she had never used before, Katherine cautiously peered around the door at the top of the stairs. Across the room a fire blazed away in the hearth. She hurried to it, warming her now-chilled body. The door opened and she looked up with a trace of alarm. While she doubted Lord Ramsey would return, it was not impossible. She did not know him, after all.

Mrs Cheney entered with a pretty blue muslin gown over her arm, together with an assortment of underclothes. A pair of blue morocco slippers similar to ones Katherine had eyed with longing while shopping dangled from one hand.

'I believe these will fit, for we are of a size. I am not as slender as you, but I daresay it will make little difference. As soon as you are dressed, come through the door on your left to my room.'

It took but a short time to slip on the pretty clothes loaned to her. Shortly Katherine, feeling very strange and not a little awkward, opened the door. There was another short flight of stairs, most likely used by the servants. Making her way to the top, she opened the door to find herself in a small room. Beyond this sitting area or possibly a writing room was a bedroom decorated in pink. Mrs Cheney hurried through to join Katherine when she heard the door click shut.

'How charming,' Gisela commented, studying the effect of blue muslin combined with corn-gold hair. 'Let me see what I can do with those curls.'

A half-hour later the two women, grown much closer through the efforts of drying and arranging Katherine's hair, retraced their steps to the saloon.

Lord Ramsey rose from his chair to greet them as they entered. 'Still raining out. You must stay here until you may safely return to town. If I may be so curious, how did you travel out here?'

Katherine gave him a wary look, wondering how he might feel about her donkey tied up beneath the oak tree. The silly animal would most likely be grazing his head off in delirious abandon.

'Donkey cart,' she replied.

He nodded. 'I noticed there are few horse-and-carriage rigs about town.'

'The doctor has one,' she offered, before

recalling that Lord Ramsey most likely possessed an elegant carriage with a pair of magnificent horses to boot, if not several.

'I see.'

Katherine blushed, something she rarely did, at the amusement in his voice. 'It is not a very large town and there is little to do unless you count a trip to the market as something exciting.'

'Is there not a fair coming up shortly?' Mrs Cheney queried.

Animation returned to Katherine, bringing a natural pink to her cheeks. 'Yes, indeed. Sturbridge Fair comes near the end of September. We actually get three weeks of drama then. I wonder the residents can bear it.'

'They still allow no plays to be performed during the rest of the year?' Lord Ramsey asked.

It was a topic dear to Katherine's heart and she waded in with less than her usual caution. 'Aside from the few plays put on by students for students, there is no theater. I long to see a play acted in a real theater someday. This year we hope for something a bit different.' Then she realized precisely to whom she spoke, and abruptly ceased.

'Yes?' Lord Ramsey settled back in his chair to study the delightful young woman

16

perched on the sofa opposite him. Her rich gold hair, now free of pond seed, was a wispy halo about her head. Those speaking blue eyes conveyed far more than she realized. That pert nose tilted up even when she glanced down, and her mouth . . . Ah, yes, her mouth was a sweetly curved pink bud when she compressed it as she did now. Said more than she'd intended, he'd wager.

'Well,' she temporized, 'do we not always hope for something a bit different?'

'I, for one, look forward to some entertainment. The country becomes dreadfully dull after a time.' Gisela tossed her brother an apologetic look. 'Not that your hospitality lacks, Philip. However, this is not London.'

'I thought we came up to rusticate a bit,' he replied dryly.

'And so we did. I am persuaded Miss Penn could be of help if we chose to do a bit of entertaining. Does one encounter trouble with precedence when dealing with the university officials?' Mrs Cheney artfully inquired.

Katherine gave her a rueful grimace. 'Indeed. The heads of houses rank by the dates of the founding of their respective colleges. In Trinity, after the master comes the regius professor and the other professors according to the dates of their chairs. I have a terrible time recalling whether Greek or

Hebrew takes precedence. They are very touchy about it, should one get mixed up. Father seldom has dinner parties, and then fortunately confines the men to ones who are easy to peg.'

'Only men?' Mrs Cheney countered, smiling a little at this delightful girl.

Here arose another of Katherine's peeves. 'I cannot believe that in this day and age the fellows and professors are not permitted to marry. Only the provost, the regius professor, perhaps one or two others, all most ancient.'

'It sounds as though you find one of the younger fellows rather appealing,' teased Mrs Cheney.

Since this was precisely the case, Katherine blushed a delightful pink again and refused to answer the gentle query. 'Well,' she managed to say, 'it means they must find a good living and give up the university post, which many find difficult to do. Rarely is it possible to combine the two.' She darted a look at Lord Ramsey, knowing full well he had it in his power to grant three of these livings.

'You have several livings in your disposal, do you not, Philip?' Mrs Cheney's eyes conveyed her amusement and curiosity.

'Yes, my dear, all well occupied at the moment.'

Katherine had hoped that perhaps one of them might have recently become vacant.

While Michael Weekes showed no inclination to move in the direction of a church living he might combine with his fellowship, Katherine aspired to such for him. The other fellows eagerly discussed the possible vacancies so that they might earn sufficient to support wife and family. All except Michael.

A plump country maid bustled in at that moment carrying a tray with a plate of tiny sandwiches and a steaming pot of tea.

'Good,' Gisela said approvingly. 'Nothing like tea to set things to right. I am certain you shall feel more the thing after a restorative cup, my dear.'

Katherine hid a smile behind her hand. Mrs Cheney sounded most motherly. Katherine wondered if she had any children, but hesitated to ask. It could be a painful subject if she had wanted children and had none.

'The rain has stopped,' Lord Ramsey observed.

'So it has. I suspect it will take some time to dry your gown, however,' Gisela added to Katherine. 'Such a tiresome thing, laundry.'

'I ought to go,' Katherine said in a subdued voice. She had relished that simply marvelous bath, and had thought it a great treat to know such luxury as being fussed over and waited upon, if only for a brief time. She was not eager to depart.

'Does anyone ever call you Kate?' Lord

Ramsey inquired in a desultory manner, as though he was only mildly curious.

Katherine gave him an affronted look. 'Certainly not.'

'What does your brother call you?'

Giving a sigh that might be interpreted as being long-suffering, Katherine replied sedately, 'Kitty.'

'Hm. Feline. Yes, I can see that.'

'Philip,' declared his sister, sounding shocked. 'What a thing to say to a stranger.'

'Oh, not quite.' He flicked Katherine an intimate smile that sent shivers down her spine. She recalled how she must have appeared when she crawled from the pond, her gown clinging to her body in an indecent way, exposing every curve and angle of her from head to toe, including a bosom she considered indelicately bountiful.

Swallowing nervously and thinking that Lord Ramsey had a most peculiar effect on her, Katherine said, 'Occasionally things happen that speed up the process of becoming acquainted.' At his look of amusement, she wondered what she had said that brought that expression to his face.

'Since you are interested in the theater, you must see Philip's collection of memorabilia. Did you know we have our own stage at Fairfax Hall?' Mrs Cheney said.

Katherine stared at Lord Ramsey, eyes wide with surprise. 'Really?' Mely had never mentioned this in her gabbling about the hall. 'I truly ought to get home,' she murmured with half-hearted propriety.

'You run the house for your father? Dear girl, what a charge on your shoulders. I know, you must come another day and spend some time looking over the theater and Philip's collection. Perhaps your father would care to view the library? And do not worry about your gown. I am certain we can arrange to return it to you once it is dry. You know the humidity during rainy weather.'

'It stopped some time ago, Gisela,' reminded Lord Ramsey in a dry aside.

'Yes, well, I feel Miss Penn knows very well what I mean, having to tend to a household,' Mrs Cheney concluded.

Katherine rose from the sofa, extending her hand first to Mrs Cheney. 'Thank you ever so much for looking after this very bedraggled girl. I have no doubt I would have caught my death had I not had that marvelous bath and dry things to put on, not to mention that excellent tea.'

'You enjoyed the bath, did you? I do, too. Soothing — in a sensuous way.' Lord Ramsey smiled, raising one eyebrow.

Katherine's mouth went dry at his look.

She suddenly decided it was far better that she escape from this house and that man, than to remain talking with his lovely sister. Lord Ramsey cut up her peace of mind far too much. Why, he completely drove Michael from her memory. Kate, indeed. Did he believe her an incipient shrew who needed taming?

'Good day, Lord Ramsey. And thank you for your kindness.' She was taken aback when he uncurled himself from his chair and made to follow her out the door. ''Tis not necessary to go with me, sir,' she protested.

'Nonsense,' he replied. 'I must see how you get that goose back to the cart. Is it quite docile?'

Feeling more at ease discussing an impersonal topic, Katherine nodded. 'Usually. He enjoys a ride in the cart so I anticipate little trouble. I expect he has had a glorious time paddling about in the pond.'

'Bring it again.'

'Tomorrow,' inserted Mrs Cheney promptly. 'Come for tea at two in the afternoon. Do bring your father as well.'

'Gisela, did I ever do this to you?'

'No, dear, but then you did not need to, did you?'

At sea as to what they meant, Katherine stepped from the saloon to the attractive stone terrace, then headed toward the pond. The first thing to do was retrieve Gabriel.

Lord Ramsey appeared at her elbow, seemingly bent on assisting her in her quest. This time, the goose came promptly, evidently having consumed its fill of pond seed and other delicacies.

When they reached the cart after a leisurely stroll — for Gabriel refused to be hurried — Katherine paused and curtsied politely. 'Again, I thank you for your gracious hospitality, Lord Ramsey. It was exceedingly kind of you to be so good to someone who, after all, trespassed.'

'Not at all. Stray, perhaps, never trespass. You will come tomorrow, will you not? Do not permit my sister's somewhat whimsical sense of humor to put you off.'

'I shall with pleasure, sir.' His sister was not the only one with a frivolous wit. Katherine thought of how envious the beautiful Mely would be at a second invitation to the hall, and smiled. It was nice to have this special treat even if his lordship made her feel all quivery inside.

'I intend to learn more of your interest in the theater.' After undoing the reins from the tree and handing them to Katherine, he turned to leave. Then he paused, adding, 'And do not forget what I said about strays.'

With that puzzling remark he strode off toward the hall, his long legs eating up the yards in a hurry.

Katherine sat in quiet bewilderment for a moment, then absently urged the donkey to a trot. Scattered drops of moisture cascaded down from the beech trees as she continued down the lane to the main road.

At the turning, her face cleared as she recalled what he had said to his sister earlier about strays. Any that wandered on to the land was his. So where did that place her?

2

Mely shifted impatiently on the wooden bench that overlooked the slowly flowing Cam, flashing a pert look at her dearest friend. The two girls sat in the rear garden of the Penn house, cozily situated beneath a pergola that once upon a time had boasted a drapery of climbing roses. It was all Katherine could do to keep the structure upright now, but she loved the view and pleasant shade it offered, and so persisted in her efforts. Today, the late-summer sun warmed them while they shared a fascinating gossip.

'I scarce believe that you, of all people, should meet Lord Ramsey. Tell me, what did his house look like?' Mely queried, her eyes searching Katherine's face for evidence that she had magically altered as a result of this momentous occasion.

Closing her eyes in reflection, Katherine said, 'My impression is one of light and charm. For you must know that I spent most of my time attending to his lordship and Mrs Cheney. We went through a breakfast room decorated, near as I can remember, in pale green and ivory. I was hurried up to the plunge bath so as to not drip over the floor any more than necessary, so I cannot tell you about the furniture, other than I recall it seemed richly dark.'

'And her bedroom?' inquired the avid listener.

'It was a luscious shade of pink. Everything in the room seemed to bloom with pretty chintz roses — from pillows on her bed to the draperies and covering of two chairs and a chaise lounge. She insisted I sit down before a charming dressing table while she brushed out my tangled hair.' Katherine exchanged a rueful look with Mely on the difficulty of dealing with Katherine's short but unruly tresses.

'Well, I believe she turned you out remarkably pretty,' was Mely's thoughtful reply to that remark. 'I do not recollect I have ever seen you look so nice.'

'The dress helps, I suspect,' Katherine said dryly, fingering the delicate blue muslin in what she knew to be the very latest style. There appeared a hint of jealousy and pique in Mely's comments. Although the vivacious brunette might be a friend, Katherine was not blind to Mely's faults.

'Your hair, as well, though.' Mely complacently patted her brunette curls. 'That particular shade of ripe corn must be trying when choosing clothes.'

'Oh, I doubt it presents any greater difficulty than brunette.' Katherine inhaled sharply, aware she had just snapped back at her friend. Was there a trace of Kate the Shrew in her, after all?

Mely opened her eyes wide at this riposte, then returned to her questioning. 'What was the hall like?'

'Very nice. A lovely carpet runner went along the length of the hall and down the stairs, so that we made no noise at all when we came back down to the saloon.'

'No paintings? What did it look like?' Mely probed.

'Mely, I thought your mother has visited there? Surely she told you everything.'

'Not as well as you do. So?'

'Some paintings — one portrait and several landscapes. That pretty green color also covered the walls in the staircase hall, with lovely white plasterwork decoration. You know the sort, garlands of fruit and flowers. I fear that when we went into the saloon all I noticed was the magnificent view from the windows looking out to the Gothic Tower. It is very romantic. Although,' Katherine added, 'there was a very comfortable sofa facing the fireplace. And I believe there was a

Gainsborough hanging above the surround.'

'I do not suppose I would have observed any more than that, what with his lordship sitting close to me.'

'He was in a chair across from where I sat,' corrected Katherine.

Her vivid recollection of Lord Ramsey was not one she wished to share with Mely. While he was not at all what one would usually describe as being handsome, he possessed a great charm of address if one overlooked his tendency to levity.

Katherine was born with a twinkle in her eye, or so her father proclaimed. She enjoyed the silly and ludicrous and adored a good chuckle. But she expected a man of Lord Ramsey's consequence to be more serious in his approach to life. Ramsey revealed a shocking bent toward frivolity and wit that Katherine was not at all accustomed to hearing. Indeed, all the gentlemen she knew, save her younger brother, behaved with exceeding propriety. Dull to be sure, but proper.

Which made Lord Ramsey's reference to strays all the more difficult for her to comprehend and analyze. If she took him seriously, as she would any other man she had met, she would think he intended to capture her for his own. And that was patent nonsense, she reflected somewhat sadly. Lord Ramsey had managed to put Katherine in a horrid confusion, and she was not accustomed to such a strange, dizzying sensation.

'And you go back tomorrow?' Mely intruded into Katherine's mental wanderings with her persistent curiosity. 'I must say, I think it vastly unfair for you to have this access to such an elevated gentleman. I would fare much better, given the chance.'

Mely undoubtedly had no notion as to how conceited she sounded. In her view, she merely stated the truth, her position as the town's incomparable. This complacency now irked Katherine. While her own mirror didn't flatter her, she knew she was no antidote. 'I shall strive to be worthy of the advantage, you may rest assured.'

Mely gave her girlhood friend a confused look. 'There are times when I simply do not understand you, Katherine. You admitted Lord Ramsey is a handsome man. Yet I doubt if he gave you more attention than that odious pet of yours.'

Gabriel wandered close to the girls, bestowing a narrow look at Mely, quite as though he prepared to nibble at her new morocco slippers.

'Go away, you nasty creature,' Mely hastily drew her feet beneath the hem of her gown.

Gabriel merely hissed at her, then waddled toward the river, obviously hoping to find something tasty. One glance was all it took to realize that eating provided Gabriel's one great interest in life. He was enormously plump. Every time he invaded the kitchen garden, the cook threatened to roast him. Katherine tried to keep the peace as best she could, but Gabriel did not make it easy.

Katherine was saved from further interrogation by the eruption of Teddy into the tranquility of the garden. At the sight of Mely he came to an abrupt halt in his precipitous dash. 'Oh. You are here,' he declared most unnecessarily. His look accused Mely of trespassing in his domain — a lowering attitude to be sure, and one the beauty was quite unaccustomed to receiving.

Mely rose from the bench, apparently deciding that she would garner no more tidbits of life at Fairfax Hall from Katherine now that her pest of a brother had arrived. He was the one male who had never appeared to succumb to Mely's charms, and she could not forgive him this failing.

'Well,' Mely drawled, with a glance at Teddy to see if he noticed her new pink muslin gown trimmed with pretty lace, 'I expect you will make a mull of the entire opportunity. For you are nearly on the shelf, are you not?'

'How astute of you to remember my age, dear girl.' Katherine grinned at Mely's puzzled expression. 'I daresay I shan't perish if I do not wed within the year.' She followed Mely toward the garden exit.

Katherine stifled the desire to say no eligible man existed in Cambridge that she would have as a husband. Michael Weekes was unattainable at present. Unless . . . she might convince Lord Ramsey to provide Michael with a living, or something. She wondered if Lord Ramsey needed a secretary. Had not her father said something about the excellent money one of the former fellows now earned in that position?

Her sense of the ridiculous coming to her aid, Katherine continued, 'Papa must have someone to look after him, for I could never leave him alone.' She omitted reference to the well-known fact that her father rarely appeared about the house and could well take care of himself, if it came to that.

'And I have not the faintest idea of how to go on,' added her incorrigible brother, who quickly twigged to his sister's feelings. 'It is important to have a sense of family,' he added in a tone of righteousness.

'I daresay you have the right of the matter in that respect, Theodore,' Mely snapped back at the young man, who so persistently ignored her. 'I wonder how you manage to get through the day.' She gave her skirts a twitch, then flounced from the garden in quick steps.

Teddy watched the garden gate swing close, then turned to face his sister. 'Honestly, Kitty, how you can tolerate that widgeon is more than I can see. What a vixen she is.'

'She does not mean to be cruel. While a trifle spoiled, who can deny that she is the loveliest girl in town?' Katherine led her brother back to the pergola, gently pushing him down on the bench. What she wished to discuss she would rather not have the entire household know.

'Can't hold a candle to you, in my opinion,' Teddy declared loyally. 'All that pink and white gives me a royal pain.'

An impatient wave of her hand silenced him. 'Never mind Mely. She is upset because I am to return to Fairfax Hall to have tea, and she longs to see the inside of the place, not to mention flirt with Lord Ramsey. They invited Papa, and I have no idea as to where he secludes himself. Be a love and find him, will you? I must inform him of the interesting particular that he shall at long last have access to the wondrous library at Fairfax Hall. You know how he has wished to go there.'

Teddy's face grew thoughtful. A golden

curl flopped over his brow, giving him a poetical look that drove him to do all sorts of things to prove his masculine abilities. His eyes began to dance with mischief. 'For a price. I will locate our dear, absent-minded father if you will agree to put on this play you wrote. It's dashed good, Kitty,' he added earnestly. 'The best you have written yet.'

'Mely would never understand it,' Katherine replied in a roundabout manner.

'That peabrain? The only thing she comprehends is how to cast out lures to all the men. I hope the one she eventually traps in her net gives her a lot of trouble and is a pinch-penny to boot,' Teddy declared with disgust.

'The gentleman doth protest too much, methinks,' Katherine said, delighting in teasing her brother and hoping to draw him away from the subject of her play.

'Cut line, Kitty. If you worry about what Papa might say, you know he never pays attention to the plays performed. We can have the author kept a secret if you like. You will see Lord Ramsey's theater tomorrow, I wager. While Papa is deep in the library, you can sound out his lordship in regard to sponsoring us. I want a chance to do this. Please, Kitty. For me?'

Katherine's gaze met his, then slid away to

focus on Gabriel at the edge of the river, just inside the small fence that kept him from swimming away. 'Very well, I shall think about it. I make no promises, mind you. I do not wish to create a conflict for Papa by doing this. You know as well as I that there is strong opposition from the university to any theater, not to mention the fair. For all we know, it might be canceled this year.'

'They would have a riot on their hands,' prophesied Teddy. 'I misdoubt they want such a view of events elsewhere in the country. Aye, you may well raise an eyebrow at me. I do not spend all my time in foolishness.'

'I never said you did, though I confess I have wondered at times when I saw you sneaking into the house in the wee hours of the night.'

'What were you doing up at that time?' Teddy gave her a nudge in the ribs.

Enjoying the bantering, Katherine lightly punched her brother on the arm, saying, 'I thought I heard a thief and meant to fetch you to defend us all.'

'Ho, that's a good one. Pull the other. What do we own to keep from a thief, pray tell? No jewels from Mama to be sure, as Papa sold them ages ago. He said them to be frivolous and that you would never wear such.'

Since this had been a sore point with

Katherine, as she had dearly longed for the pearls and other pretty things her mother had possessed, she grimaced, glaring at Teddy. 'Enough. You hurry off to urge Papa to come home in time to go visiting tomorrow. He shan't like having to travel in the donkey cart, thinking such transport beneath his dignity, but it cannot be helped.'

Theodore Penn rose to his full height, grinning down at his sister from his elevated position. He was a gangly youth with the promise of great handsomeness to come. Indeed, the poetic locks and smiling blue eyes had drawn the eye of every young woman in town. A bit of time and the awareness of his attraction would make him a devastating young man.

Katherine sighed, knowing full well that while sufficient money existed to set him up, there was not a penny to spare when it came to her. Her father did not believe in educating females nor in giving them an independence. Katherine had read everything of interest in his library, but dared not utter a word to reveal what she had learned. He would undoubtedly declare her scandalous and might even cast her off to fend for herself. She could be a governess, perhaps. Or a teacher in one of those boarding schools for young ladies. The image of Lord Ramsey popped up in her mind to mock her. Michael Weekes did not. Had she given it consideration, she might have thought it decidedly odd that he remained ignored as a possible savior.

How did her father expect her to find a husband when she looked the veriest dowd? As a doctor of divinity, she imagined he expected her to have her mind above such things as pretty clothes. Not so.

She watched her brother hurry up the streets, then she returned to the house, fingering the fine muslin in her hand as she walked. The delicate sort of fabric that one might draw through a ring appealed immensely to her touch. And the slippers she could not resist wearing just for a few hours were the softest she had ever had on her feet. No doubt her father would declare that any man worth his salt would not be taken in by fine feathers. Papa had never been around when Mely flirted with any handy male, dressed in her delicate pink muslins and batting long lashes.

Michael had paid little attention to Mely, other than answer questions put to him. He rather ignored her. Katherine suspected he liked the food at the Penn house and enjoyed Katherine's housewifely talents. Any look he gave Katherine was approval for her direction of the meals and ability to act hostess for any guest in the home, more's the pity.

Unhappy with the direction of her thoughts, Katherine hurried out to the kitchen to confer with the cook regarding the dinner to be held later in the week. Her father had invited the provost and his wife to dine, and Katherine had a hunch he would include a few other men, informing her later about the change in numbers.

He was not mean, she assured herself, rather absentminded and preoccupied. He needed a good wife to see to his wants. Katherine devoutly hoped that she would not be required to tend to him the rest of his life. She much preferred to look after a husband and children of her own if only she might find the right man. After her kitchen conference, Katherine wandered into the neat parlor.

'Daydreaming again, Katherine?'

Startled, Katherine quickly turned to face the older woman who served as a companion and chaperone of sorts. She was a spindly woman of sharp tongue and sight. Her wispy gray hair peeped from beneath her prim white cap of plain, sturdy muslin. Smoothing down her starched white apron over her serviceable round gown, she advanced upon Katherine.

'Cousin Sophia. You quite surprised me.'

Katherine ventured a smile, wondering what mood her father's distant cousin possessed today. She refused the title of aunt, for she said it made her feel ancient.

'Finished chatting with Amelia Bonner already? Either she gave up easily or you stood up to her better than usual.' Cousin Sophia ventured a thin smile.

'Teddy came home.' Katherine didn't see fit to explain her conversation with Mely to the older woman. The two simply could not see eye to eye about anything. Katherine could understand this, as Cousin Sophia declared men to be of no interest and Mely thought them divine creatures placed on earth for her amusement.

'And Amelia went into a taking because Theodore refuses to make a fool of himself over her,' Cousin Sophia said dryly.

'I rather suspect the day will come when he will tumble over some pretty thing,' Katherine said by way of reply.

'And where will you be then, I wonder? I know what I shall do. When you are older, I intend to return to my cottage by the sea and grow flowers.' Cousin Sophia had made a point of reminding Katherine about her desires nearly every day. Not that Katherine might forget the matter with such frequent hints.

'I think it is a great piece of nonsense that Papa insists you remain here when you dearly want to return home. As though I cannot manage by myself after all you have taught me,' Katherine graciously replied, trying to defuse what she feared would be another oration on the subject of the thoughtlessness of men in general and her father in particular.

'Did you agree to produce your play? I suspect your brother will not let you rest until you do.'

'I promised to consider it. He wants me to approach Lord Ramsey about supporting our efforts. We need a sponsor, for finances if nothing else.' Katherine longed to ask Cousin Sophia what might prompt Lord Ramsey to say such foolishness as declaring all strays were his to keep and then instructing her to remember it. As if she might put such ridiculous words from her mind. How would she manage to face him tomorrow with Papa along?

'I quite like it, you know. 'Tis a fine bit of nonsense, although your father would never understand it. I declare, how that man can have fathered you two is more than I can understand. You must take after your mother's side of the family. Are there any of her relatives living yet?'

'Great-aunt Harriette resides in London.

How I would love to visit her, but Papa declares her a wicked old woman and I must not go.'

'Pity,' replied Cousin Sophia. 'She might have been the making of you, or at least helped you find a husband. I fear that is the only path for you. You are far too pretty to become an eccentric.'

At this piece of silliness, Katherine grinned and shook her head, giving Cousin Sophia a hug. 'I surely hope so.' One was enough in the family, although this thought remained unspoken.

'And I will wager that Great-aunt Harriette is not in the least wicked,' Cousin Sophia concluded before she marched back into the house lest she acquire a bit of sun on her face.

Katherine snapped her fingers at Gabriel and waited until he waddled to her side. 'Do you wish to go with us tomorrow? I expect you would like another swim in that pond.' The goose gave her a curious look. 'And Cousin Sophia said I am too pretty to be an eccentric. She neglected to mention my habit of talking to you, my friend. The beauty of our conversation is that you never talk back.' Nor, Katherine added silently while she strolled up to the house, did Gabriel utter smug remarks designed to make Katherine feel homely or unwanted. 'On the shelf' was a term that Katherine could do very well without hearing, at least until she felt she warranted such. Which she admitted lurked not all that far off.

Her expression brightened as she discovered Michael Weekes in the drawing room. That he patently sought her father and not her did not particularly bother Katherine. He was here.

'Ah, Miss Penn, good day to you. Might you have any notion where your father could be found? I particularly desire speech with him.'

Katherine shook her head while she studied Michael. Why had she not observed before that his eyes seemed a bit too close together? And his hair was a rather uninspiring brown. The image of Lord Ramsey flashed in her mind: his vibrant good looks, rich brown hair, and very nice gray eyes. Michael possessed a penetrating voice, however. Heretofore Katherine had thought it an excellent thing for a man who often preached. Now, she reflected that a deep, rumbling sort of tone — such as Lord Ramsey used to such effect — could accomplish wonders. It certainly had affected her. She got goose bumps merely thinking about it, not to mention what he had said.

That bit of nonsense she pushed to the back of her mind to be reexamined later.

'Papa has not been around much lately. I suspect he is preparing for Sturbridge Fair. A certain amount of paperwork and arranging always demands his time.'

Michael gave her a skeptical look. Did he know what her father did with his days? Katherine truly wondered. Although the college now required that professors actually give lectures on a fairly regular basis, she couldn't prove it. How tempting to sneak into the lecture hall and listen sometime. If he found her out, there would be the devil to pay, but it might be interesting, even so.

Just then the front door slammed and Teddy popped around the door, giving Katherine a saucy grin. 'Hullo, Mr Weekes, Katherine. Papa's on his way home, utterly entranced with the prospect of perusing the contents of the Fairfax library. I neglected to find out how you managed such a thing. You ought to do it more often. It put Papa in a jolly good mood.'

Katherine gave Teddy a despairing look, then glanced at Michael to see how he reacted to Teddy's comments.

Michael smiled, his crooked front tooth coming to Katherine's notice. She had thought it charming when first observed.

42

'How providential, Miss Penn. Your father will enjoy his visit to Fairfax Hall very much. What a thoughtful daughter to consider him thus.'

Katherine felt a glow of pleasure. How very rare to get any manner of encomium from Michael. This was to be treasured. To be sure, it was not of the same variety as the remark regarding strays, but far more to the point.

The front door slammed again. Cousin Sophia's voice mingled with that of Julian Penn. Katherine watched as her father entered the room.

A striking man, with blond hair containing no trace of gray, he was not given to fat; indeed, he had the figure of a younger man. But, then, he was only forty-nine. His usually vague blue eyes now sharply focused on his daughter, and he smiled with delight.

'Weekes, has my good Katherine told you the news? I am to have access to the library at Fairfax Hall.' Julian Penn rubbed his hands together with anticipation.

'He did not invite you to take up residence, Papa,' reminded Katherine with affection.

'Most fortunate, indeed, sir,' Weekes replied humbly.

Cousin Sophia had trailed into the room after Julian and now offered a comment. She said with a certain amount of asperity, 'If he had this much interest in seeing to Katherine's future, she'd be wed by now.'

Katherine wished she might disappear. Why, oh, why did Cousin Sophia feel it necessary to harp on this subject? What a blessing that neither of the men seemed to hear her.

Mr Weekes took advantage of the opportunity to question the doctor of divinity about his problem, something to do with a translation, as far as Katherine could make out, naturally being excluded from the conversation.

'Katherine,' Julian Penn said abruptly, 'set a place for Mr Weekes for dinner. We have much to discuss.' The two men went off down the hall to the one place where Julian might be found when at home, his study.

'You might as well give up on that one, Katherine,' Cousin Sophia said in soft tones. 'He will never see you as a woman. All he thinks of when he looks at you is the conformable daughter and what an excellent manager you are for your father, not to mention the good meals to be had here. Although, I wonder if he might believe you to be a way to your father.'

'Well, that is a fine way to talk, I must say.' Katherine gave Cousin Sophia an indignant look, but very much feared her estimation of Michael Weekes quite correct. Katherine resolved to do her best to draw some manner of response from Michael during dinner. Surely once the men had concluded their discussion, Michael's attention might be captured.

If only Lord Ramsey had that living or position available. Perhaps if Katherine could stir Michael to some sort of interesting reaction to her womanly charms, she might put forth the effort to snare such for him.

Lord Ramsey had seemed to appreciate her attributes, she quite vividly recalled. His knowing grin off into the distance while she had rung out her skirts offered one example. The sotto voce comment about preferring to assist her himself returned as well. While she wasn't entirely sure about that one, it was close enough.

She sighed with longing for something she did not have, just what she could not say. But the delightful verbal sparring with Lord Ramsey had given her a dissatisfaction with Michael Weekes. She scolded herself for disloyalty and went off to prepare their long-suffering cook for the extra guest, not to mention Julian Penn, for dinner.

Tomorrow Katherine would see Lord Ramsey once again. Surely her memories of him were enhanced by foolish romantic nonsense. Yet somehow a part of her hoped it would not be so.

3

Katherine studied her collection of gowns, briefly wishing she possessed the assortment Mely undoubtedly owned in her wardrobe. She paused in the act of slipping her violet kerseymere over her head to wonder what sort of reaction Mely might get from Michael Weekes. It was positively disgusting how Mely could turn every male, with the definite exception of Teddy, into treacle.

A tap on Katherine's door was followed by the entrance of Cousin Sophia. The older lady studied Katherine for a moment, then said, 'Well, 'tis not so bad an idea, to attract Mr Weekes. To be honest, I think you might have greater success with Lord Ramsey.' She joined Katherine by the looking glass to adjust the delicate lace collar that trimmed the modest neckline of the gown.

Katherine gave her a dismayed stare. 'You think Mr Weekes so hopeless, then? Am I addle-brained to imagine a future with the gentleman? For, indeed, I believe him very amiable and gentlemanlike.'

'That shows a want of confidence, my girl. I shouldn't wonder but what you could do better than Mr Weekes as a partner. I think you should rather attract his lordship. 'Tis a good thing Amelia is not included in that invitation tomorrow. She would flirt her way into his life in seconds.'

'Cousin Sophia,' Katherine cautioned in a voice that revealed how often she had heard similar sentiments expressed and had little patience with them.

'Do you not wish Lord Ramsey to support you in the matter of the play you and your brother wish to produce during the fair? You must put your best foot forward, Katherine. Tomorrow you ought to wear that pretty sea-green muslin with the dainty embroidery on the skirt and sleeves. I vow, even your father might notice that.'

Katherine ignored the reference to her father and his lack of interest in his children. She felt he had not actually turned away from them, but rather become absorbed in his studies since the death of their mother.

'I am most interested in the costumes and scenery. However, I suspect Teddy wants to do more than merely produce. He appears torn between the desire to direct and act. Indeed, he muttered something about going off to see Miss Eliza O'Neill to try to persuade her to play my heroine. I shall believe that when I see it.'

'Well, you know that many London actresses and actors happily drive out here to appear during Sturbridge Fair. Nevertheless, you shall require financial backing. Plays are not produced without what Theodore calls blunt. Money is a must, and goodness knows you have sufficient for the necessary, but no more.' Cousin Sophia threaded a violet ribbon through Katherine's hair, still brushed as Mrs Cheney had cleverly fixed it.

'Yes,' Katherine murmured in total agreement, then her mind shifted. 'I wonder what happened to Mrs Cheney's husband. She has been a widow some two years. Although she has put off wearing her blacks. She was dressed in a delicate lavender and wore a cap, albeit a becoming one, of lace. She does not seem old, you know. Although after being around her, I would suppose she is nearer to forty than I first thought. There must be quite a few years between brother and sister.'

'Amelia's mother informed me that Mrs Cheney became widowed when her husband died while traveling on the Continent. Something to do with brigands, I believe. And I also learned there are ten years between Lord Ramsey and his sister. She is thirty-nine,' Cousin Sophia concluded in her precise manner.

'She certainly does not look it. Do you

know,' Katherine added thoughtfully, 'that makes her only ten years younger than Father. Does Mrs Bonner also know why Mrs Cheney did not assume her rightful title?'

'Probably did not mean all that much to her, my dear. Not everyone feels it to be important.' Cousin Sophia glanced at the little clock that graced the mantel over the small fireplace in Katherine's bedroom. 'Dear me, we had best get down to the drawing room. Dinner will be ready and Cook will have a spasm if we are late.'

Katherine paused before the mirror one last time to check her reflection. She thought she looked well enough to stir something within Michael Weekes. But what?

Neither gentleman was in the drawing room, a fact that did not surprise either lady. Cousin Sophia bustled down the hall, returning in minutes with Julian Penn and the distracted Mr Weekes.

Studying Michael Weekes provided Katherine with something to do between bites of the delicious meal. She sat across from him at the table. He continued to converse with her father about the translation of a particular phrase from Ovid. Katherine might have offered her opinion, having read that particular portion and reached her own conclusions regarding the meaning. But both men would be horrified to think that a young lady should have even a nodding acquaintance with Latin, much less an idea on Ovid, so she held her tongue. How excessively tiresome to be so hedged about with restrictions, she reflected. She longed for someone who could share her curiosity about the world, not to mention her love of the ridiculous.

Could Michael serve as the hero in her version of the current rage of the theater, the gothic melodrama? Those close-set eyes bothered her. How could she have failed to notice them before? she wondered, totally perplexed.

'Pass the salt, Katherine,' Cousin Sophie said in a soft voice. Then still more quietly she added, 'And stop looking at our guest as though he were a horse and you contemplated buying him. I fully expect you to ask to see his teeth at any moment.'

Katherine blushed, for she suspected she had stared at Mr Weekes far more than was seemly. 'I am sorry, Cousin Sophia. I was thinking, you see.'

'I rather suspected such, my girl.'

At that point Julian Penn turned to his daughter, his face for once most congenial. 'I am indebted to you, Katherine. How did you manage to arrange for my perusal of the

Fairfax collection?'

'Actually you owe part of the treat to Gabriel. Had he not been along, chances are that I would not have fallen into the pond, nor met Lord Ramsey and his sister, Mrs Cheney, much less entered the house.' Katherine exchanged amused glances with her brother. Both well knew that Papa barely tolerated her pet. Katherine attributed Gabriel's longevity to his ability to hide from the cook.

'Harrumph,' grumbled Mr Penn, not liking to concede anything good to the ill-tempered bird. 'Explain a deal better, if you please.'

'I went out to collect some wildflowers to press. My supply was quite low, and I wish to make a number of framed arrangements with the hope of selling them at the fair.' At Teddy's frown, she defended her pursuit. 'There are any number of young ladies who enjoy this pastime, and mine turn out exceedingly well, if I do say so.'

'And?' prodded her patient father.

'His lordship came out to see what I was doing. I had not thought him to be in residence, for I had heard nothing from Mely about it. Anyway, his dog jumped up on me and I fell into the pond. Naturally the gentleman wished to see me properly cared for, so he turned me over to his sister.'

'You had tea?' he prompted.

'After a bath and dry clothing.' At the raised eyebrows from both men, Katherine explained, 'The pond weed had gone to seed, you see. It was all over me.' She ignored the snide little chuckle from Teddy's direction.

'And during the tea the subject of the library came up and they were certain your scholar father would wish to study it?' her father concluded.

'Something like that,' Katherine murmured by way of a reply. She did not have the heart to tell him that she had been invited first, and he included as an afterthought. For one thing, she doubted either of the men would believe such a thing. A professor had an elevated opinion of himself. Besides, she had a fondness for Papa, and his little vanities were to be tolerated.

'Well, now, you see, Mr Weekes? A good daughter can be of assistance.' Mr Penn gave Mr Weekes a jocular look.

'I doubt I shall have the felicity of knowing the same, what with the strictures against marriage for the university fellows,' Mr Weekes replied. 'Until the officials adopt changes in the rules, I shall have to continue my solitary way.' He might have added that he cared not to leave the comfortable life of a fellow, but he remained silent on that score.

'You have ten undergraduates in your care, do you not? What a great responsibility to tend not only their minds but their manners and discipline as well,' Cousin Sophia said at this point, sounding most impressed.

Teddy jumped into the conversation, guessing something of his sister's thoughts and how little she could say. 'Do you intend to be a fellow of the college for a long time, sir?' Teddy was mindful that a university fellow had a certain amount of influence. Although Teddy had nothing to do with them directly, he had heard that the fellows did a good deal of gossiping — like a bunch of old hens, in his opinion.

'For the present I have no thought to alter my chosen path.' He glanced at Katherine, but no visible sign of heartfelt longing on his part appeared.

Katherine wondered if she ought to intercede on his behalf with Lord Ramsey. But, then, Mr Weekes could hardly tell his lordship that he was perishing for a living in some nearby church in order to enter the holy state of matrimony. If only his eyes hadn't become so close-set. She could scarcely credit they had been that way all along, yet common sense told her that it had to be the case.

'Well, we shall finish our discussion over a glass of port. Ladies?' reminded Julian Penn.

Teddy hastily popped up from his chair, leaving the last bite of his sweet uneaten in his haste to exit the room. Outside the dining room, he muttered to Katherine, 'I have no wish to be quizzed on my knowledge of Ovid.'

'How do you expect to pass your tripos if that is the case? Part of the examination will center on Greek and Latin. I imagine you will do well enough in mathematics. But when it comes to theology, well,' Katherine concluded, unable to imagine her brother as a clergyman — or a teacher, for that matter. Once he acquired his bachelor of arts, he would be equal to Mr Weekes. He would then hear lectures by a master of arts. Eventually he must take the dreaded oral tripos examination.

'Don't be a clunch,' Teddy replied. 'I intend to make my way in government. As regius professor Papa has a connection with the Prince Regent. And don't he always see the Duke of Gloucester when he comes to visit? With the duke as the chancellor of the university, I should think it would be a prime advantage for me. And Lord Palmerston is one of the university representatives in Parliament. I rather thought to see if I might work under him, you know.'

'I am impressed, Teddy. I had no idea you

had made so many plans. Although I feel certain you are taking a good bit for granted,' Katherine concluded sagely.

Her brother gave her a superior look, then sauntered out the front door, off, she suspected, to chat with his fellow students, or worse yet, get into some deviltry. She would be profoundly thankful when he outgrew all the rigs and rows so frequently entered into by the undergraduates. If they were not tipping over lampposts, they were off to the cockfights. The dons, finished with their tutoring for the day, spent their evenings playing cards and gossiping.

Unable to alter anything, Katherine gave up on Mr Weekes for the night. Yawning hugely, she slowly walked up to her room to spend some time wondering what the morrow would bring. She gazed into the looking glass, thinking herself to be a sorry comparison to Mely, with her lively brunette curls and dancing eyes. Perhaps Katherine ought to learn how to flirt?

★ ★ ★

After lunch on the following day she gathered up the freshly laundered blue muslin, giving it a wistful look as she did. When would she have the opportunity to wear such a fashionable gown again? The allowance from Papa covered, as Cousin Sophia had said, the essentials. Her gowns received refurbishment quite often, new ones rarely bespoke, although she knew her father made quite an excellent living as regius professor. He seemed to have the peculiar notion that she required no more money to sustain her today than she did as a babe.

Teddy burst through the doorway, his excitement most obvious as he spoke. 'Dash it all, Kitty, why did you not include me in the invitation? There is a pair of prime goers pulling a smashing carriage.' He held out a package, which Katherine found to be her old yellow muslin, washed and ironed to new freshness.

'How thoughtful!' Katherine was thankful that she would not have to listen to her father complaining about driving in the donkey cart, even if Katherine had two donkeys in tandem to draw it.

Mr Penn quite naturally accepted that the carriage had been sent to fetch them as a mark of esteem for a man of his position. It would never have occurred to him to consider that Lord Ramsey might have the slightest interest in his daughter. Indeed, it would have been a preposterous notion.

The mellow red brick hall was more

imposing from the front, the broad pediment of Portland stone over the door elegantly carved with the Ramsey coat of arms. Katherine hoped she appeared graceful as she stepped from the carriage, then walked along with her father up one of the staircases to the impressive oak door.

Kendall, the dignified butler who had traveled up from London with his master, led them through the entrance hall. Katherine thought Teddy would appreciate all the sporting pictures hung on the walls. Not able to pause to examine them, she suspected they were some of the finest examples to be found.

A charming Mrs Cheney greeted them as they entered the saloon she appeared to favor for tea. Katherine proffered the pretty blue muslin with her heartfelt thanks. She then trailed along across the room, looking about her with an interested eye to detail. The happy thought that she might relay her description to Mely's avid ears had earlier entered her head.

'We are delighted you were able to join us for tea this afternoon. I know how busy you must be, Mr Penn,' Gisela said as she drew Julian Penn along with her to the sofa. The blue muslin had been given to the butler to dispose of, and Gisela Cheney turned her full attention to Mr Penn.

Amused at the flash of frustration that crossed her father's face at this delay, Katherine wondered where his lordship might be.

'No Gabriel today?'

Katherine whirled about, smiling in amusement at the notion of Gabriel driving along in so fine a carriage as had been sent for them. 'Hardly. His appreciation for the finer things does not seem to extend beyond the pond, sir.'

'I am pleased you are no worse the wear for your fall in the water yesterday.' He advanced upon her, his hand extended to warmly clasp hers.

'Fie, sir, what a poor thing you must think me if a little wetting would send me to my bed.' Katherine beamed up at him, for he was a very nice height, even as she wondered at the effect of his touch. She had shaken hands with Mr Weekes any number of times, and never had this trembling seized her so. Not to mention the startling result of gazing into those warm gray eyes. Indeed, she felt quite shaken.

They consumed the lavish tea in leisurely style. Julian Penn relaxed to a degree, charmed by the attentiveness of his hostess. She exhibited that delightful ability to draw out her guests that the most amiable of ladies possess. Julian had not been around such grace in some time, or at least noticed it.

'You must be pleased to see your daughter has grown to such a fine young woman,' murmured Gisela to Mr Penn as they watched Katherine speak in earnest conversation with Lord Ramsey about the coming fair. 'I imagine you have received many offers for her hand.'

Julian seemed clearly taken aback at these words. He peered at his daughter for a moment before replying. 'No, I cannot say I have. Ours is a small community and Katherine has always been a bit . . . '

'Unusual?'

'Precisely. She shows a marked tendency to levity that few of the gentlemen here esteem.' He exchanged a glance with Mrs Cheney before returning his gaze to his daughter.

'What a pity. She would shine in London, I vow. There is a luminous quality about her — an inner radiation — as it were — that quite enchants the viewer.'

Julian Penn obviously had not considered his daughter in that light. He studied her while sipping the last of his tea, a thoughtful expression on his face.

'Come, sir,' declared Lord Ramsey. 'I believe you are interested in the library. My sister will gladly show you the way. I suspect that once you get there, you will scarce know the rest of the world is around.' His smile took any sting from the words. They all rose from their seats as he added, 'I shall escort Miss Penn to the little theater room I have had built on to the house.'

The scholar said nothing to this arrangement. Not interested in Mrs Cheney, nor persuaded that Lord Ramsey was being other than polite in regards to his daughter, he turned his mind toward the pleasure offered by books. Casting a puzzled glance at his girl, who suddenly appeared to have aged considerably, he gallantly offered his arm to Mrs Cheney. Shortly he stood in the enormous and excellently lit library, gazing upon rows and rows of treasure. As predicted, he forgot all else and began to scan the volumes, seeking the special books he knew to be there.

Katherine paused in the saloon after her father and Mrs Cheney had disappeared around the corner. She strolled closer to the window, studying the effect of the Gothic Tower in the distance.

'It seems to attract the eye, does it not?' inquired Lord Ramsey, totally unaccustomed to being ignored by a young woman — single or otherwise — for a mere folly. 'The Chinese Bridge is directly below; you can just make out the top of the railings. It gives added atmosphere to the tower. Did you know the head gamekeeper inhabits the place?' He came close to her, pointing out just what he meant by showing her with his hand.

'I wonder how one could best achieve that same effect for scenery,' she mused. 'It has such a wonderfully decayed look to it.'

'Scenery? As for a play?'

'I have agreed to the production of a play I have written,' she replied, not daring to look at him. 'I expect there will be many who fail to understand the point of it, for it is a satire on the present craze for the gothic.'

'I see.' His brow cleared.

He was far too near, Katherine decided. It was unseemly for a gentleman to stand so close. Her breath seemed to be strangled and she cleared her throat. 'It presents a lovely landscape.' Reflecting that she had best approach the subject her brother would wish discussed, she turned from the entrancing prospect of the folly to the owner. 'You said something about a theater, sir.'

'Ah, yes,' he answered, seeming happy to reclaim the attention of the young and very lovely guest. 'This way.'

Katherine accepted his arm and walked at his side. They went the opposite direction her father and Mrs Cheney had taken. From the entrance hall they walked through what appeared to be a small sitting room.

The vaulted ceiling of the room they now entered was lavishly decorated with gold leaf and the walls painted with scenes of muses. Katherine restrained a gasp. She thought it an admirable, if somewhat extravagant, place to hold theatrical productions. But then, she had never been to London and presumably the theaters there were of great elaboration. Realizing her host expected her admiration, Katherine very prettily declared, 'I do like it. May we see the stage?'

Undaunted by this faint praise, for he had seen her delight as she scrutinized the room, Philip took her hand and assisted her up a flight of steps to the broad wooden stage. The oak floor was highly polished, far better than the usual, Katherine imagined. She freed herself from his hand, then began wandering about, poking into the recesses, looking up at the ropes and pulleys that controlled the scenery. What an entrancing experience for one who loved the theater.

'You have not seen one of your efforts produced before?' He watched as she paused, her head gracefully tilted to one side in amusement as she smiled back at him. Her eyes, so very blue and sparkling, were full of mirth at the very notion.

'Hardly. Our house is not given to the likes of this grandeur.' She gestured to encompass the entire room. 'And I fear I do not have access to a theater.'

'A play is not real until it has been experienced by an audience, I once heard someone say,' he said while strolling over to her side.

Katherine glanced at the plump Cupid painted on the wall at her side, then back at him. 'I daresay an actress said that. I find my imagination can summon up a very good cast of characters for me when I read a play. But, then, I so rarely get to see a performance that I must rely on that rather than on reality most of the time.'

'Pity we cannot use this stage during the fair. What do you intend to do?' He drew up a stool for her, then one for himself. They edged on to them, Katherine feeling a bit like a little girl on hers.

'Teddy — my brother Theodore, that is — wants to erect a theater off Cheese Row. Have you ever been to the fair?' When he shook his head, she explained, 'The fair is laid out in a gridlike manner. All the streets have acquired names over the years. The longest one is Garlic Row, but there is Cheap Side, Soper's Row, and Brush Row, to mention a few. The various booths and stalls range along these in much the same order each year. I fear the fair is not as important as it once was. It is said that once Sturbridge Fair was the largest and most important in all of England.'

He smiled at her earnestness, for she had the look of a little girl reciting her lessons. She resembled no schoolchild this day, nor had she yesterday when he had observed her excellent form draped in clinging, wet muslin. Today the sea-green gown she wore brought luster to her hair and made her eyes look entrancingly mysterious.

'But I prose on, sir. I vow I become the veriest prattle box when it comes to the fair. You will attend this year?'

'Naturally. If only to see your theatrical production.'

Katherine's face fell as she considered what Teddy wanted her to ask of this man.

'Do I detect a problem?'

Katherine nodded shyly, feeling all sorts of emotions but daring as she considered how to frame her request.

'You seek a patron, perhaps? Someone to oversee and help finance the play? What sort of receipts do the plays get? Would a backer be likely to reap his investment in return?'

Grateful that Lord Ramsey had such a practical bent of mind, Katherine nodded eagerly. 'Oh, yes. I investigated and found it to be a sound venture. If only my subject draws the crowds. Some will see it a mere gothic. I hope others will discern the satire concealed within. Either way, it ought to do well enough,' she concluded modestly.

He gave his jaw a considering rub, mostly for her benefit. If financing this production meant he would have access to the lively young woman at his side, it would be money well spent. If he actually reaped a return, it would be more than expected. 'I believe it would prove to be an interesting time. Late September, did you not say? It is early August, so we would have to step lively.'

'Oh, lovely,' breathed Katherine thankfully. 'I had hoped, you know, but I never did truly expect . . . ' Her voice faded away as she met his gaze. Uncomfortable with the feelings stirring within her, she slid from the stool, giving her skirts a practical shaking. 'I made the necessary copies of the script, and we have several players in mind. Teddy thinks to journey to Norwich to meet Eliza O'Neill, the actress. He hopes to persuade her to play the heroine. I misdoubt his ability to convince her, but one never knows what may happen, does one?'

'How true.' Philip also slid from his stool, took her arm to escort her back to the main part of the house, discussing along the way the various things that needed to be done. They strolled the length of the house until they reached the immense library, fully as large as the theater.

'Time to leave already?' The dismay in Julian Penn's voice brought gentle laughter to all three, who now watched him, book in hand, as he frowned back at them.

'You have my word that you may have access to the library anytime you please.' Philip considered this offer a stroke of genius, for he could see how pleased Katherine Penn looked at his proposal. It also meant that he and Miss Penn could work on the plans for the play unhindered by proprieties, for a father is considered the best chaperon in the world, even if he is buried in a book.

They walked out to where the carriage now awaited them. Katherine dawdled a bit, turning to Lord Ramsey, her appreciation shining forth from her eyes. 'How kind of you. You must know how happy he is to think he can read all those books and not miss anything in haste.'

Philip felt the veriest fraud as he disclaimed any nobility of action. He stood a few moments as the carriage disappeared from view in the direction of Cambridge, holding the copy of her play that she had slipped to him before she entered the carriage. Then he rejoined his sister in the house, reflecting that the following six weeks would provide a lively time for them both. Of course there were obstacles to overcome, but Philip felt these a mere trifle. What could possibly deflect his intention during the fair?

4

The River Cam flowed leisurely past the copper beech where Katherine and Cousin Sophia sat taking advantage of a rather nice morning sun. Rain threatened from approaching clouds and Katherine hated to go indoors before utterly necessary.

'Actors seem a rather unsavory lot, do they not?' Cousin Sophia queried gently. She took another stitch in the complicated piece of needlework she had nearly finished. It was a collection of exquisite flowers done on linen in the finest of stitches. Cousin Sophia was as precise in her stitching as in everything else.

'Teddy declares them all to be great guns, at least the men. I suspect the actresses may be something else entirely. Although I really do not know, one does hear stories.' She gave her relative an appraising look, then continued. 'You realize this places me as one of them . . . so to speak. I may well be classified as a rogue and vagabond too, if Teddy and I become associated with the theater.'

'That act was done away with in 1788, was it not?' Cousin Sophia replied vaguely, referring to the Licensing Act of 1737, which attempted to curtail theatrical productions and branded all persons associated with the theater in any manner as rogues and vaga-bonds, promising dire penalties upon them. The players and agents had managed well to circumvent that restriction over the years.

'No matter,' Katherine said testily, 'the feeling lingers on, especially in Cambridge at the university. The notion of acting as a respectable profession seems beyond con-sideration. It might help if the ladies, in particular, would mend their ways,' she concluded thoughtfully.

'I suspect that gentlemen make that rather difficult. They make offers to those ladies that must be very hard to refuse,' Cousin Sophia said dryly. 'After all, actresses do not earn so very much, do they?'

'The leading ones do well enough, I sus-pect,' Katherine said, exchanging a guarded look with Cousin Sophia. 'Taverns and theaters top the university list of diversions liable to corrupt the students. As if they needed any help in that.' She held up her hand in warning, her eyes now fixed on the garden gate. 'We have company. Mely joins us. She will be full of questions, I vow.' Silent looks were exchanged, but no time for words of caution from Katherine. Not that she need have worried. Anyway, Cousin Sophia was more apt to listen than speak. She had once remarked she learned more that way.

'What a charming scene, my dears. 'Tis a pretty picture you present to the eye.' Amelia Bonner found a small wood bench and tugged it close to where Katherine sat seemingly absorbed in mending a torn flounce on her favorite yellow muslin.

'Rain before long,' Cousin Sophia muttered to no one in particular.

'I trust you had a simply charming day at Fairfax Hall yesterday? I could not come over before because Mama would have me assist in entertaining. We have so many parties it grows tedious.' Amelia patted her pretty curls and smiled complacently at the two women. 'But, then, you are fortunately spared all that bother. So thoughtful of your father.'

'True,' Katherine replied quietly. 'Some men think nothing of burdening their households with political parties to advance their positions. Not that I believe your father guilty of such, mind you.' But he was, in Katherine's opinion. Mr Bonner continually ingratiated himself with his superiors. He was a toad-eater of the first degree.

Amelia's smile grew a bit thin as she studied Katherine as though to see if that bland smile concealed a malice heretofore unnoticed. Brightening, she continued. 'Tell me everything.'

'He sent a lovely carriage,' Cousin Sophia offered in her dry, papery voice. 'Teddy quite envied them as he had no chance to drive behind those grays.'

'And?' Amelia begged, her eyes as round as buttons.

'Mrs Cheney served a delicious tea, with those tiny sandwiches Papa loves so much and a divine apple tart,' Katherine added.

'And?' Amelia prodded.

Katherine exchanged a quick glance with Cousin Sophia, then continued. 'Papa perused the library to his heart's content — or at least as time permitted. In fact, Lord Ramsey has given him free run of the place.'

'Oh,' Amelia breathed in an envious sigh. 'What about you? Surely you did not sit admiring the view all that while, although I am sure the view is all that is admirable, for it must be, must it not?'

'Lord Ramsey took me to see his theater,' Katherine replied in a tranquil voice that belied the sudden tumult in her pulse at the very memory. She omitted their discussion of the view of the Gothic Tower and her play.

'You must tell me every detail. I think it is vastly unfair that you alone should see the place, Katherine. You do nothing to warrant such attention.'

'She breathes, does she not?' inquired Cousin Sophia mildly.

Amelia paid no heed to Cousin Sophia. She rarely did, seeming to believe the older woman all about in her head. 'I await your description, Katherine.'

''Tis a large room with a high ceiling touched with gold. Murals of the muses decorate three of the walls. Across the far end of the room is a very good stage with all the things one needs, I suspect, for a production.'

'And what would you know about that, pray tell?' Amelia inquired pertly. She gave Katherine another one of her envious, almost sullen looks. 'I declare it is most unfair.'

'One must be prepared to make the best of any situation,' Cousin Sophia inserted sternly. 'For all you know, Katherine petitioned him for a change in the university rules pertaining to the fellows. You are aware, are you not, that Lord Ramsey is a high member of the governing body of the university?' Cousin Sophia's voice flowed as mild as milk, but nevertheless contained a thread of something that stopped Amelia from answering back as she must have wished.

'I had forgotten that you are quite taken with a certain fellow. How is Mr Weekes,

Katherine? Did he not dine here recently?'

Wondering how Mrs Bonner had gleaned that bit of information — for Katherine had said nothing to anyone — she said, with as much calm as possible, given the provocation, 'Indeed, he was here the evening before last. He finds it desirable to consult with my father frequently, it seems.'

Katherine gave Mely a coy smile, implying that there could well be another reason Mr Weekes would visit the Penn household. It was against her nature to do this, but of a sudden Mely's presumptions annoyed her. In addition, Mr Weekes had irked Katherine with his lack of appreciation of her careful preparations for his visit.

'Do you not fear that Mr Weekes will take it most unseemly that you involve yourself with the theater, Katherine? You write those little plays and quite dote on the performances. After all, there is something of an odor about actors and actresses, I believe. Not that I have ever known any,' Amelia decried in modest accents, 'but I have heard tales, you know.'

'I can well imagine,' Cousin Sophia commented dryly. 'Your dear mother seems remarkably well informed about nearly everything.'

Amelia smiled with gratitude at this recognition of her dearest mama. 'That she does. So you deemed Lord Ramsey's theater charming, dearest Katherine?'

'Lovely, quite, quite lovely. You know, Mely, Lord Ramsey must feel the theater to be all the thing, or else he would never construct one at his home. I daresay he is more fashionable and up to date than are we provincials.' With that little barb planted neatly in Amelia's peabrain, Katherine gathered up her needlework. 'I believe the rain is about to descend. We had best go into the house.'

Drops began to fall as the door closed behind them.

'Join us for nuncheon, Amelia,' Katherine invited as she neatly disposed of the yellow muslin. 'We shall be just the three and may continue our coze.'

Miss Amelia Bonner was deep in reflection, for she answered this invitation with the most absent of manner. 'Indeed, I shall.' She continued to think, furrowing up her pretty brow in a way to horrify her mama, then said, 'I suspect you have the right of it, Katherine. We must be careful not to offend Lord Ramsey with overly pious pronouncements about acting and the like.'

With a supreme effort, Katherine kept her face perfectly calm. 'How clever of you to come to that conclusion. Although the town and the university are forever at daggers drawn, it would never do to add to the problem.'

'What about your papa? How will he accept your interest in the theater? And when do I get to read your play?' wailed Amelia as they strolled to the pretty breakfast room to sit down to the excellent nuncheon prepared by Cook.

'Papa,' Katherine replied with a deal of caution, 'presents a problem I still puzzle over. Perhaps he will be so taken up with the Fairfax library I shall not see him for weeks. That would admirably solve the dilemma most neatly.'

She had not been best pleased that Amelia had learned about her writing. Teddy had blurted out the truth of the matter one summer day while the three had strolled along the path by the river. He had been distressed to hear Amelia mildly criticizing his dear sister and had championed her cause a bit too ably. Amelia had protested she would never breathe a word of the secret. Katherine wondered. There had been no gossip yet, but that did not mean the truth might be allowed to slip out at a crucial moment.

'You would never say a word about it, would you, Mely?' Katherine inquired with seeming casualness. 'His lordship might not like it.'

'And what does his lordship have to do with it?' Amelia replied as quick as could be.

Katherine bit her lip in vexation. She was no better than Teddy. For a peabrain, Mely was remarkably fast to catch on to some matters. There was nothing to do but reveal just enough to satisfy her. 'He intends to sponsor a production.'

'Oh,' Amelia cried, 'that will mean you must consult him about the costumes and scenery and everything. Does he have the say about the people who act in the play as well?'

'Why? Do you intend to audition?' Katherine laughed at Mely's horrified expression. 'I tease, dear girl.'

'Well, and I think it a very poor sort. You must know that Mama would never permit such.'

'I think you would do well,' Cousin Sophia commented. 'You are a pretty girl and well able to express emotion.'

Katherine choked on a bite of muffin and had to be pounded on the back. She took a long sip of water from her glass before giving her relative a scolding look.

'Enough. I shall have to give some thought to the costumes,' Katherine said at last when she could speak. 'Perhaps Mrs Cheney can assist me. She must be well up on what is in the London theaters.'

'Lord Ramsey would know as well,' Amelia added slyly.

'Amelia, my love, you overstep.' Katherine smiled at her friend with affection, for in spite of the little jealousies shown from time to time, they had been friends since their childhood.

The shower had ended by the time the ladies had concluded their meal. Amelia bid her friends good day with what must have been mixed emotions. She had promised not to reveal the support given by Lord Ramsey to Katherine's theatrical venture, and that must have made her tongue fairly itch.

When Julian Penn entered the house shortly, he nodded to Katherine as he instructed her to order the donkeys and cart made ready.

'Do you go out to Fairfax Hall this afternoon? I would drive with you, if I may.'

'It is not necessary for you to come along with me,' Mr Penn protested, looking askance at his daughter.

'Mrs Cheney has offered to assist me with a dress, Papa,' Katherine replied mildly, hoping her father would not question the notion of a near stranger doing such a thing.

Mr Penn studied his daughter, taking in her plain round gown of green India mull. 'You could do with a few new gowns, my girl.

Have Mrs Cheney tell you what the latest fashion might be and order three or four. She looks to have superb taste.'

'And what do I use for money?' Katherine boldly queried. It had long been a sore point that her allowance had not been raised when Teddy got an increase every year on the basis of his needs at university.

'What do you get now?'

Not imagining he had forgotten for a moment, Katherine reminded him.

'Hm. I suppose you must have more. Tell the seamstress to address her bill to me.'

Amazed at this turnabout, Katherine grabbed her pelisse from the peg in the hall and followed her father out of the house to the street, where shortly the donkeys placidly trotted up to them. Gabriel waddled up to the cart, casting inquiring looks at Katherine. She scooped the goose up, placing him in the back, then took the reins, for she had far more patience with the animals than her father, and they set off for Fairfax Hall in high spirits.

'You found Lord Ramsey to be agreeable company?' Mr Penn inquired, although his tone implied he expected nothing less.

'Yes, Papa,' Katherine replied dutifully. 'I admire Mrs Cheney as well. It must have been a dreadful shock when brigands attacked and killed her husband. It happened in Italy, I believe.'

Mr Penn nodded sagely. 'I have heard the crossing of the Alps into Italy can be most hazardous. She is young to be left alone. There are no children to comfort her?'

'None that I know about, although there might be some away at school. She is nine-and-thirty, Papa, only ten years younger than you.'

'Is that so?' came the thoughtful reply. 'She is a remarkably lovely woman for her years.'

'She has a delightful sense of humor as well,' added Katherine, recalling the teasing banter between brother and sister. 'How fortunate she has an agreeable brother to support her in her time of need.'

'She has put off her blacks,' Mr Penn commented as their cart entered the grounds of Fairfax Hall. The donkeys had moved quite smartly for Katherine, as they usually did. Only for Mr Penn did they balk and prove annoying.

'Lavender becomes her. I am glad you did not prevent me from tagging along. I should hate to miss a *tête-à-tête* with her.' Katherine omitted mention of Lord Ramsey. Not that she was averse to seeing him again. She dare not reveal it to her father, however. He would think it improper and she would most assuredly have remained at home.

Mrs Cheney greeted them in the entrance hall, her hands extended. 'I was just wishing to see you, my dear,' she said to Katherine. 'How obliging of you to come at the thought.' Her eyes lighted up with inner laughter and Katherine's heart warmed to her.

'I need not tell you where you must go, sir,' she greeted Mr Penn. 'If there is anything you require, please do not hesitate to ask. I took the liberty of placing a carafe of lemonade next to the decanters of claret and port in the library, should you become thirsty. I imagine reading can at times be dry work.'

'Indeed, good lady. I thank you for your gracious consideration.' Julian Penn bestowed a look on Gisela Cheney that surprised Katherine. He actually appeared to see Mrs Cheney as a woman, wonder of wonders.

The two ladies watched him as he marched off in the direction of the library, then Mrs Cheney took Katherine's arm and led her to the saloon.

'My brother has taken himself off on a tour of the farms. There is always so much to be done, you know.'

'He is well liked by the people on his land, I have heard. Not all landowners do as well by their people.'

'There, I knew you were a woman of

uncommon sense. Come, we shall have a coze by the window that looks out on the folly. It is my favorite view, for it constantly reminds me of what I have escaped.'

'Escaped, my lady?' The odd choice of word startled Katherine into giving voice to her reaction.

'Please call me Gisela, my dear. Although a good deal older than you, I long for a confidante and friend. Say you will do that for me?'

Touched by the thread of sadness that had suddenly crept into Mrs Cheney's voice, Katherine immediately nodded. 'Of course, Gisela.'

'You may well wonder why I say escape, for it is a most peculiar word to choose. My husband, God rest his soul, became obsessed with those quaint ruins he found in Europe. I rarely saw him, following our marriage. Reports by indifferent mail are less than pleasing to a wife. He would not take me along with him, for I lost our only child the very first trip and he never forgave me that. I ultimately came to bless those ruins, for they brought me peace. You see, there was something strangely wrong with his mind. I believe it fortunate we had no children, for the child might have inherited his aberration along with his wealth.'

'Good heavens,' exclaimed Katherine in a soft, sympathetic voice. 'I am sorry.'

'I rarely speak of it, but I wanted you to understand why I happily remain here in the country. In London there are too many who recall and gossip.'

Katherine thought of Mrs Bonner but said nothing.

'Tell me about your plans for your production of the play during the fair,' Mrs Cheney said with a bright smile.

An eruption in the hall brought their heads around. Through the open door Katherine could see her brother and Lord Ramsey in conversation as they entered the house together.

'The separate copies are done and the play ready to cast,' Katherine replied while trying to keep her mind on the matter and not look at his lordship. 'Most of the performers will be local. Theodore believes he might be able to obtain the talents of Miss O'Neill for the heroine. He plans to take a copy of the script to Norwich for her to read. I suspect the offer of ample money will have a greater result.'

'What about costumes?' With great interest Gisela watched Katherine's delicate rise of color as Philip entered the room.

'Costumes,' echoed Teddy. 'I just mentioned that to Lord Ramsey, and he said something about his attics.'

'Famous,' Gisela declared, clapping her hands together with delight. 'I gather this is one of those plays that occur in the obscure past?'

'Naturally, for it has castles and specters, not to mention veils that sway most mysteriously.' Katherine chuckled at the grimace that crossed Lord Ramsey's face.

'Skulls and weird moans as well?' Gisela laughed up at her brother. 'This promises to be spine-chilling indeed. We shall have to station several stalwart young men with a generous supply of vinaigrette for the vaporish.'

'It has a sensible ending,' Katherine was prompted to say. 'Have you read *Mansfield Park* by Miss Austen? It was released in May this year. I believe she pokes a bit of fun at these gothic novels in her book. I do the same in my play, for you must know they are so very silly. All these goosish damsels crying buckets of tears and jumping at the very least noise. Not to mention those fantastical castles with more weird things happening than one can credit.'

'Oh, to be so sensible,' Gisela declared. 'Let us hope there are sufficient people who want to be terrified.'

'This is supposed to be a money-making

venture, I trust,' Lord Ramsey said dryly.

'Costumes,' reminded Teddy, eager to leave a subject fraught with potential difficulties.

'We had best make our way to the attics, I suspect,' Gisela inserted smoothly. 'Katherine, since you know the characters, you shall have to dictate the choices and we can only hope to alter as needs be.' Rising from her chair by the window, she took Katherine's hand and led her toward the entrance hall. 'Come along, gentlemen,' she commanded in a very nice way. 'We shall have need of your assistance, for costumes can be very heavy.'

'Not to mention dusty,' Lord Ramsey said in an aside to Teddy that was clearly heard by the ladies who marched up the stairs ahead of them.

When they reached the attics, Katherine thought she had never seen such a well-ordered place of storage. Neat trunks lined part of one wall and stored furniture was arranged in another area. Leather hatboxes intrigued her, as did a large box labeled 'feathers.'

While Lord Ramsey and his sister discussed which trunk might be the best to open, Katherine sought out her brother.

'Teddy, how do you happen to turn up here?' Katherine inquired in a dulcet tone that did not fool her sibling in the least.

Theodore Penn had been most aggrieved when he found himself left out of the visit to Fairfax Hall. More than anything he longed to make the acquaintance of his lordship. He had heard Lord Ramsey was a splendid rider to the hounds. Teddy had contemplated an invitation to join that select group that Ramsey rode with, and had cast caution to the winds. Never one to stand at formalities — at least not outside the university — he had saddled his horse and ridden off to seek his sister and the *entrées* he desired.

'Well, you see, I thought you might have need of me,' he replied with an ingenuous smile.

'See that you say or do nothing to give his lordship a disgust of you,' she admonished, not having the heart to scold Teddy when she knew full well how he enjoyed anything to do with the theater and production.

'Papa is safely occupied in the library, is he not? We must contrive to keep this from him if we can.' Teddy may have intended to speak softly. He failed.

Ramsey had overheard this last remark and frowned. 'Do you anticipate trouble with that quarter?' He knew the attitude of the university all too well; he had to listen to the prosing of the various professors far too often.

'Well, actually we have never approached him on this particular matter, sir. We felt prudence to be the better course, if you follow our thoughts,' Teddy replied earnestly.

Turning to Katherine, Lord Ramsey gave her a concerned look. 'Does this present a serious problem? I'll not have you placed in jeopardy.'

'Philip,' Gisela cried in dismay, 'you will not frighten the girl. She has written a play — which I hope to read this evening — and intends to produce it during the fair. It is hardly a situation of enormous difficulty.' She thought a moment, then added, 'If you like, I can sound out her father. He will likely tell me more than the rest of you.'

Lord Ramsey rubbed his chin, thus getting a smear of dirt across it. 'And how is that, pray tell?'

'I shall use my feminine wiles,' Gisela declared triumphantly. She then chuckled at the face her brother made, and turned to the chosen trunk.

Within an hour they had selected a variety of gowns and coats suitable for the characters in Katherine's play. She was ecstatic at the richness of fabric, the beautiful lines of the garments. They would have cost an enormous sum of money had she tried to purchase or make them.

'I vow the actors and actresses will wonder ere they see this bounty,' Katherine declared to Gisela. 'Such elegance is not often seen, especially where they must supply their own costumes, as is sometimes the case, so Teddy tells me.' She studied her brother while he helped to gather the clothing in neat piles for the servants to fetch later. 'Although where he comes by all his knowledge I cannot imagine.'

'There is a morning coach to London with a return the same evening, is there not?' Gisela said innocently.

'You mean . . . ' whispered Katherine, incensed that she had been excluded when Teddy knew how much she longed to go to the theater.

'I rather suspect so,' Gisela said with a rueful face.

Katherine was silent while the four made their return trip to the lower floor. The ladies paused in Gisela's room to freshen up while the two young men continued to the saloon.

Katherine turned to her new friend. 'I worry that the costumes may be damaged seriously beyond repair. I imagine they will get hard usage.'

'They are merely rotting away in the trunk, my dear,' Gisela said, soothing Katherine's ruffled feathers with an offer of some lovely cologne.

When the ladies joined the men, Lord Ramsey ushered Katherine to a chair by the window, inhaling with appreciation. 'Quite superior to pondweed.'

Katherine chuckled at the memory, then gestured toward the pond. 'Gabriel makes a return visit. I fancy he longed to come, for he came up to me as we were to enter the cart. Do you suppose that is possible?'

Ramsey bent over to study the face tilted up at him, fixed her with a warm gaze, and shrugged. 'Anything is possible, have you not learned that yet?'

'Anything?' Katherine made a reflective face, then smiled. 'I shall cling to that thought, my lord.'

'You do that, Miss Penn.'

'Philip, I am well aware that we all observe the proprieties of society, but do you not think we might call you Philip rather than that odious title all the time?' Gisela suggested.

He shrugged again. 'Only if I may call Miss Penn, Katherine. And her brother, Teddy, of course.'

'Naturally,' replied Gisela, looking remarkably smug. 'That is settled, then. I shall like that. I get excessively tired of being Mrs Cheney-ed to death.'

Sounds heard in the hall indicated that Mr

88

Penn had decided he had spent quite enough of this day closeted in his lordship's fine library. By the time he reached the front door, Gisela skimmed along the hall to halt his departure.

'Join us in the saloon, sir, please do. We have been having such a delightful visit. How pleased I am to make the acquaintance of your children. You have done a very fine job of raising them by yourself. It cannot have been easy for you.'

Clearly startled to receive the unexpected sympathy, he paused in his steps, obviously reflecting the past years. 'You are very kind. I had not considered it as such, but I did have help, my cousin, Sophia.'

'Ah, yes. She is the lady who longs to return to her garden by the sea.'

Amazed that Mrs Cheney had learned so much in such a short time, he permitted himself to be led to the saloon, where they had a good talk.

Before they left, Gisela said to Mr Penn, 'I fear the gentleman who usually preaches our Sunday sermon has taken ill. Would you consider taking his place? I should very much like to hear you.'

Evidently flattered at such a request, Mr Penn nodded graciously and promised to attend to the matter.

Katherine and Teddy exchanged worried looks.

Seated behind, Gabriel honked grandly, having relished his bout with the gardener's son who had fetched him from the pond.

5

'Perhaps he will come down with a putrid sore throat and shan't be able to speak next Sunday?' Katherine said with little hope that her unkind wish might be granted.

'No such luck,' Teddy muttered in reply as he kicked at a tuft of grass along the riverbank at the foot of the garden behind the Penn house.

'He has a nice voice,' Katherine said in an attempt to be generous, 'and a very elegant mind.'

'That is what I fear, his elegance of mind. Last time he spoke he had an awful sermon. Nattered on above an hour. Dreadful! I tell you, Kitty, there must be something we can do.' He glanced at where she stood, as though hoping for some manner of miracle from her.

She shook her head. 'I see nothing but what we had best attend divine services, and support him as a good son and daughter ought.'

'You ask a great deal,' he said with a morose sigh.

'It is the very least we can do,' Katherine replied virtuously, wrapping her shawl about her more tightly, as though a chill had swept along the Cam.

'I expect you have the right of it.' He shoved his hands deeper into his pockets, considering the coming Sunday with about the same enthusiasm with which one faces the tooth-drawer.

'However, other things require our attention. We must consider auditions for the roles.'

He brightened, nodding in agreement. 'There's that chap who played the hero last year, the one you thought so good? I saw him the other day. Might be a good choice for our hero.' His enthusiasm caught him up from the doldrums into which he had fallen.

'I believe his name was Ninian Denham, was it not? Tall, flaxen-haired, with dark-brown eyes?' Katherine grinned at her brother as she remembered the part the young man had played. 'I suspect he might do well. He has the requisite poetical looks.'

'I still say I ought to be allowed a chance at the part,' Teddy grumbled as they turned toward the house.

'You cannot direct *and* act. You have not the experience. I shall give you all my support, but we are mere babes when it comes to something like this. I have tried to garner all the information I could, but there is nothing like actually doing a thing, you must know. Besides, if you can tell Miss O'Neill that you have such a handsome, experienced actor to play against, she might look more favorably upon the part.'

He sighed, this time with resignation. 'I imagine you are right again. You frequently are. Have you begun the scenery sketches? You are dashed clever at that sort of thing, although your watercolor landscapes seem a bit dreary.'

'They suffer very much from cows, little boys, and rain, if you must know. One tries, but sitting about in nature can have the most dire results.' The twinkle in her eyes belied her complaining accents.

'At least falling in the pond at Fairfax Hall brought a few blessings. Do we consult with Lord Ramsey tomorrow?' His eagerness was plain, even if he pretended otherwise.

'I thought we might see him, yes. The days flow by, and there is so much to do. Papa wants to visit his library, fortunately. I can tag along out there with little or no suspicion. Papa believes me in a fair way to becoming a bosom bow to Mrs Cheney, even though we must be nearly twenty years apart in age.'

'Old enough to be your mother.'

'But very, very nice, and ever so kind. Which is more than I can say for his lordship,'

Katherine concluded, thinking of the little darts from Lord Ramsey. What a pity one of the clerics who held a Ramsey-bestowed living didn't go aloft to his maker so Mr Weekes might be set forth as a suitable candidate. Not that she actually wished an old man ill. But some of the clerics were dreadfully ancient and gave the driest sermons in the world. Which thought brought her back to the coming Sunday. 'I wonder if we might stuff cotton wool in our ears?'

'Now who's daft in the head? Oh, you mean church. I suspect we must take our medicine.' He grimaced at the very thought of the coming sermon.

The two wandered up to the house to join Cousin Sophia in the sitting room, where she worked at completing her elegant piece of needlework.

'It looks quite, quite lovely,' Katherine said with enthusiasm.

'I shall require a new piece of canvas and more wools tomorrow. Shall you keep me company when I shop?'

Katherine exchanged a guarded look with her brother. 'We promised to visit Mrs Cheney.'

'And Lord Ramsey,' added Teddy.

Cousin Sophia placed her needlework in her lap, giving the two young people a shrewd stare. 'Something is up. I shall not ask, but I expect you will want a chaperone with you?' She tilted her head and smiled.

'You merely wish to know what is going on,' Katherine replied.

'Your play,' Cousin Sophia replied calmly. 'You shall have to cast the roles and ready the scenery, not to mention arrange costumes. That castle will be difficult to simulate.'

'How neatly you frame us, Cousin,' Katherine laughed, then gave the older woman a little hug.

The lady smiled, darting glances at the two. 'What do you plan?'

'Since the title is *Castle of the Black Forest*, I want something gloomy enough to make the ladies tremble with anticipation.' Katherine placed her hands together before her, as though to plead with a villain.

'Your heroine has enough foolish fancies to do the lot in, I think,' inserted Teddy, barely suppressing a grin.

'Well, and she is foolish. Of course I believe that anyone whose sensibilities are so delicate that they swoon at the least shadow or collapse into tears at the wave of a drapery is a peagoose.'

'Pity you cannot have Amelia play the part,' Cousin Sophia commented dryly.

'Mely would fit it admirably,' Teddy agreed.

'Did someone mention my name?' Amelia Bonner inquired as she entered the room. 'I told dear Mrs Moore I would see myself in, for we are all such old friends.' She studied their faces with great curiosity. 'Your housekeeper is so busy,' she added by way of explanation.

Katherine thought Mely was well on her way to becoming just like her mother. There was little one might do about such a thing, however. Unless one was given to teaching lessons, and Katherine had enough on her plate at the moment, thank you very much.

'Did you enjoy your visit to Fairfax Hall?' Mely quizzed like a persistent little bird. 'But what a silly question. Of course you did, for who could not? I vow I should simply swoon were I to receive an invitation to tea there. It must have been vastly pleasant for you. My Katherine, you are of a certainty moving about in elevated circles. Soon you will have no time for your ordinary friends.' Her smile was polite, but Katherine detected a waspish note in that sugary voice.

Since Katherine suspected that were the tables to be turned, Mely would cut her as quick as a cat could wink its eye, Katherine felt few qualms in not extending any sort of invitation to join them, not that such would be proper — thank heavens. Only Lord

Ramsey or Mrs Cheney should do that, and with any luck at all, their paths would not cross. If Mely learned more about the play, their lives would be in greater jeopardy.

'I think the least you might do is include me, Katherine. After all, we have been friends since we were in leading strings. I would never dream of repeating what I know about your little play, but . . . ' She batted her dark, feathery lashes at Teddy, who began a retreat toward the door and safety, muttering vaguely about something or other he had to do.

Katherine looked at Cousin Sophia with dismay. She had felt secure, thinking there was little Mely could do to push her way into the group. Now it seemed Mely had figured out her own path. Katherine bowed to the inevitable.

'I feel sure Mrs Cheney would welcome an extra hand with the costumes. You sew such exquisite stitches.' This fortunately was true. Amelia did the most perfect stitching Katherine had ever seen. She could be depended upon to alter costumes in secrecy, were she included, and her work would hold up well. 'All the clothes we found in the old trunks are in need of touches of repair. Mrs Cheney's maid would be overwhelmed with the job, so we had planned to do our share.'

'You, Katherine? Sewing? Hm, you do well enough, but you need more patience,' Amelia stated in a rather arrogant manner.

Since her words were true, there was no cause for Katherine to be annoyed. Perhaps it was the smug manner in which they were spoken that irritated her.

At that moment Teddy stuck his head around the corner. 'Katherine, you must help me with that job I mentioned earlier. I know it is a bit messy, but Mely is welcome to come if she doesn't mind a bit of dirt.'

Amelia threw up her hands in horror at the very thought of dirt. 'No, I thank you, Theodore. Another time.' She curtsied to Cousin Sophia, then fled the house, having accomplished what she desired in jig time.

'Pity you did not think of that before she invited herself along to Fairfax Hall with us tomorrow,' Katherine said. 'What is it I must do that will soil my hands?'

'Nothing. I merely said that to frighten her off. You know how she hates a dab of mud. I thought we might round up a few actors for auditions. Care to join me now?'

'Gladly.'

The two left Cousin Sophia putting the final stitches in the tapestry and headed to the area of town where they knew the actors liked to linger.

★ ★ ★

Lord Ramsey hastily guided his team into position before the inn, then left his carriage and pair in the hands of his groom. He had observed Miss Penn with her brother, and felt this was a rather unsavory area for the two.

He strolled along the walk, peering into each door, wondering what business they might have here. Of course it might be something to do with the play, he supposed. Then he halted as he caught a glimpse of the two young people in the dim recesses of an inn.

Katherine spoke with a devilishly handsome man. Not that Ramsey considered those angelic blonds with sad dark eyes to be an example of masculine perfection. But he understood some ladies did. He entered the inn, making his way to the rear.

'Good day, again, Miss Penn, Theodore.'

Teddy's flashing eyes forgave Lord Ramsey the slip, but also cautioned him against repeating the error of calling Teddy by his given name. It was bad enough for a fellow to look like a poet without having a die-away name to boot.

'What a surprise,' murmured Katherine, noting how Lord Ramsey put the hero completely into the shade. Blond good looks could not compare with his lordship's aristocratic grace, not to mention dark locks and warm gray eyes. Even Lord Ramsey's physique was superior. Katherine fleetingly wondered what it might be like to be clasped in those arms as her hero would be required to hold the heroine.

'Ought you be here?' Lord Ramsey gestured to the surroundings, which admittedly were not of high quality.

She tilted her fine nose in the air ever so slightly, giving Lord Ramsey a look that she hoped conveyed there were limits to what controls he might exercise over her, even if he were sponsoring their theatrical efforts.

'We were just going into a room at the back for more privacy. I have a copy of the script with me. This gentleman was about to read a few lines for us,' she said with a nice flair of speech.

Ramsey shrugged, then with a wave of his hand indicated they proceed — with himself for company.

Katherine had been afraid he would accompany them. She wondered if all playwrights had this difficulty with the backers of their productions. If he interfered, it would be terribly difficult to deny him his say. Katherine feared she was not as resolute as she ought to be.

'Gisela read your play,' he said in an undertone.

'So soon?' Katherine paused to glance at his face.

'She enjoyed it very much. At least I think so. She giggled so much it was difficult to tell.'

Katherine compressed her mouth, fighting back a grin. 'If our audience feels the same, we are made.'

'Have you mentioned this to your father as yet?'

'No, and please do not tell me that as a good daughter I ought to inform him what I am doing. You have some influence with the university. Can you not convince someone that there will be no harm, at least in our production?'

'I fear that my connection had best be kept silent.'

'Oh, dear.' Katherine frowned, causing Ninian Denham to stop his reading. 'Nothing to do with you, Mr Denham. Please continue.' To Lord Ramsey she whispered, 'Let us hope we can keep Mely quiet — for your sake as well as ours.'

When the handsome young actor completed his reading of the requested lines, Katherine applauded. 'Fine, fine.'

Her brother looked at Lord Ramsey, who

reluctantly nodded his agreement. Although Mr Denham proved to be an excellent actor, Philip had mixed emotions about his working closely with Katherine for any time at all.

'The part is yours, Mr Denham,' Katherine said with pleasure. 'Keep the script. If my brother succeeds in his endeavor, you shall have a very good actress to play against. Until she arrives, I shall take her part.'

'Miss Penn, do you think that wise?' Lord Ramsey objected.

She turned to face him, her hands clenched at her sides. 'If we obtain Miss O'Neill, we cannot afford to pay her salary for weeks on end, even were she free to come. She has commitments, I am sure. I know all the lines and how I want Mr Denham to play the part.'

'Dash it all, Kitty, I thought I was to direct the play.' Teddy gave her a look that bordered on pouting.

Katherine wondered what she had done to deserve Teddy, Lord Ramsey, and Mely, each bent on having his or her own way. Turning to Mr Denham, she suggested they meet soon to rehearse.

'Why do you not use the theater at Fairfax Hall, Miss Penn? That way few, if any, will hear of it.'

He looked immensely pleased with himself,

thought Katherine, as she considered his offer.

'Fine,' she replied, showing her reluctance a little. She set a time, then watched the actor depart.

'Who or what is Mely?' Lord Ramsey demanded once the door was closed.

It was Teddy who chose to answer. 'She's a friend who has learned about the play. Amelia Bonner is not only a peagoose, but she's a prattle box to boot.'

'And you fear her?'

'I had to agree that she can work on the costumes out at Fairfax Hall, my lord. It seems the hall holds a fascination for her.'

'I suspect she wants to meet you and your sister as well,' grumbled Teddy with strong resentment at the silly young woman who had pushed her way into his and his sister's project. 'I warn you, her mother is the greatest gossip in town.'

A rap on the door brought a surprising response. Outside the door several people Katherine knew performed in the annual Sturbridge productions stood waiting to enter the small room where Mr Denham had read.

'Auditions?' a pert young miss said.

'For an ogre of a count and a serving maid.' Katherine laughed. She had kept her cast of characters short, knowing full well that paying a large number of actors might be a strain. Even with Lord Ramsey aboard, she did not wish to change anything.

Before the afternoon was out, the cast was complete. Katherine, Teddy, and Lord Ramsey strolled from the inn after appeasing the landlord by buying a round of ale for all involved.

'Miss Penn, I cannot like you being so closely involved in the rehearsals,' Lord Ramsey declared — rather piously, Katherine thought.

Looking at him, she could see he was greatly displeased. 'Cousin Sophia has volunteered to assist. She will play chaperone.'

'Only play? I think I had best be around as well.' He smiled down at her with the expression of one who has just won a round of play in a hotly contested game.

'You leave Amelia and Gisela alone to mend costumes?' Katherine darted a smug glance at him, to be met with a cool stare that quite disconcerted her.

'I trust Gisela can handle Miss Bonner.'

'You act as though you do not trust me with Mr Denham, sir.' Katherine was annoyed, even as she knew it most likely improper for her to be working with Mr Denham. 'I assure you that merely because he is an extremely handsome man does not affect me in the least. I shall play my part as though he were a brother.' While her voice remained admirably calm, shaking only a trifle, she seethed inside. How dare he take over her life, or imply that she might foolishly tumble into an infatuation with an actor.

'Well, I best be off early in the morning,' Teddy said out of the blue. He had not been paying attention to the tense conversation between his sister and Lord Ramsey. Rather, he stood deep in thought regarding his trip to Norwich and the coming interview with Miss O'Neill.

'You wish to go alone?' Lord Ramsey inquired, seeming to indicate he might be willing to accompany Teddy.

Katherine was torn between suggesting that Lord Ramsey go along with Teddy, thus hurting her brother's feelings, and the alternative of having his lordship looking over her shoulder. She remained silent, not wishing to dishearten her brother.

'By Jove, yes. You know, Kitty, I might not be back by Sunday. Sorry to miss services and all, but that's how it is.' Teddy looked excessively smug.

Katherine longed to punch him in the arm, but standing on one of the busier streets in Cambridge was not the place to do so. 'I am persuaded that you selected the time well, from your point of view, at least.' She said nothing more, loyalty to her father preventing her from warning Lord Ramsey what she feared they were in for on Sunday.

'Oh, Katherine,' came a fluting voice from across the way. The three turned, with Teddy excusing himself immediately on a vague pretext. Since Amelia didn't want to see him anyway, she was only mildly vexed to see him dash off.

'Amelia Bonner, Lord Ramsey,' Katherine said in an undertone. 'The one we must placate.'

Lord Ramsey's lips twitched slightly at the dry inflection in Katherine's voice. A devilish twinkle crept into his eyes and he gave Katherine an amused glance before facing the beautiful young woman who approached.

'Ah, Miss Bonner.' He bowed low over the beauty's hand, smiling into those limpid eyes with a nicety of manners. 'You do us honor. Miss Penn and I were just discussing the coming days. Do say you will join us. Perhaps we might begin this Sunday? Divine services, then dinner?'

Katherine almost choked. Mely made a point of attending the service where the most young men were sure to be present. She would not enjoy hearing Mr Penn speak in the least, for the undergraduates were sure not to be there.

'I would be honored,' she declaimed in the

grandest of manners. She tossed a victorious smile at Katherine before departing their company some minutes later.

* * *

Friday proved to be one of those days Katherine would rather forget. Mely made herself agreeable, but proceeded to take over the mending of the costumes in an officious manner that set everyone's teeth on edge in short order.

Mrs Cheney found every excuse in the world to absent herself from the saloon where the women worked. Mostly she went to the library to check on Mr Penn with the flimsiest of pretexts. Katherine envied her the talent of making those excuses sound exceedingly reasonable. But, then, Mely was so content to be at Fairfax Hall helping dear Mrs Cheney that Katherine doubted if she paid any true attention to them.

In truth, Katherine was pleased that Mrs Cheney and her father seemed to get along so very well. They had a brief chat during nuncheon discussing a topic of mutual interest. Katherine kept busy keeping Mely away from them, but thought they enjoyed it excessively, which was more than she might say for dealing with Miss Amelia Bonner.

On Sunday Amelia and Mrs Bonner joined Katherine and Cousin Sophia at divine services in the little church not far from the gates of Fairfax Hall. A short parade of children filled the front pew.

Lord Ramsey and Mrs Cheney moved forward to greet the visitors. Mrs Cheney explained thus, 'I teach a Sunday school every week, you see. Poor little things know not how to read or write. The older children attend the charity school in the village.' The kind expression in her eyes clearly revealed the depth of her compassion for the tots. 'I am hoping we can find a teacher for them so they can learn all week, some woman of good reputation.'

The organist began the prelude and there was no further conversation.

The sermon proved as dreary as Katherine feared. Her father seemed to feel he preached at a group of students, for he used the longest words and most incomprehensible allusions to be found. She stifled a sigh. Glancing at Lord Ramsey, she noted his eyes appeared glazed, and she felt pity for him. Mrs Cheney looked angry, which Katherine thought an unusual reaction to a boring sermon. At her side, Cousin Sophia appeared to doze.

They assembled at Fairfax Hall following the close of service. During a most agreeable dinner, the subject of the sermon was neatly avoided by an alert Katherine and Cousin Sophia, who had been cautioned earlier.

Amelia and her mother expressed their delight at being included in the gathering. Indeed, Amelia chattered on like the worst of magpies. Her performance of the day before was surpassed, in Katherine's estimation. Lord Ramsey wore an expression of great forbearance.

Mrs Cheney stayed strangely silent during the meal. Katherine attributed her quiet either to a reluctance to participate or a dislike of the toadying Mrs Bonner. Usually Gisela was a delightful companion, and her conversation charming. Katherine noted that Mely had not been invited to the informality of using Gisela's first name. Her observation soothed her somewhat.

Upon conclusion of the excellent meal, the group strolled out to the saloon, Mrs Bonner exclaiming over the splendid view of the Gothic Tower. Amelia appeared to be mentally cataloging the contents of the room. Katherine found her separation from Lord Ramsey gratifying. She still nursed her ire at his behavior while in town.

Katherine sensed her father awaited praise

for his fine words at church, for he dropped one or two subtle hints. Lord Ramsey obliged.

'Interesting sermon, Mr Penn. I do not recall ever hearing that topic put quite that way before.'

Before Mr Penn could reply, Gisela spoke. 'And I hope you never do again, dear brother.' Her eyes flashing, she rounded upon Katherine's father. Although her voice was controlled, her words were not. 'And just who were you trying to reach with your fine, high-sounding words today? Farmer Jones? The Widow Dabney? Or perhaps Mr Willowby and his good wife, who barely know how to read their alphabet? What word of the gospel was in that sermon to touch their hearts, pray tell?' she lashed at the astounded man. 'People showed their taste rather than their piety. Not a few fell asleep; most fortunate people they were, too.'

'Madam,' he began, with an appealing glance at Lord Ramsey.

'I am not finished, if you please.' Mrs Cheney placed a deterring hand on Mr Penn's arm. 'When Jonah attempted to evade the call of the Lord, it must have had a meaning for us all. I did not hear a clue from you, sir. Not a syllable did you reveal of God's purpose for Jonah, nor the lesson to be learned from him. I heard a lot of nonsensical rhetoric that might sound fine in a classroom, although I do not see how you keep from boring the students to death. I was heartily bored myself.' Her eyes flashed her scorn, but she still did not permit a defense from Mr Penn.

'The Lord called a man, who then resisted him,' she stated in her lovely voice, now fervent with emotion. 'Jonah needed to be taught a lesson. He was. He learned his salvation comes from the Lord, and so he was told to preach to the Ninevites. He did, and the people repented of their sins and were spared. Do you think one soul was brought to knowledge of the truth from your words today, sir? Could you not have just talked to the people, simply told them the needful as you might to a friend?'

The room was silent. Lord Ramsey took a step forward, his hand reaching out to his sister.

Katherine drew close to Cousin Sophia. Mrs Bonner stood with her mouth unattractively open, while Amelia glanced at Lord Ramsey, as though trying to gauge what her own reaction ought to be.

Mr Penn stood very still.

Mrs Cheney suddenly took note of the shocked faces around her. She uttered a muffled cry behind a hand that flew to cover her mouth, and ran from the room, her skirts whirling about her legs as she hurried toward the staircase.

'I do beg your pardon on behalf of my sister, Mr Penn. She has not been herself for some time.' Lord Ramsey looked torn between attending to his guests and following his upset sister.

As much as Katherine agreed with Mrs Cheney, she felt it necessary to support her father. 'Perhaps we best leave.'

'Tomorrow?' Lord Ramsey sent an appealing glance to Katherine, who evaded his look. She had not quite forgiven him the fuss he had made over Mely the other day, nor the interfering manner he had adopted toward her and her play, and this still illogically added to her sense of injustice.

'Perhaps,' she replied coolly. 'Thank you for the kind invitation, Lord Ramsey.'

The subdued party walked down the front steps to where the carriage shortly drew up before them. Lord Ramsey had seen to it they were conveyed home in style, and for that Katherine repented of her sour thoughts.

'Well,' blurted out Mely once they sat in the carriage, 'I must say I think that was ill-done.'

'Mrs Cheney was upset, Amelia,' Cousin Sophia said in a soothing voice.

'Unforgivable,' Mrs Bonner declared in an aggrieved tone.

'I trust we shall not hear a word of this about town, Martha,' Cousin Sophia said in a voice that brooked no denial. 'I would hate to nose it about that you dye that pretty hair of yours.'

'But I do never,' declared the shocked Mrs Bonner.

'I know that,' replied Cousin Sophia complacently. 'But think what a good bit of gossip it would make.'

'Well!' Mrs Bonner subsided into silence.

From Mr Penn not a word was heard. Katherine suspected he remained unaware of the softly spoken words within the carriage between his cousin and the greatest gossip in town.

It must have been a terrible blow to her father to hear what was after all the truth as most of the world would see it. Katherine placed a comforting hand on his sleeve, and gave him an encouraging smile. He merely stared at her as though he didn't know her.

Katherine took a deep breath and wondered what the days to follow would bring. Dare she even think of the play? She pushed Lord Ramsey from her mind for the moment.

6

A storm had moved in during the night and the day was a dreary, wet one, fit for Gabriel and the ducks.

Katherine shook off her hooded cloak and handed it and her exceedingly wet umbrella to the Fairfax butler before following him through the hall to the saloon. She had not intended to come here today. In the early hours of the morning she had recalled the words and manner used by Lord Ramsey, and her anger had returned fourfold. His attitude and distrust rankled. Only the note from Mrs Cheney, pleading to see her, persuaded Katherine to change her mind.

She paused just inside the saloon, studying the figure at the window pensively staring out toward the Gothic Tower. A hasty check of the room brought the happy information that Lord Ramsey was nowhere to be seen. 'Gisela?' She could hear the tension in her own voice and wondered if Mrs Cheney could as well.

Mrs Cheney whirled about, then rapidly glided toward Katherine, her hands outstretched. 'What a wretched creature I am.

Can you ever forgive me for what I said yesterday? Or can your father? I expect he will never wish to see my face again.' Her fervent declaration stirred Katherine to compassion. The high degree of Gisela's distress readily evidenced itself in her failure to observe Katherine's damp, sorry condition.

Tears glistened in Mrs Cheney's eyes, her expression truly one of repentance as she searched Katherine's face. 'Come, we shall have a cup of tea and I will try to explain, for I owe you that much, I believe.'

'Please, I . . . ' Katherine tried in vain to protest, very torn. She wondered whether she actually wished to know what was on the older woman's mind. Katherine smoothed down her dark-green kerseymere and seated herself as close to the fire as possible, having been chilled to the bone during her drive.

'I insist, my dear,' Mrs Cheney replied in the nicest possible way while plumping herself on to the sofa.

The tray must have been requested in advance, for within minutes of her tug of the bellpull, the butler entered bearing all that was necessary for a completely delicious tea.

Watching as Mrs Cheney went through the motions of pouring, adding lemon slices, offering biscuits, Katherine wondered, her curiosity greatly stirred. She had searched her brain last night for a possible clue to such outrageous, quite unladylike behavior. Nothing had come to mind.

On the trip home her father had withdrawn from her and Cousin Sophia, which Katherine supposed was not surprising. It had been a devastating attack on what was closest to his heart: his intellectual abilities and public image. Once home, Katherine and Cousin Sophia had promptly entered the house. Julian Penn had turned from them and the comforting words they might have offered, and stalked away. Presumably he had gone to the common room at Trinity to console himself with a glass of port and conversation with one of his cronies. Katherine did not hear him return home before she drifted off to an uneasy sleep.

By morning's light she had found no intelligent explanation forthcoming, which meant that whatever it was had more to do with irrational emotional feelings than with logic.

When the note from Fairfax Hall had come, her first reaction had been negative. Only a second reading had persuaded her to accept, a behavior endorsed by Cousin Sophia, who wanted Katherine to get to the bottom of the unusual behavior.

Now Katherine wondered.

At last the moment arrived. Mrs Cheney sat, her face troubled as she stirred her cup of tea, the spoon gently clinking against the china cup. Beyond the room, the rain fell in a mizzle, the tower now a ghostly ruin in the distance. The butler had stirred the fire before he departed, sending showers of sparks dancing up the chimney and heat into the room. Katherine inched closer to its drying warmth.

'You see,' Mrs Cheney began, 'I had come to admire your father very much over the days he had been coming here. He has a wonderful mind, such depth of knowledge. Whenever I visited with him, I felt I spoke with a man of truly great dimensions. I fear I began to place him on a pedestal.' She bowed her head for a few moments, took a sip of what must by now be rather cool tea, then continued.

'The day that silly little girl was here, I fled to where he worked in the library whenever I could. I suspect it was as much to be with him as to escape her inanities. She is a shocking peagoose, is she not?'

When Katherine allowed a small smile to escape at this truism, Mrs Cheney breathed a sigh, then again forged ahead with her explanation.

Katherine shivered and wished she had

brought a shawl with her. She had not precisely gotten soaked, but rather damp and chilled, on her drive to the hall. A draft curled through the room, and Katherine stifled a longing to sneeze.

'So, when we attended divine services Sunday, I waited in high expectations. I felt your father would be so different from my husband. For my husband was ever one to prose, and always spoke as though he were preaching from Olympus to lesser mortals below. Not that he expected us to understand him, mind you. It seemed to me that he desired to proclaim himself superior in his use of speech, to set himself apart and make the rest of the world conscious of his superior mental accomplishments. Do you know that he forbade me the use of my title? No Lady Gisela Cheney in his household, if you please. It upset my brother very much, I fear. Nor were our parents happy. You know the earl and his countess spend the winter in Italy?' she said in a moment's digression.

She fell silent a moment, first looking into the flames, then back at Katherine. 'I felt betrayed when I heard your father speak. I had anticipated so much more, you see. And there he stood, talking down to us poor souls just as my dead husband was wont to do. I fear I lost my sense of reason for a brief time.

What I said to Mr Penn was unforgivable, I know. But I wonder, do you think he might find it in his heart to . . .

The remainder of her sentence was lost as Katherine at last gave in to her body and sneezed, not once, but several times. Fortunately she had managed to locate her handkerchief first. She glanced at Mrs Cheney with a look of apology. 'So sorry.'

'My dear, you are shivering,' Mrs Cheney exclaimed. 'How thoughtless of me.' She put her cup and saucer on the tray, then jumped up to place a hand on Katherine's arm. 'You must be chilled through. I shall never forgive myself if you take ill.' She thought a moment, then laughed, a shaky little laugh, to be sure. 'I believe the best remedy is a warm bath. Poor girl, you seem ever in the need for hot water when you visit us.'

At that Katherine chuckled, recalling quite vividly the first day she had met Mrs Cheney and Lord Ramsey. He was not in evidence today. Since the weather was far too inclement to be out and about with tenants and the like, Katherine could only believe he wished privacy for his sister and her confession. Whatever the reason, she assured herself she was grateful not to confront him.

'Come. The water ought to be yet quite warm and it will take but minutes to add hot to it. The sooner, the better. I shall place some herbs in it as well. Nothing like a bit of lavender and chamomile to soothe the body and take away the aches.'

Needing no urging to engage in a delightful bath once again, Katherine shamelessly permitted herself to be led up the back stairs to the plunge bath. She sneezed several times on the way, causing Mrs Cheney to hurry her along until they were nearly at a run.

Once in the bathroom, Mrs Cheney saw to the addition of the hot water herself, then left the room to locate the required herbs.

Katherine watched the flow of steaming water into the tile-lined bath, marveling that water could not only be piped into the house, but heated first as well. It truly was a modern miracle.

By the time Mrs Cheney returned, the water had reached the desired temperature. 'For,' she explained, 'we do not wish you to become a boiled lobster, merely warm.' She poured the fragrant oils into the water, gestured to the neat pile of towels, then left.

Feeling quite decadent, Katherine stripped her damp clothes off, then eased into the water. A light tap on the door preceded a young maid, who whisked the garments from the room while discreetly avoiding a glance at the woman in the bath.

It proved far better than her first experience. This time, Katherine genuinely needed the healing heat. The aroma of the herbs seemed to ease that desire to sneeze, and she felt her chest clearing of the tightness that had threatened.

Since there seemed no need to rush, for Cousin Sophia expected her to remain some time and Katherine doubted if either Mrs Cheney or Lord Ramsey would mind should she take her time about the bath, Katherine luxuriated to her heart's content. She vowed if she ever became rich — a most unlikely occurrence, she admitted — she would build such a bath and enter it every day.

It was not until she observed her skin beginning to puff and wrinkle that she reluctantly decided she had best get out. Steam had brought additional warmth to the room, and Katherine felt no chill at first. When she looked about for her clothes, she realized that in order to dress she must return to the adjacent room, where a cozy fire burned to further warm her. Such comforts were only to be envied.

Wrapping the largest of the towels about her, reveling in the softness of the Turkish pile, she slipped from the bathroom to find her clothes awaiting her neatly draped over a chair near the fire.

After briskly rubbing herself dry, she was about to set aside her towel to don her stays when she heard the rattle of the doorknob. Katherine hastily wrapped the towel about her, although she expected it was merely Mrs Cheney coming to check on her.

Rather, Lord Ramsey began to enter the room. He paused in the act of removing his coat, a near-comical expression of dismay on his face as he discovered the room to be occupied. 'Excuse me. I had not realized there was someone here.' He adjusted his coat, backing from the room as he spoke. 'The pond again? I hope Hector was not responsible.' The dog had not been in evidence of late.

'The rain, sir.' She sneezed, less violently this time.

A frantic clutch at her towel kept her almost decent. However, she did not miss the warm gleam in Lord Ramsey's eyes as he surveyed her lightly covered self before discreetly closing the door behind him.

Drat the man! How odious of him to come here just when she reached for her stays. She crossed to check the door and found no lock, explaining Lord Ramsey's entrance.

What he might think of her now was beyond Katherine to imagine. Would he view her with distaste? The very thought prompted her to rush into her stays, demure shift, neat petticoat, practical hose, and respectable kerseymere gown. All were dry and warm and contributed to a feeling of well-being. This was marred by the irrational anger she felt toward his lordship. Now he would be convinced she was no better than she should be. Life simply was not just. She paused before she made to return downstairs. Would this cause him to refuse his support of the production?

When she joined Mrs Cheney in the saloon, a fragrant herbal tisane steamed away in a pot. The brother and sister were quietly chatting while seated on the sofa before the fire. They rose as Katherine entered the room. Although ostensibly gliding forward to greet Gisela, Katherine was very aware of the man who so angered and intrigued her.

'Katherine, my dear, I trust you feel more the thing? I had Cook prepare an herbal drink for you. I believe you will be the better for it. And I persuaded Philip to join us. Even time in the steward's room can become tedious. Records, you know.' She smiled warmly at her brother, thus missing the guarded look on Katherine's face.

'Record-keeping is a necessary thing, I expect. Or do you work on a history of the Fairfax family, my lord?' Katherine chose to meet Lord Ramsey's gaze at this point. While that warm glow lingered, there was no sign of any other emotion she could identify. Not that there wasn't something lurking in those eyes, for they had a decidedly naughty twinkle in them that she found improper while at the same moment wished to explore. Such contradictory feelings prompted her to abruptly seat herself on the chair by the fire.

The gentleman remained blessedly silent about their brief encounter. For this, Katherine decided she could almost forgive him that wicked little gleam in those beautiful gray eyes of his. It was uncomfortable to realize that he had seen more of her than any man alive. She could not help but wonder which way his feelings might lean as a result and how it would affect his support.

'I thought it might be interesting to do a history, for one has not been attempted before. Fortunately there are excellent records kept here for me to use.'

'Tiresome work, at least,' interposed Mrs Cheney.

'It has its moments,' Lord Ramsey replied quietly.

Had not Katherine raised her eyes at that minute, she would have missed that curve of his lips, a reminiscent curve that coupled with the gleam in his eyes to quite unsettle her.

How utterly odious of the man to make her feel guilty for what was, after all, quite innocent. She resolved to turn her mind to higher things and gave her attention to Mrs Cheney.

'I am sorry that the trip has proven hazardous to your health, dear Katherine. But I cannot begin to tell you how glad I am that you came.'

'I, as well,' Lord Ramsey added, smiling at his sister.

When Katherine was unable to prevent herself from darting a glance at him, she found a look of sincere appreciation on his face. She relaxed, thinking herself perhaps out of the woods, so to speak.

'About your father . . . ' Mrs Cheney began, then her voice drifted away.

'I fear I cannot say what he will think, or do, for he left us at the door last evening and went off. I expect he retired to the common room at Trinity to surround himself with the old familiar and comfortable essence of what he is and knows. Perhaps he had a glass of port with one of the other professors or fellows, maybe a hand of cards. Or it might be they merely sat and discussed something that distracted him from what he did not wish to dwell upon for the moment. He will face your accusation eventually.'

'Dare I ask how you feel about what Gisela said?'

Katherine looked at Lord Ramsey again, then nodded. 'I suppose I am not the most loyal of daughters, but I could not help but feel just as Gisela. I knew what to expect and I ought to have cautioned you, I fear. But it was very difficult and awkward for me to say anything. Do you recall the remark Teddy made before he left us for Norwich, the one about being sad to miss divine services? He was happy to escape. It is not a pleasant thing, I must confess. I revere him, but Papa is a dead bore.'

At which words, the tension broke and Lord Ramsey gave a small chuckle. He rose from the sofa to stroll to the window. 'I trust he will return to use the library again?'

'I cannot say.' Katherine glanced at Mrs Cheney, then back to her lap, where her hands smoothed out her skirt. 'I hope this will not alter our plans for the play. May we yet rehearse in your theater?' If Lord Ramsey denied the use, it would mean Katherine was free to rehearse whenever and wherever she pleased and was possible. And with whom, as well.

'Oh.' Mrs Cheney jumped up and walked to the door. 'I have your play, my dear. I will find it, for my maid will never know where to look. I wish to show you a part I particularly enjoyed. I will be but a few moments.'

The silence in the room deepened after she left. Katherine rose from her chair, walking slowly to where a pianoforte stood at the far end of the room. Idly, she allowed her fingers to pick out a melody while flicking glances at Lord Ramsey from time to time. It perhaps was not well done of her to boldly touch the instrument, but she could not bear to sit in silence with his lordship after what had happened earlier. That he should see her so disturbed her greatly.

'Will you play something for me?'

How, she wondered wildly, had he managed to get from the window to her side in seconds? Calling upon the strength that had seen her through countless evenings when she was required to entertain her father's company, Katherine seated herself on the stool and began to play.

Why she drifted from an imposing church hymn by Bach to a romantic tune she had composed, she never knew. It was as flowing and dramatic as any Gothic tale might be. Indeed, it could be a musical theme for her play. She had poured the yearning of her heart into it. The piece concluded, she wondered what evil imp had urged her to perform it for Lord Ramsey.

'Lovely,' breathed Mrs Cheney who had returned unheard while Katherine was playing. 'Wild and tempestuous, but undeniably lovely. It's like a storm in a glade that tears the autumn leaves from the trees, preparing the sheltered spot for the tranquility of winter.'

'I do not recognize the music. It is contemporary, of course, but who?' He remained close to Katherine, a sensation she found overly disturbing.

'No one of consequence, sir.' Katherine rose from where she sat, crossing to join Mrs Cheney. She avoided looking at Lord Ramsey, for she held the ridiculous notion he might read her mind. 'You found my play, I see. What was it you wished to point out to me?'

Seeing that Katherine was not to be drawn into a discussion of the unusual music she had performed, her hostess politely opened to the part of the play that had particularly delighted her, and began to discuss the backdrop requisite for the scene.

Relieved to be so easily allowed to pass by her error, Katherine entered into the discussion with enthusiasm. Her sneezes gone and her chest feeling more normal, she thought she would be able to return home suffering no ill effects.

Before long she considered it time to depart. Rising to make her farewells, she was surprised when Lord Ramsey joined Gisela and her on their walk to the door. Her little cart awaited her, the donkeys standing placidly in the falling mist.

'I have enjoyed the afternoon,' Katherine declared with polite enthusiasm. There had been unsettling moments, but those she preferred to ignore.

Lord Ramsey frowned as he looked out the doorway to where the cart awaited. 'I fear you will catch your death if you drive home in that vehicle.'

'I am not such a poor honey as that,' Katherine said with a touch of asperity. It might have served better had she not sneezed at that moment.

'Hot bricks and an extra blanket may help, but I have my doubts,' he said with a resigned tone of voice. 'Will you promise us that you will not take any undue risks going home and promptly warm yourself once there?'

'I imagine the best thing would be to stay with us,' Gisela said thoughtfully. 'I ought to insist, but I cannot think what your father would say when he learned of the matter.' She looked as though she might burst into tears at the thought of the discord she had created by her hasty, though sincerely meant, words.

'It would be far better, I agree. I feel Miss

Penn has had quite enough of the Fairfax family for the time being.' Lord Ramsey revealed nothing of his thoughts on the matter.

Once Kendall arranged the cart with heated bricks, the butler bowed her out with formality, holding a huge umbrella over her while handing her the nicely dried-out one she had brought with her. He tucked in a blanket about her with a fatherly air, then watched her depart.

Katherine glanced back at the windows. Gisela waved once, then disappeared. Of Lord Ramsey she saw nothing.

There were no other vehicles foolish enough to be on the road, so Katherine had ample time to reflect upon the afternoon and all that had happened. She had detected a coolness of attitude in Lord Ramsey before she left. He had returned to calling her Miss Penn. Her ire rose as she considered possible reasons. He had not wanted her to remain, she felt sure of that. Then, a conceivable explanation for his behavior came to her. Oh, that Lord Ramsey could believe her so foolish as to succumb to the blandishments of the actor Ninian Denham!

With this ridiculous thought floating around in her mind, Katherine arrived home in a state of annoyance unrivaled in memory.

Cousin Sophia met her in the hall, rightly judged her mood, and guided Katherine into the drawing room, to push her on to a chair by the fire with no nonsense permitted, first removing her hooded cloak. 'Amelia was here not long ago.'

Diverted momentarily from the tirade she was about to issue, Katherine asked, 'What did she want, as if I did not know?'

'That girl is about a subtle as a dead pig,' Cousin Sophia declared. 'She said she simply had to see you; then, when I said you were away from home, she poked and pried. She is just like her mother. Worse I could not say about her.'

Katherine moved forward to warm her hands, giving a watery chuckle as she did. 'I wager we may have a spot of trouble with her.'

'A spot? More like an entire barrel, I should say.' Cousin Sophia sniffed in disdain, then grew alarmed as Katherine emitted a dainty sneeze. 'What's this? Are you taking a cold?' She bustled over to give a tug of the bellpull; then, not waiting, she hurried off to the hall to issue instructions to Mrs Moore for a soothing draft.

'I knew I ought not go this afternoon,' Katherine explained. 'The weather worsened, and although I now know better what

131

prompted Mrs Cheney to act in the manner she did, I fear there are other complications we had not anticipated.' Katherine eased off her shoes, then stretched her feet toward the fire. She was thawing out. Hopefully the weather would improve before the fair.

Mrs Moore entered with a tray holding a steaming herbal tisane. Katherine sipped at it, allowing the warmth to spread throughout her.

'I know I shall be fine. I had a sneezing spell while at Fairfax Hall and Mrs Cheney insisted I take an herbal bath. You know I am never ill.'

The front door slammed shut. In moments Mr Penn came into the drawing room, his coat flapping about him as he strode across the room.

Mrs Moore disappeared after a few whispered instructions from Cousin Sophia. Katherine studied her father, wondering what was going on in his head.

'Miserable day,' he commented, eyeing Katherine's stocking feet with a raised brow.

'I was out and got chilled. Should you like an herbal drink? Peppermint is rather nice, I think.'

'Port is better,' countered Mr Penn as he shed his coat and joined Katherine by the fire. 'What a time I have had of it. Young

132

fellow was with me today. Made me feel an ancient, larding his talk with 'you know, sir,' until I wanted to order him hence.'

She was surprised to hear him complain like this. He usually said not a word about his day at the college, nor anything of the people he dealt with.

'I miss your mother at times like this,' he admitted to Katherine's further astonishment. 'She was a comfort on days such as these.'

''Tis a pity, Papa,' murmured Katherine, trying to understand what had happened to her usually taciturn father.

'I could have talked to her about yesterday. She would have understood,' Mr Penn continued in a reflective tone.

Katherine studied him briefly while sipping her tisane, then ventured to say, 'I feel certain that Mrs Cheney would perceive more of your feelings than you know.'

Instead of flaring up in indignation, which Katherine fully expected him to do, Mr Penn merely looked at her and shrugged. 'Do you, indeed? Well, I misdoubt she or her brother will wish to see either of us again.'

'No reason for that, is there?' Katherine took a cautious breath, then continued, 'Actually I saw them earlier today. I spent the afternoon at Fairfax Hall. Mrs Cheney wished to explain her hasty words to me, and she hopes to convey her sentiments to you as well. It seems she had put you on a pedestal and you tumbled rather badly.' Katherine omitted any reference to Lord Ramsey. He was a topic best left alone.

'What say you, my Katherine?'

'About your message at divine service?' Katherine avoided his eyes, not wishing to make her thoughts known immediately to one who often read her too well.

'Ah, you need say nothing, my girl. That averted countenance tells me all. Did Sophia really go to sleep?'

'I did,' said that lady as she entered the room in time to hear the last few remarks. 'You were a dreadful bore, Julian. Perhaps in the end Mrs Cheney did you and all of us a service.'

This was more than Julian could be expected to bear. He rose from his chair, gave his cousin a narrow look, then quit the room.

'That was not well done,' Katherine said softly. 'He told me that he misses Mama.'

'And so he should. It would not have hurt him to marry again. Goodness knows you needed a mother, and a woman would have told him the needful long ago.'

'And you might have been tending your gardens these many years,' Katherine snapped back, then instantly repented her quick words.

'I have never said I regret my time with you, girl. I will not deny I would like my peace again, however.' She bestowed a fond pat on Katherine's shoulder, then gave the doorway through which Julian Penn had passed a troubled look.

Mr Penn remained at home for dinner, but the subject of Sunday was not brought forth again. Katherine went to bed with an uneasy heart. She had no better idea as to what Lord Ramsey might do about the play. Each day brought them closer to the date of the fair. They needed to reserve a space. Teddy was likely to be gone for a week, so she must make the arrangements. Or, better, Lord Ramsey. But they needed money and how she hated to approach him for the amount necessary. Would he think her accustomed to asking gentlemen for sums of cash?

The following morning Katherine was relieved to find her health no worse for her outing. The day was fine and she thought about setting out once again to look for a few of the late wild-flowers that might have survived the rain.

Mrs Moore entered the breakfast room with a missive in her hand. ''Tis from Fairfax Hall, if I make no mistake. For you, Katherine.'

It had taken years to persuade Mrs Moore to call her Katherine after being Kitty for so long. To be called Miss Penn was unthinkable.

Katherine accepted the crisp cream note, folded in thirds and sealed as though it were a letter going to China. The housekeeper was correct. As the good lady had not lingered to catch the news, although most likely she wanted to know, Katherine did not inform her she was right.

Cousin Sophia differed. 'Well, spit it out, girl.'

'We are all invited to Fairfax Hall for dinner tomorrow.' The two women exchanged dismayed looks. 'Think you that Papa will accept?'

Unvoiced was Katherine's concern. What if he did?

7

There was no one in the Penn house more surprised than Katherine when her father had accepted the invitation from Fairfax Hall. She had been certain that he would toss it in the fire and utter a few pithy words about those in high places who tried to impress their opinions on others.

He had glanced at it, grunted, then stared at his daughter sitting in her chair in the breakfast room, a cautious expression on her face. 'You enjoyed your time there, did you not?' he inquired.

Katherine had replied, 'Yes, Papa. Mrs Cheney is all that is kind and dear.' Katherine had not seen fit to comment on his odious lordship.

'Hm,' he had replied while tapping the stiff cream paper against the palm of his hand, watching the ebb and flow of color in his daughter's face. 'I should like to see what Mrs Cheney has to say for herself, I believe.'

Katherine knew that she must have sat there looking for all the world like a fish out of water. Never had she expected her father to be so reasonable. Unless he intended to berate Mrs Cheney for her words. No,

Katherine decided, her father's manners forbade such behavior.

And now the three of them, for Teddy had still not returned from Norwich, sat in the elegant carriage sent from the hall, driving rapidly toward what Katherine fervently hoped would be a pleasant dinner party.

'Thank goodness we managed to escape the Bonners this evening,' Cousin Sophia declared in a fervent voice.

'I hope you shall not be disappointed. Since Mrs Cheney thought Mely to be a peagoose, I doubt we shall be afflicted with their company,' Katherine replied, a smile lighting her eyes.

'Mrs Cheney has no opinion of Amelia Bonner? Perhaps she has more sense than I thought,' Julian Penn reflected quietly from his corner of the carriage just as they drew up before the house. He brushed down his best jacket of dull blue cloth with modest brass buttons before getting out.

They were ushered into the house with all due ceremony. Kendall was the London butler to perfection, causing even Mr Penn to cast an approving eye on him.

'I am so pleased you could join us this evening. Time in the country is enlivened by good company,' Mrs Cheney said in her charming way.

'The pleasure is ours, good lady,' responded Mr Penn politely, quite obviously studying his hostess while maintaining a wary regard. Yet he seemed ready and willing to make his effort to reach an understanding.

Katherine hoped that he would not put Gisela out of countenance with his fixed regard.

'It pleases me that you suffered no ill from your visit with us the other day,' Lord Ramsey said as he turned to greet Katherine after making her father welcome.

'I warmed myself by the fire as bid, and Cousin Sophia saw that I swallowed a tisane she uses for incipient colds. It proved most beneficial.' Katherine eyed him with care, wondering whether she would be in charity with him, come the end of the evening.

They strolled along to the drawing room, a place Katherine had heretofore not seen. Cousin Sophia issued a faint gasp as they entered, for the room was indeed beautiful. Yellow silk-hung walls reflected the light from the many candles and torcheres. The exquisite pale aquamarine of the ceiling echoed the rich velvet that covered the chairs and settees with a French touch of opulence. Katherine particularly liked the delightful painting in the arch above the chimneypiece. The theme undoubtedly had something to do with music, but the gamboling cherubs really gave no clue. However, it charmed her, and her face lit up with a winsome grin.

She glanced at Lord Ramsey, who had suddenly turned up at her elbow, and said, 'Very captivating, my lord.'

'I thought you might appreciate the carved swags of foliage and flowers about the room, but do you find that sentimental piece appealing? My father got a bit carried away when he ordered the renovation of the room.' His eyes teased her, and Katherine wondered why she always had this ridiculous sense of floating when he drew near her.

He had moved closer to her while he spoke and she now felt difficulty in breathing. She tried to recall that she wished Lord Ramsey to procure a good living for Mr Weekes, but somehow her intentions slid from her mind.

'Come along with me for a moment.' He glanced at the others. 'I wish to discuss a few things with you that are best kept just to us.'

A sense of doom threatened Katherine. He would now tell her that he intended to withdraw his support. She just knew it. 'Of course,' she quietly agreed.

Cousin Sophia nodded when informed of Lord Ramsey's desire to show Katherine some drawings in his book room.

Walking swiftly at his side through a room

done mostly in red, then across a long room that stretched from the front to the back of the house that Katherine assumed to be the gallery, they entered a charming room with masses and masses of books. She guessed it provided extra shelving for an overflow of books from the library, for a glimpse of that room revealed its shelves to be full. Small wonder her father acted like a child in a toy shop when offered the opportunity to peruse the contents of the library at Fairfax Hall.

'I could have brought these out, but I suspected we had best conceal this project from your father for as long as possible.' He pulled a sheaf of drawings from a folder on a small desk near the fireplace. One by one he spilled them out on the mahogany surface of the table in the center of the room, revealing a brilliant collection of scenes, all of which she recognized as background for her play.

He picked up a branch of candles, setting it on the table to provide better light for her.

Choosing the first sketch, she studied it, then looked up at Lord Ramsey, incredulity shining from her eyes. 'How did you know this is precisely what I had in mind for the first scene? This is definitely the woods where Belinda is abducted.' She quickly pulled the next watercolor from the pile, breathing in with pleasure as she examined it. 'Ah, the castle. One can almost smell that dank, fetid air, feel the cold stone walls. And the sensation of impending doom clearly hangs over the setting.'

Lord Ramsey crossed his arms over his chest, his attitude one of lordly expectancy.

At the next drawing she frowned. 'I had not thought the bedroom in the castle to be quite so sumptuous. Do you really believe he would indulge himself so?'

'He is a hedonist, is he not? A pursuer of happiness for himself, if not for others? A man devoted to pleasure would enjoy such a room, I believe.'

Katherine's gaze was caught in his gray eyes for a few moments, then she forcibly returned her attention to the drawing in her hands, hands that trembled ever so slightly. Did Lord Ramsey revel in the quest of pleasure? That notion brought all manner of forbidden thoughts to mind. 'You seem to know a great deal about a man in such circumstances. I had thought billowing silks and velvet cushions more in line with a seraglio, based on what I have read.'

'I was unaware anything of that nature would be included in the reading list for a professor of divinity's daughter.' An insinuation lurked in his voice that she could not like in the least, for it sounded amused, in a superior persuasion, of course.

Katherine refused to rise to his bait. For one thing, she had no intention of revealing her reading list to him or anyone else. It would be shocking and proclaim her a bluestocking of the worst sort. 'You must admit, this is not what might be expected in a remote castle where a maiden has been abducted. Her hero will have a time rescuing her as it is.' Katherine studied the lavish bedroom, wondering what it might cost to produce. That a woman might not be spending time in here was debatable, as she would be captive and resistant.

'You feel that a woman would be attracted to such an exotic surrounding? That she might feel reluctance at leaving this?'

Since there was no way that Katherine might safely answer this improper question, she chose a different direction for her questioning. 'How difficult will these be to construct?' She tapped her finger on the harem-like bedroom of the wicked count.

'You approve of them, then? I thought the ladies in the audience might find them attractive in a naughty way.' His voice revealed a trace of lingering amusement mixed with anticipation.

It would have been cruel to disappoint him after such painstaking work on behalf of the play. And his investment, she reminded herself at once. 'They are splendid. You must know how very good they are. Did you do them, or did you have a professional draw them up for you? They would be shockingly expensive to create, I fear.' Regarding what ladies might think, she prudently remained silent.

'No problem, my dear girl. I dabble a bit in drawing and the like. As to construction, I shall show you what I've devised after dinner.'

With that tantalizing bit of information Katherine had to be content. They returned to the drawing room as Kendall entered to inform them that dinner was served. No questions as to where they had been were forthcoming in the ensuing stir as the others rose, moving toward the door.

Lord Ramsey escorted Cousin Sophia and Katherine while Mr Penn offered his arm to Mrs Cheney.

Katherine glanced back to take note of the wary looks exchanged between the two. If matters might be patched up there, the subterfuge necessary in her frequent travels to Fairfax Hall would be greatly reduced. She felt it quite necessary to rehearse with Ninian Denham. She was not sure if Lord Ramsey would continue to uphold this portion of their agreement.

The atmosphere in the dining room was congenial. Although vast in size, there was a charm and warmth about it. What seemed like yards of polished mahogany was dotted with place settings, glittering crystal candelabra, and masses of late-summer flowers in low arrangements to facilitate conversation. Katherine observed the viscount's coronet and initials incorporated in the plasterwork on the ceiling, the details highlighted by the abundance of candles in the wall sconces. Had he ordered this, or his father before him? She knew the Earl of Fairfax preferred to live in his principal residence south of London. It was an unexpected vanity.

Just how much did this touch of pride reflect the taste of the man at her side? Katherine tried to ascertain something more of his nature from darted glances during the meal.

To her right Katherine could hear polite conversation flowing unabated between Mrs Cheney and Mr Penn. It was undoubtedly reserved and did not seem to offer a great deal of hope, yet Katherine knew that Gisela intended to make her peace. Katherine prayed it might be achieved, and soon. However, the very presence of her father at this table was a step in the right direction.

The meal was well prepared and elegantly

served, yet she found it not ostentatious, such as one might have found at the table of a man bent on impressing. Of course, Gisela most likely had the arranging of the dinner, yet it said well for both of them and Katherine found her estimation of them increased.

Rather than return to the elegant drawing room, they strolled to a small, more intimate drawing room near the entry to the house. Katherine walked over to admire the painting above the mantel, which turned out to be a very pretty Gainsborough of a young woman.

'My aunt. Rather charming, is she not?' Lord Ramsey announced in a clear voice that anyone in the room might hear. In a soft aside, he added, 'Shortly we shall leave the room so that I may show you what I have done.'

Surprised at this touch of mystery and intrigue, Katherine gave him a look and a discreet nod.

Across the room, Mrs Cheney sat facing Mr Penn with a determined look on her face. Katherine tried not to be obvious in her efforts to overhear what was being said. She so hoped all would go well.

'I hope you will forgive my hasty tongue this past Sunday,' Mrs Cheney said in her clear, pleasant voice. 'It was unforgivable of me to presume to take you to task in what is, after all, your calling. You must think me exceedingly forward.'

Mr Penn studied his folded hands, which rested on his lap, then looked at the earnest and attractive woman who sat comfortably close. His expression was troubled, his voice low as he spoke. 'No, you had the right of it, my good lady. Even my daughter could not deny I was a prosy old bore — put Cousin Sophia and who knows how many others to sleep. One forgets, you know. I am so far removed from the everyday world that it is easy to lose sight of the needful.'

Mrs Cheney waited a moment, as though hoping he might be more forthcoming. He wasn't. As a forgiveness, it lacked a certain something, but it was far better than nothing and certainly more acceptable than hostility.

'My brother expressed his hopes that you might continue to use his library. He is making use of the book room at present. I believe he intends to do a history of the family, such as it is.' She gave him a tentative smile and seemed a bit anxious.

'A worthy cause, madam.' Mr Penn had a kindly yet thoughtful expression on his face. It surely revealed no antipathy for the Fairfax family. Indeed, it could be viewed as almost encouraging.

Mrs Cheney relaxed a trifle, then turned to

Katherine. 'Play something for us, will you?'

The pianoforte had been moved from the saloon. Katherine eyed it with misgivings. She had no intention of repeating her previous *faux pas*. She considered it an error of taste to indulge oneself in the wild music she adored. Rather she would play the acceptable. Nodding obediently, she crossed and seated herself before the keyboard.

The Bach hymn she had played before rolled forth with magnificent pomp. Other equally polite music followed, the sort no one might take exception to in the least.

'You play for others, but not for yourself this evening, is that it?' Lord Ramsey queried in that soft rich tone he used when trying not to be overheard.

Katherine flashed him a look of feigned surprise. 'I seldom have the luxury of playing for myself, sir.' She glanced at her father and Mrs Cheney. Cousin Sophia she discounted, as that lady approved the uninhibited sound that flowed when Katherine played her own music. Said it reminded her of the ocean.

'I see.' He considered her a moment, then assisted her from the piano when she concluded a final piece. To Cousin Sophia, he remarked, 'I want to show Katherine what I have done toward our joint effort.' The look he gave her was significant, and since Cousin

Sophia was anything but a slow-top, she merely smiled and nodded.

Unwilling to interrupt her father and Gisela, who sat in what appeared to be harmonious conversation, Katherine left the room with Lord Ramsey.

Minutes later found them entering the theater. They walked along toward the stage. Light from the branch of candles in Lord Ramsey's hand sent flickering shadows dancing over the murals, making the figures on the walls seem almost alive.

Katherine shivered. Her thin muslin, which had seemed quite appropriate for a dinner at Fairfax Hall, was not the proper item for prowling about the deserted theater.

'Here, hold the candles while I find you a shawl. I know there is one around here somewhere. Since we managed to stave off a cold, it would be the height of foolishness to risk it again.'

Katherine accepted the candelabrum, standing where he pointed while he hunted about in a large box. He fished out a lovely length of heavy silk and draped it about her shoulders with a flourish.

'Thank you,' murmured a subdued Katherine.

He gave her a dissatisfied look, then crossed the stage to the wings. Katherine watched him, mystified by his silence.

In moments a creaking sound like that of a wheel being turned accompanied the appearance of the first scene, the woodland where the fair Belinda was to be attracted to, then abducted by, the villain. It was astonishingly simple in execution, yet effective for all that.

'You see, the actors can be at the side, yet not seen by the audience until the right moment.'

'What a splendid invention, sir. Far better than any I have seen in all these years. But,' she wondered, 'can this be set up in the crude theater at the fair? We shan't have the facilities there that you have here.'

'Not to worry. My head carpenter feels he can manage the matter with no problem.'

'How much does he know?' She gave him a suspicious look, hoping this escapade was not to filter through the town and thus reach her father's ears in time for him to put a stop to it.

'He knows to keep his tongue between his teeth. He values his job far too much to be a gabble-monger.'

'I would never have you turn him off because of this.'

He gave her an exasperated look. 'You cannot have it both ways, Katherine. If you are a bit soft, they will take advantage of you.'

'I expect you are right,' she muttered, her

150

face downcast while she felt rather stupid. Fancy telling his lordship how to manage his estate.

He crossed to her side in moments, tilting her chin up and looking into her eyes as revealed in the flickering light. He took the candelabrum from her and set it on a nearby table. 'Katherine . . . '

There was promise in that whisper. She searched his eyes, for what she didn't know. They were shadowed and she could tell little from what she could make out. But it was something that made her heart beat far too fast and her palms feel clammy. How lovely to hear her name on his lips once again.

He touched her mouth with his, a much-too-fleeting yet warm touch that revealed a hint of the promise in his words. Katherine felt bereft when he drew back to look at her. She felt his hands clasp her shoulders, pulling her toward him. Was this what she wanted? Would his opinion of her be confirmed? She remembered that gleam in his eyes when he had interrupted her dressing the day of the rain.

'Philip?' She wanted to feel his arms about her, she realized with a shock. Most of all, she desired the touch of his mouth again, and this time for not so brief a spell.

'Well,' came the matter-of-fact voice of

Cousin Sophia as she advanced upon the stage.

Katherine listened to the faint curse that escaped from Philip and wondered what might have happened had Cousin Sophia not taken it upon herself to follow them. Why had she waited so long? And why enter just now?

'Are you testing the scenery to discover if it will add to the mood?' The older woman clambered up on the stage with surprising agility. 'I should say you have done very well. 'Tis a spot conducive to young love, I vow.' She looked about her at the woodland set, then wandered back to where the wheel that worked the scenery was located. 'Hmm, this is a fancy bit of invention.'

'Your Cousin Sophia is an amazing woman.' Philip's comment was spoken in a not-altogether-complimentary tone.

'Yes, she is. I can only be grateful that she undertakes to look after me when she would rather be elsewhere. I suspect I must find myself a home one of these days so she can be free of me.'

'A home?' He gave her a startled look, then turned to study Cousin Sophia. 'Is there someone in mind?' He would know Katherine could not set up her own establishment. 'Or do you intend to put on a cap and do for your father?'

'I am not past praying for, sir. There are difficulties, you see,' she snapped back, just as though Mr Weekes had spoken with her and the details remained to be ironed out between her father and the fellow.

Lord Ramsey's laugh disconcerted her. She flounced to the stairs, marching down them with firm steps.

'You approve of the scenery, I take it,' he said with a mocking bow.

Katherine refused to be outdone by him. She curtsied low and elegantly. 'Was there any doubt, sir? I feel certain you have solved all problems. Your sketches are splendid. What more can I say?' She waited, hands on her hips, feeling like the shrew he once thought her to be.

He sauntered toward the edge of the stage to where the equipment for raising and lowering the oil lamps used to illumine the stage was housed. Neatly avoiding the footlight board, he bowed to her. 'Such flattery, my dear Katherine. If only your actors can do the scenery justice, I shall be happy.'

Caught up short, Katherine became sober, dropping her hands and advancing to where he stood above her. 'About the actors. It will not be long before they must rehearse together, both my play and the comedy. May

153

we continue to use this stage?' She waited for him to blast her for her impudence.

'All of them?' He laughed. 'By all means. Bring the lot when next you come. The weeks are short and I would see them know their parts well.' He jumped from the stage, apparently forgetting about Cousin Sophia, who was still pottering about the rear of the stage behind them.

'Fine,' Katherine murmured, relieved he would make no fuss, although she could simply not understand why he grinned at her in that odious manner.

'I wonder if your brother is having any success in luring the lovely Miss O'Neill to our production.' He spoke in that odd drawl she had heard before, one she didn't like in the least.

'It depends,' Katherine replied with spirit, 'on how much money he can dangle before her. There are some women who regard that as prime motivation.'

'And how do you feel, my lovely Kate?' Philip advanced upon her again, his hand reaching out to lightly caress her cheek.

'Money?' She trembled at his touch. 'It helps to provide food and a roof over one's head, does it not?' Deciding it was time she be practical, she turned away from him and walked toward the door. 'Coming, Cousin

154

Sophia?' Philip could see to the candles.

At the door, she waited for her chaperone to join her. Sophia clumped down the stairs and marched up the aisle to where Katherine stood in silence, trying not to watch Lord Ramsey.

'Thought I'd see if you needed me. You did,' Cousin Sophia said as they walked through the hall.

'What are Mrs Cheney and Papa thinking by now?' The dismay she felt rang in her voice.

'They were deep in a discussion about Jonah when I left. I suspected I'd not be missed.'

Philip caught up with them as they entered the small drawing room, taking note of the pleasant picture his sister made with the older gentleman. She was animated, flushed with pleasure, and quite obviously having the time of her life.

'It is late, Papa. We had best head for home,' reminded Katherine gently, for she hated to interrupt this agreeable conversation after all that had happened.

'We can talk again, madam,' Mr Penn said, bowing nicely to his hostess. 'I confess I have enjoyed myself prodigiously, in spite of our few disagreements.'

Katherine exchanged a worried look, first

155

with Cousin Sophia, then with Philip.

'Well, I expect it is rather unusual for a woman to presume to argue with so learned a gentleman.' Gisela glanced up at Mr Penn, fluttering her eyelashes in a demure manner.

'You will come again to use the library?' Lord Ramsey inquired in his more lofty way.

'I should be delighted.' Mr Penn looked as though he were contemplating something quite different than dusty tomes, however.

Cousin Sophia tugged at his arm, drawing Mr Penn toward the entrance hall. Katherine followed. She handed the borrowed shawl to Philip, along with a provocative look.

Kendall assisted Katherine into her pelisse. Within a very few minutes the three Penns were back in the carriage and on their way home, farewells floating on the cool August evening air.

★ ★ ★

Far off in Norwich young Theodore Penn relaxed at the White Swan. He had found it was where the Norwich Company had established their headquarters, and it had proven a most convenient place to get access to Miss O'Neill while the company paused here on their tour.

Not that he did more than speak with her.

Her dragon of a father constantly hovered about her, never allowing her a moment to herself, it seemed. It was dashed odd. For Teddy had heard all these stories about actresses, how free and easy they were with their favors. Miss O'Neill was as prim and proper as a dowager duchess of the *ton*.

However, to listen to the actors reciting their lines, arguing over interpretations, was first-rate entertainment, a heady experience for him. He strolled about, watching the scenes being painted, flats refurbished for the coming productions. The company would also set up during Sturbridge Fair in competition with Teddy.

Of course, he remained quiet about his intentions as best he might. He found it distinctly interesting to discover what the opposition expected to offer. He had heard that Miss O'Neill was to earn a prodigious amount per week at Covent Garden the coming season when she parted ways with the Norwich Company.

London actors viewed the freedom offered during the fair with enthusiasm. For the provincial players it provided attractions they seldom experienced in any other of the circuit towns they traveled through.

Teddy hoped Miss O'Neill — and her father — could be persuaded to join his effort. It might take another day or two, for it proved dashed slow work. But he reflected he had never had so wondrous a time in his life, and he didn't mind the delay at all. If only he succeeded.

8

'You are a silly goose, Gabriel,' Katherine sang to her pet the following morning. It was a beautiful day and she felt wonderful. Wisps of clouds brushed across the cerulean sky. In the garden the apricot tree espaliered against the brick wall drooped, weighted with fruit. Soon she must pick it and help Cook to preserve it for the winter. Gabriel left off nibbling at the weeds among the annuals and waddled close to where Katherine sat at the edge of her flower bed.

Across the river Katherine could see masses of goldenrod and hare bells, meadow-sweet, and tall spikes of purple loosestrife. She thought nature's garden superior to her own efforts. But, then, she had Gabriel to assist in her work, which was definitely a mixed blessing.

She permitted the goose to place his head on her lap, a rare sign of affection. He settled down and Katherine continued to gaze at the scene across the river while her thoughts took her elsewhere.

Several days had passed since the dinner at Fairfax Hall. Her father had resumed his visits, although somewhat curtailed in length. He never mentioned what he did, but Katherine was satisfied that he went.

She continued rehearsing with Ninian Denham, assuming the role of Belinda in place of Miss O'Neill. Of Philip, little was seen. He had popped in to watch Katherine in a scene with Mr Denham, then left. He gave no clue to his feelings, his face a bland mask, she thought with asperity. Odious man. In the ensuing days she had not forgotten for an hour the feelings he stirred in her. How it shook her to realize that she was so susceptible to a kiss.

The arrival of her brother so early in the morning was a surprise.

'Teddy, you are up betimes this morn.' She shifted, thus disturbing Gabriel, who took off in a huff.

'Dash it all, Kitty, good days like this are few at this time of year. Lord Ramsey has invited me out to see the progress he is making with the flats. He has a design for the theater booth as well.' Teddy leaned up against the copper beech, watching as Katherine weeded her bed of annuals, now in full bloom.

'Thank goodness you managed to convince Miss O'Neill to perform with us. We shall need the money to compensate Lord Ramsey for all he does. Or ought I say his head carpenter?' she added with a touch of irony.

''Tis Ramsey who is the brains. He's devilishly clever, Kitty. Think of all the devices he has dreamed up for our production. Let me tell you, the Norwich Company would like to get their hands on what he's done. Clever, clever man.'

'I am sure you are right,' she murmured, thinking his lordship was too clever for his own good. Katherine managed to contain the annoyance she felt. She had not been invited to view the flats, nor anything else, for that matter. The woodland set still stood in place on the stage where they practiced. She wondered about the sumptuous scenery for the final act, where the hero would climb through the window to rescue the hapless Belinda. Good grief, but that character was a widgeon. Katherine could only hope that Miss O'Neill could breathe some sympathy into her.

'He is that pleased we are to have Miss O'Neill. Did you know that she was given five hundred pounds' worth of diamonds after her last season in London? These few months with the Norwich Company will be her last, I expect. She ought to go on to higher and better things.'

'With her dragon of a father as well?'

Katherine had been amused at the story of Eliza O'Neill and her protective father. Katherine was not so green that she hadn't heard tales about actresses and their gentlemen friends.

'I think he has some maggoty notion of splicing her to a peer. As if anyone connected to the theater would have such a chance,' Teddy scoffed.

Katherine nodded her agreement, rather bleakly, had Teddy taken notice. He didn't. Instead, he straightened and sauntered toward the gate, saying, 'I will toddle on now. Must check on those costumes again. That Mrs Cheney is a great gun, Kitty.'

'That she is,' Katherine replied, although she doubted her brother heard her, for he was already through the gate and most likely setting off toward Fairfax Hall by now.

The gate remained ajar because Amelia Bonner had passed Teddy and decided to pay her respects to Katherine.

'Such a lovely day, is it not?' Amelia inquired in her high, fluting voice. She drifted across the grass to stand at Katherine's side, her newest walking dress of pale-blue India mull displayed to advantage in the soft afternoon sun.

Katherine stiffened, then rose, brushing down her skirt as best she could after removing her gardening gloves. 'How nice to see you. Fine weather for a walk.' She stayed where she was, not wanting to bring Mely into the house on a Saturday when the cleaning was in progress.

'Does your father preach at the Fairfax church on the morrow?'

Not really surprised at the question, Katherine nodded. 'He has been asked to fill the pulpit again. The need is still there.'

To say that Amelia was surprised was mild. She provoked Katherine, even as she admitted Mely had reason to feel as she did.

'I should think Lord Ramsey might have any person he wished to speak there.'

Katherine smiled, nodding graciously at her longtime friend and combatant. 'You are absolutely correct.'

This left Amelia with little more to say on that subject. 'I shall attend chapel tomorrow. They have a shorter service, no sermon, and good music.' There were usually a large number of handsome young men there as well.

Katherine made no reply to this teaser, so Mely launched into a series of bits and scraps of gossip while Katherine reflected that Mely was wasted on Cambridge. She ought to be in London with the *ton* at her disposal. What a hash she would make of that elite group in a trice.

'How do matters proceed at the hall?' Mely whispered, looking about her as though a spy might be lurking in the shrubbery.

'Well enough. I have heard them read their lines and can but pray all will be well. The man who plays the evil count is an impossible nodcock. I hope that Teddy will cope with him before the fourteenth of September, when we are to open.' The words made her shiver with dread of that event.

'It is not long, is it,' Amelia replied brightly. 'You sound as though you wish us ill, Mely.'

'Never,' replied that young woman judiciously. 'I only hope you understand what a revelation of this rather scandalous undertaking will do your chances of being Mrs You-know-who.' She bestowed a virtuous look on Katherine, then took leave of her, much to Katherine's relief. Mely in long doses was too much for a body to survive right now.

How lowering to her spirits to realize that Mely was undoubtedly right. Mr Weekes would look elsewhere for a bride, someone who could bring money, name, and spotless reputation to him. Neither could she dream of an alliance with Lord Ramsey. He was of higher birth, greater wealth, and could well manage to find a young lady of unexceptional background. Of course, he might offer Katherine a slip on the shoulder. This thought so enraged her that she pulled up a marigold before she realized what she was doing.

Disgusted with her stupidity, she tossed the weeds and the lone marigold away, then entered the house after picking a few flowers. Mrs Moore and the daily maid had the place as neat as a pin. Katherine sought a vase, then arranged the hastily chosen bouquet of daisies and China asters she had selected.

'Katherine, love, do you recognize that young man in front of the house?' Cousin Sophia inquired in puzzled accents. 'I vow, there is something familiar about him, but I cannot place it at the moment.'

She peered around the sheer curtain in the front room to where a gentleman of fashionable dress and elegant manner paid the driver of a hackney. Katherine hurriedly joined her, disapproving of the act even as she looked.

The horse that pulled the hackney was a retired Newmarket racehorse, and the poor animal looked as though he would rather be anywhere else but before the vehicle, even if it gleamed with polishing. He stood impatiently as a small mountain of luggage was removed from the boot and stacked awaiting a servant.

Then the visitor turned and Katherine gasped. Here was the handsome count of her play. He looked angelically beautiful, yet capable of intrigue. Evidently of the dandy persuasion, he dressed in the height of fashion, his hat tilted at the precise angle, the proper number of fobs dangling below his elegant waistcoat. Oh, he certainly didn't belong at the Penn house.

'He must have the wrong address,' Katherine said, giving voice to her thoughts.

'I feel certain I know someone who strongly resembles him. Let me think,' Cousin Sophia insisted while Katherine left the window and crossed to the hall.

Mrs Moore ushered in the young man and sent someone to fetch his baggage. She brought him down the hall to where Katherine stood waiting.

'Mr Exton to see you, Miss Penn.' Mrs Moore flashed a curious look at the new-comer, then disappeared, aware she would find out his identity eventually. Little went on in the house that the servants didn't know right away, if not beforehand.

'Sidney Exton at your service. I am charmed to meet my Cousin Katherine at last. I have heard much of you from our great-aunt, Harriette Winstanley.' Hat held behind him, he bowed over Katherine's hand

with what she fondly considered an irresistible manner.

Enchanted with his address, not to
mention his appearance, Katherine decided
she had been mistaken about him. Oh, he
might have the requisite looks for the count,
but he was far too nice for the evil business.
She smiled and bobbed a polite curtsy.

'Please join me in the drawing room. Shall
I send for Papa?' She led the way into the
room, gesturing toward the sofa, while she
took a chair close by.

'Do not disturb him, I pray. I know he
must be a very busy gentleman in his high
position at the college.'

Much in charity with the visitor, Katherine
set about making him welcome. Cousin
Sophia entered and Katherine introduced
her. She merely nodded graciously, all the
while studying Mr Exton with a keen gaze.

'Cousin Sidney is from London,' Katherine
explained to Cousin Sophia.

'Came up here to rusticate, did you?'
Cousin Sophia inquired in a less-than-warm
tone.

Seeming amused by the older lady, Sidney
Exton smiled, shaking his head. 'Not at all.
I've never been to Cambridge, being an
Oxford man myself. Thought it my duty to
look up my relatives. There are precious few

of us left, on my side of the family at least.' He gave Katherine an inquiring look.

She felt obliged to explain. 'There is Teddy — that is, my brother, Theodore — and myself. And Papa, of course. Cousin Sophia is residing with us until I marry.'

He looked gratifyingly alarmed at this news. 'I am desolate to think you might be lost to me now that I have found you, dear cousin.' One of his dark curls flopped over his noble brow in a charming way, making Katherine's heart flutter a bit. While it might be true that Mr Exton was shorter than Lord Ramsey, he was infinitely more eligible. And his eyes were not as close-set as Mr Weekes's either.

'Oh, that day is far enough away,' Cousin Sophia declared bluntly.

Katherine thought that the dear lady did not have to make it sound quite such an implausible happening. She turned to their newly discovered relative and said, 'I am not without gentlemen friends, you see. One must be selective.'

Cousin Sophia gave a snort of disdain for that nonsense, leaving Katherine longing to box someone's ears.

'I hope it is not inconvenient for me to visit with you at this time?' Cousin Sidney looked politely anxious.

That explained all the baggage that Katherine had seen piled outside. 'Why, no, I suppose not.' Lest her welcome seem cool, she smiled encouragingly at Mr Exton while she tried to recall if her father had invited anyone to visit during the coming days.

'I thought I might stay for the fair. 'Tis only a few weeks away, is it not?' Mr Exton looked first at Katherine, then at Cousin Sophia for confirmation of what any ninny ought to have known.

Katherine gave a faint frown. If this new cousin was installed in the house, there was little she might do to keep her secret. She glanced at Cousin Sophia, believing she saw a similar concern on that lady's face. 'I do not think it will be a problem.' Inspiration struck. 'However, I am busy helping Mrs Cheney of Fairfax Hall with a project that requires a great deal of my time. And Teddy is on the go every minute, it seems. He is still an undergraduate, you know, due to get his degree before long. And we never know when our dear father may come home with a surprise guest. So you are welcome to stay with us, but I fear we cannot extend our customary hospitality at this moment. I feel sure you will understand.'

'Merely look upon it as sharing with the family,' Cousin Sophia added dryly.

'I should like that above all things.' The look he sent Katherine from his hazel eyes was enough to make any female feel desirable and pretty. Katherine glowed.

'Why, Katherine, you naughty girl. You did never say a word about having such elegant company coming.' Miss Amelia Bonner entered the room in a flurry of trailing ribbons, not to mention eyelashes aflutter over her pretty blue eyes.

'Miss Amelia Bonner, Mr Sidney Exton, up from London.'

Sidney rose and bowed over Mely's hand with the aplomb of a diplomat. Katherine believed that his attention to herself had been considerably nicer.

'London,' breathed Miss Bonner as though Katherine had just said Cathay. Her curtsy was a perfection of demure propriety combined with charming flirtation.

Katherine wished she could manage it as well. Mely's coquetry might earn her a bit of civility from Mr Exton, but if she thought she was going to walk off with Katherine's prize guest right under her nose, she had another think coming.

'My cousin is to spend the coming weeks with us, until the fair. Is that not lovely?'

Amelia gave Mr Exton a predatory, rather feline glance. Katherine gave her a bland smile. Never mind that Lord Ramsey put this new cousin in the shade without half trying. Katherine needed someone to boost her wounded vanity and Mr Exton looked the perfect one to help.

He performed the task admirably. Smiling fondly in Katherine's direction, he then turned to Mely with a polite face. 'I will wish to spend as much time with my cousin as possible, Miss Bonner.'

Belatedly Katherine remembered her play. Drat it all, she was going to have to foist her new cousin on Mely, after all. And she knew that young lady would make the utmost of the situation. Still, Katherine consoled herself that Mr Exton had wanted to spend time with her first.

Heroically Katherine sighed. 'I cannot believe I near forgot Mrs Cheney and the work we do. Perhaps I may rely upon you, dearest Amelia, to show my cousin a few of the sights about town?'

'The Bridge of Sighs?' Mely smiled at Mr Exton, a dreamy sort of smile that usually turned every male in sight into blancmange. 'And a lovely walk along the river? And you will want to view the Round Chapel, of course.'

Mr Exton looked rather dazed at this turn of events. He cast a bewildered glance at

Katherine, who gazed helplessly back at him.

'There is precious little that Miss Bonner does not know about our town.' Katherine thought of all the gossip that could trip off Mely's tongue, including the business about Katherine's play, and she clenched her teeth. If Sidney Exton was at all inclined toward tittle-tattle, he would get his ears filled from dear Amelia's sweet lips without trying.

'I say, Kitty, Ramsey has the greatest new idea . . . ' Teddy came to a fast halt inside the drawing-room door. His eyes grew wide at the stranger seated on the sofa with both his sister and Amelia Bonner looking like two cats about to pounce on the same mouse.

'Cousin Bertrand is your father, I believe,' Cousin Sophia declared abruptly. 'Actually he is a second cousin. He was the Penn who went heavily into the Exchange, did he not? Lost a fortune, as I recall. Down in the hatches, are you, my lad?' She tilted her head as she studied the faintly flushed countenance of the young man across from her. 'Could happen to any one, I expect. We are none of us free of the danger of improvident parents.' She glanced benignly at Amelia Bonner when she said this, and Katherine was required to clear her throat of an unexpected obstruction.

Embarrassed by her relative's possibly wounding remark, Katherine tried to smooth things over. 'When we are free, we shall be pleased to escort you about. Theodore, our cousin, Mr Sidney Exton, has come to visit with us for a few weeks. I told him that I am unfortunately occupied with assisting Mrs Cheney at Fairfax Hall. And you, poor dear, are up to your ears in lectures and what not. Amelia will help us out, though. Will you not, Mely?' Katherine hoped that that widgeon caught the threat in Katherine's voice and paid heed to it.

'Do you attend divine services with the family tomorrow, Mr Exton?' Mely said, her blue eyes flashing coyly and far too flirtatiously at him. 'Mr Penn is such an articulate speaker. You will be simply awed.'

Katherine exchanged grim looks with her brother.

'I should think we would be gudgeons were we to permit him to be on his own. Sunday is a dashed dull day in Cambridge, y'know,' Teddy inserted helplessly. 'Besides, we are invited to stay on after services.'

Wishing she might have the privilege of kicking her brother on the ankle or any other available spot, Katherine clenched her teeth while hoping that Amelia Bonner did not have the crust to intrude upon what was, after all, an invitation not extended to her.

Amelia tilted her head, rising from her

chair with a show of reluctance. Her fifteen minutes, the time allotted for a social call, were up. 'I shall go to chapel tomorrow. But perhaps later . . . ' She curtsied to them all in a very pretty manner.

Teddy elected to escort her to the front door.

Katherine devoutly hoped that her brother redeemed himself by reminding Mely of the bargain she had made.

★   ★   ★

If Mr Penn was astonished by the arrival of a nephew he could not in the least recall, it was not evident in his manner. He was all graciousness, even as he assured Katherine and Theodore that he would welcome the visit to Fairfax Hall on the morrow following divine services.

Katherine hoped for the best and prayed the worst would not occur. Perhaps Mrs Cheney would approve of Papa's sermon. And the fish in the river might fly by then as well, Katherine reflected.

Cousin Sophia took her aside following dinner, while the gentlemen remained at the dining table to exchange stories and sip the excellent port Julian Penn had stored up. 'What shall you do?'

'I do not know for sure. He could not show up at a worse time,' Katherine cried softly in vexation. Another month and she would have been free to do as she pleased, without the play to worry about. 'I should not like him bearing tales back to Aunt Harriette. Although I have never met the lady, I have quite enjoyed her letters over the years. She has a delightful wit.' Not to mention wicked. Katherine had always managed to conceal those letters from the rest of the family.

'Hm.' Cousin Sophia seemed to be searching her brain for something. 'We had best keep him occupied. When you must go to the hall, I shall take him about. If that Amelia Bonner shows up, I shall make a point to be along. Anything to further your cause, dear girl.'

The look of astonishment on Katherine's face delighted Cousin Sophia, for she chuckled heartily. 'I know full well what was going on in your mind. I merely thought to dampen the sugar a bit, you see. It would never do to make him think we pushed you at his head.'

'Of course not,' Katherine murmured, agreeing completely with that notion. 'Tomorrow will be a test of sorts. Good heavens,' she suddenly declared. 'He will be with us at the hall. I had best warn Lord Ramsey and Mrs

Cheney.' Katherine always referred to them by their correct titles to others, even though she had been invited to be more informal. It had never seemed proper to her to be so familiar. It seemed to her that Philip was a good deal inclined to levity and failed to bestow his position with proper consequence. Then, as she turned from Cousin Sophia and crossed to the sofa, she realized she had been thinking about Lord Ramsey as Philip for several days now. It would never do, of course. But there appeared little harm in it as long as she contained her foolish daydreams to herself.

Katherine ought to have known that Cousin Sidney would fade in comparison once he got near the elegance of Lord Ramsey. When the two met just before services the next day, she could see immediately that Sidney's collar points were too high, that that clever nip in his waist was a bit too much, and that his manners, which she had thought so nice today, were overly unctuous. He simply could not hold a candle to Philip. Drat it all, anyway.

Nonetheless, Katherine bestowed a sugary smile on Lord Ramsey while clinging to Cousin Sidney's arm for dear life.

'You must join us after services, Mr Exton,' Gisela said in a cordial manner while she glanced from him to Katherine and back again.

Remembering the need to caution Lord Ramsey, Katherine managed to get next to him as they strolled into the pretty little church. While Sidney paused to admire the perfectly splendid monument to one of the Fairfax ancestors, she whispered to Lord Ramsey to exercise all care when around Sidney. She wanted no more complications and certainly no talebearing.

'Dear girl, what do you take me for? A flat? I am well aware of the need for secrecy. How shall you manage with him under your nose . . . so to speak?'

'I do not know,' she confessed. 'Why did he have to turn up now?' she murmured, thus ruining her pretense of a flirtation.

Lord Ramsey beamed a smile at her that shook her to her toes.

Then the organ began to play and they all took their seats. Katherine braced herself when her father rose to speak. She was delightfully surprised when he addressed the small congregation more like friends, or at least like people he had met once or twice. His message was simple and appeared straight from the heart. Cousin Sophia stayed awake, listening with all evidence of amazement.

Following the service, they waited for Mr Penn to join them. Gisela looked exceedingly smug and Katherine said so. Or at least she implied it to her.

'I have had a word or two with your father this past week. He did very well, did he not?' Gisela resembled nothing so much as a proud mother.

Cousin Sophia poked Katherine in the back, whereupon Katherine closed her mouth. She gave the older lady an indignant glance, but Sophia was all innocence.

The small group strolled across the beautiful lawns up to the hall, where Kendall appeared to open the doors for them. Katherine marveled that he didn't seem out of breath, which, considering he must have run all the way up from church to get there ahead of them, was amazing.

Gisela took charge of things. 'Come all, let us go to the saloon while we await our dinner,' She drifted across the entrance hall after leaving her shawl with Kendall. She beckoned to Sidney Exton and the flattered young man scurried after her.

'Well, how does it go on so far?' Lord Ramsay asked.

Katherine watched Gisela charm Sidney right out of his boots, and she tried to veil her annoyance. Was every other woman in the world more able to weave a spell than herself?

Recalling the question, she shrugged slightly. 'He has the second-best bedroom and seems annoyed there is no footman to wait upon his requests. I gather he manages well enough without a valet, although I would have sworn he was accustomed to the services of one,' she said, narrowing her eyes as she studied her cousin.

'And?' he prodded.

'I arranged for Mely to show him about town. I wish I could see them when she takes him to King's College Chapel. She knows every eligible young man in town and there ought to be a veritable crush when they espy her, escort or no escort.' Katherine chuckled at the very notion of the scene.

'What are his interests?'

At this query Katherine frowned. 'Do you know, I have no idea. So far he has made a point of fawning over my hand and smiling at me. Poor Teddy gets scant attention.'

Lord Ramsey grinned at Katherine and she felt all soft and warm inside for at least one full minute.

'He is playing it close to the chest, I see. Do you believe his talk about coming because he wants to get acquainted with his newly discovered cousin?'

'Well,' she said consideringly, 'he did say

that he had heard all about me from Aunt Harriette, and that sounds a plumper, for she never mentioned him to me. Yet Cousin Sophia claims he looks just like his father, the one who lost so much money on the Exchange.'

'I still cannot believe you are the daughter of an esteemed doctor of divinity,' he mused softly, although Katherine heard him quite plainly, standing as close as they were now.

'It is the lack of a mother, or so Cousin Sophia declares. Have pity on me and help me think of something.'

'If worse comes to worst you shall have to tell him the truth and swear him to secrecy.'

'Like Mely? Heaven help us.'

9

The view out toward the Gothic Tower had never been lovelier, Katherine decided. Strolling across the saloon, she left the dangerously tempting company of Lord Ramsey to stand by herself for a moment. After one of his wicked little conversations, she felt the need for restoration. Alas, her ploy did not succeed. He followed her.

'You seem drawn to the scene of your crime. Tell me, how is your pet, er — Gabriel, is it not?' The bland voice held that curious tone once again, and it got Katherine's back up. Teasing her, was he?

When Katherine turned her head, mildly exasperated that she couldn't flee his presence, she found herself trapped by his eyes, those warm gray pools of silver. 'It was never a crime, precisely,' she corrected. 'I felt quite certain you would not mind if I picked a few wildflowers that were destined to die shortly anyway. It is not as though I was pilfering from a prize garden.' She sniffed, then added, 'Gabriel is in fine fettle and a more troublesome pet I could not imagine. Unless it was a bird that persisted in molting forever and a day.'

She discovered a silly urge to giggle when she espied that mischievous look in those eyes of his. What a scandalously insouciant man he was, at least most of the time. Never would she become accustomed to that wicked streak in a man after the solemn and rather dull sort of gentlemen she encountered at home and at the college. Yet it might be an intriguing area to explore.

'When do you bring the remainder of the cast out to begin their joint rehearsal? I cannot like your spending so much time alone with Mr Denham, with only your aunt for a companion.' Those eyes cooled abruptly and his beautiful mouth firmed with his resolution.

Angry at his assumptions, yet mindful of the need to appease the sponsor of the production, who, after all, had a right to make comments, she said, 'I cannot for the life of me think why anything Mr Denham does ought to disturb you. He is a gentleman at all times. And,' she continued, 'there is no earthly reason for you to keep popping in every few minutes to see how we go on. It quite destroys the mood, if you must know.'

'And what mood is that, pray tell?' There was an oily smoothness to this question that ought to have cautioned her.

Katherine ignored that dangerous note in his voice. She had grown accustomed to it these past days, for it seemed to creep in rather often. 'Well, the hero is supposed to be in love with Belinda. It is utterly distracting when Mr Denham is trying to wax poetic over my limp hand and then you interrupt.'

'Over your limp hand? Why is your hand limp?'

He was merely curious now, she noted, relieved and yet piqued. Without giving a great deal of thought to her reply, Katherine said, 'Because it is the greatest rubbish in the world, all those silly words I wrote for the hero to gush at poor Belinda,' she replied with her usual honesty.

'Rubbish?' Had she kept her gaze fastened upon Lord Ramsey, Katherine would have observed that sparkle return to his eyes once again.

Having returned her attention to the Gothic Tower, she nodded, 'Rubbish. A woman would be foolish beyond permission to accept that spurious lovemaking for more than what it is, which is utter nonsense. I scarce have patience with the silly geese.'

'You do not find the words of love to be appealing? How do you think a woman ought to be wooed in that case?'

'Oh,' she replied, not meeting his gaze,

'flowery effusions are meaningless. It is what is done that truly matters. If a gentleman feels great affection for a lady, he ought to demonstrate it with actions, not mere words. A kiss on the hand offers little by way of consolation.'

'I must remember that,' he murmured.

At least Katherine thought that was what he said, for his words were faint as he turned to greet Sidney Exton. She was left to mull over her unguarded conversation with Philip, scolding herself for allowing him to draw her out on the subject. He had the oddest ability to lure Katherine to speak her mind without due caution. She glanced across the room to where Cousin Sophia watched. The older lady wore a contented, if doting, smile.

Gisela motioned Katherine to her side. 'Philip tells me he has gone out to the fair site to inspect the location for the theater booth. It is a generous space on Cheese Row just off Garlic Row. Does that meet with your approval?' Her voice was soft but clear.

'Actually it is quite good.' Katherine smiled in what she hoped was a reassuring manner. It annoyed her that Lord Ramsey must make these arrangements even as she knew full well that she could not, for it would surely reveal her involvement. In a town the size of Cambridge, the news would be abroad in hours.

'I trust my little Katherine is proving to be a help in your project for the poor children, Mrs Cheney,' Julian Penn said as he joined the two women where they stood near the fireplace.

For a moment both looked blank. Then Gisela smiled, nodded graciously. 'I believe we shall have the plans for the school well in hand by the time we are done. Of course my brother will design a building for the school. It remains for us to find a teacher.'

Recalling what Philip had said, Katherine inserted, 'One who is biddable and yet able to handle young people well, I fancy.'

'Indeed,' Gisela replied with a whimsical expression entering her eyes as she glanced toward Katherine.

Lest she succumb to a serious case of the whoops, Katherine turned the subject to the weather, always a safe topic, and extricated Gisela and herself from dangerous waters.

When it came time for the Sunday dinner usually served at Fairfax Hall following divine services, Katherine was surprised to find Mr Exton — or Cousin Sidney, as he insisted she call him — at her elbow.

'I claim your company, dear cousin,' he said with warm civility.

He turned to Lord Ramsey with a nice deference, adding, 'It is a pleasant thing to discover I have so attractive a relative, sir. We are fast becoming close, er, friends.' Sidney beamed a proprietary smile at her.

Katherine flashed an amused look at Sidney, thinking how far he seemed from her first image of him as the evil count. He was a harmless fribble, even if he persisted in flattering her with attentions she was not quite certain she wished. How quickly she had revised her initial perception of him, particularly after comparing him with Lord Ramsey.

'Indeed, Cousin Sidney is all that is gallant,' she responded to his kind words. She was aware that as a tribute it was questionable, for if she truly felt him worthy, she would have referred to him as civil — or, at the very least, amiable. Even if he weren't aware of the subtle distinctions in manners, she most definitely was. She suspected that Lord Ramsey was too, when she caught sight of that naughty gleam in his eyes.

They moved on into the dining room, where Katherine found herself seated between Sidney and Philip. His lordship was being his usual self-confident, yet easygoing self. She marveled that he could at once be modest, well-mannered, and considerate, while at the same time managing to make Sidney look the veriest dullard. She suspected Cousin

Sidney was a bit of a snob.

How fortunate that she had worn her nicest Sunday gown of soft lilac satin with long sleeves that gathered at the armholes and tied into divisions with pretty ribands. It made her feel graceful. She also knew the rows and rows of tucks above the hem to be the very latest thing from the fashion journals she had seen in Gisela's room when they had searched for a style best suited to Katherine's short hair. There was nothing like looking one's finest to aid in coping with a pair of males who seemed about to — politely — clash.

During the soup course she listened to the men debate the merits of Oxford versus Cambridge in the most partisan of terms. While she nibbled on oyster patties and brill with a delicate lobster sauce she heard the virtues of country life as opposed to London delights debated with languid but deceptive thrust and counter. His lordship was a trifle condescending, she thought. Yet Sidney tried. And failed, she admitted as she heard him flounder in his arguments.

Sidney's manners might be gentlemanlike, but they were by no means winning, she decided. However, she was not about to let Philip know that she felt thus. He might be of the first consequence, but that was no reason to dally with Sidney as though he were a mere nobody. Which he was, she reflected with rueful honesty.

Why had Aunt Harriette never mentioned him in her many letters? That was a question that plagued Katherine in the back of her mind throughout the remainder of the dinner even as she listened to the conversation. With no effort upon her part it went on beneath her nose like a game of battledore and shuttlecock.

'You are coming out tomorrow, are you not?' inquired Philip as they sampled the partridge and salad, mutton, beetroot, and potatoes placed before them.

Knowing he wanted to discuss the allocation of costumes and meet the other characters, Katherine nodded, her mouth being partially full of salad at the moment.

'What is it you do here, cousin?' inserted Sidney, his voice striking Katherine as a trifle suspicious.

'We are planning a school,' Katherine said, just as Lord Ramsey declared, 'Assisting me with my family history.'

'Actually, I do a bit of both,' Katherine amended after glaring at Lord Ramsey.

'Both?' It was plain that Mr Exton was now more than a bit suspicious. He turned his head to study Katherine as the plates were removed and the next course brought on.

Katherine stared at the pears and whipped cream with an absorbed gaze. 'My, does this not look utterly delicious.' Her enthusiasm sounded a bit strained, but she could only pray that Sidney dropped the subject like he ought, given his attempt to act the London gentleman.

'I am pleased you are enjoying your meal, Miss Penn,' Lord Ramsey said with that deceptive smoothness Katherine had learned to accept with prudent caution. Turning his attention back to Sidney, he added, 'It is gratifying to see a young woman who enjoys her food rather than nibbles.'

Her spoon clattered on her dish after the last bite of pear had been popped into her mouth. The morsel sank to her stomach like a stone as she fastened a politely frigid gaze on Lord Ramsey. How she longed to poke him in the ribs.

'My father,' she replied with a show of genteel good manners, 'has taught me to appreciate excellent food and not waste a thing.'

'Action is definitely the clue, I believe,' murmured Lord Ramsey by way of reply. This non sequitur totally puzzled Katherine, but this was hardly surprising. His lordship continually did that. It was his form of wit, she supposed. She simply was not accustomed to it. When a small voice told her it would be delightful to adjust to such, she ordered it be gone.

The men spent no time at port as was customary in the evening, although Katherine suspected her father missed it. She edged her way so that she stood next to his lordship and hissed, 'Are you trying to get us into a pickle? Helping with a history, indeed.'

'Would pond water have been better? I thought you had quite enough of pond weed.'

'I believe I have had more than enough of a good many things,' Katherine murmured, beginning to wonder if she was losing touch with reality.

'Well,' Philip offered in a consoling manner, 'I intend to stand by my original plan. I did tell you that all strays on my land are mine, did I not?' With that remark, he smiled from those gorgeous gray eyes and strolled off to where Julian Penn stood admiring the portrait on the far wall.

Katherine shut her mouth with a snap, deciding that there was something more than a little smoky about the viscount. If only he weren't so attractive. He was also, she sighed wistfully, a touch beyond her. She had best figure out a way to persuade him to provide Mr Weekes with a living. It would be lovely to have children, at least four, she considered. Only when she thought about them, somehow they appeared to have gray eyes and dark hair, and not one had eyes set too close together.

The remainder of the time at the hall went quickly and before long Katherine breathed a sigh of relief once she was safely on her way back to town, Sidney in tow. There had been no further dangerous conversation between Lord Ramsey and her new cousin, most fortunately.

Unfortunately, Amelia Bonner was tittupping along the path close to the Penn house when the driver stopped to permit the family to step out of the carriage.

'Katherine, my dear! I daresay you are returned from the hall. Have you had a lovely visit? Of course you have. How could you not? Dinner, too, I gather. It must have been excessively elegant. Such a lovely house. I simply long to see it again.' That she also hoped to quiz Katherine about the visit, not to mention the divine service, was nicely but imperfectly concealed.

This fond declamation was met with a wry acknowledgment from Katherine.

Sidney advanced to offer his hand, ostensibly to assist Mely around a spot of mud on the path.

'La, sir, what lovely manners you have,' Miss Bonner gushed. 'I can see our Cambridge gentlemen shall have to look to their laurels.'

How clever of Mely, to be able to bat her eyelashes while clinging to Sidney's arm and babbling inanities about gallant gentlemen, thought Katherine while exchanging guarded looks with Cousin Sophia.

'Will you not join us for a dish of tea?' Cousin Sophia offered in spite of a dark look from Katherine.

'I ought not, but then, you are all graciousness,' Mely replied in her most bubbling voice.

Having a fair idea of what was to be in store for them all the next half-hour or so, Katherine assisted Cousin Sophia into the house, then sought the housekeeper to give her instructions for a goodly tea. Katherine might not be hungry, but it would never do to present a less-than-bountiful spread when Miss Amelia Bonner came to tea. Word would be all over town in a trice that the regius professor was in dire straits and forced to economize.

When Katherine entered the drawing room, she made the unpleasant discovery that Mely was seated close to Cousin Sidney and in deep conversation. It was a moot point as to which of the two attempted to pry information from the other. Their guilty expressions told all.

Katherine hoped she might conceal her worries from them. It would not do to hand more power to Mely. What had Mely said to her cousin?

Sidney jumped up to walk across the room to take Katherine's hand. He turned to face Amelia, a rather fatuous smile on his face. 'I am quite enjoying my stay here, Miss Bonner. In my enchanting cousin, I feel I find the ideal of all womanhood.'

Mely clearly did not appreciate Sidney's declaration. 'La, sir, you are a very elegant spinner of words, are you not? I doubt if Katherine hears such from her other gentleman callers. Who is it now, Katherine, dear? Last I knew Mr Weekes claimed your interest.'

'It is difficult to recall. Cambridge is overflowing with males, as you well know, Mely.' Katherine gracefully extricated herself from Sidney's clasp, turning to welcome Cousin Sophia and the tea tray at the same time.

Since she was not attending, she missed the annoyed look that settled upon Sidney's face and the calculating expression that flitted across the pretty Miss Bonner's countenance.

What had Sidney and Amelia Bonner been discussing when Katherine entered the room? She wondered at the guilty expression on Mely's devious little face. As Cousin Sophia had said, the girl was as subtle as a dead pig. So what was she up to now? Surely she was not piqued because Sidney seemed to exhibit a preference for Katherine rather than the darling of Cambridge?

'Miss Bonner told me all about your project, dear Katherine,' chided Cousin Sidney in injured tones once the housekeeper had departed the room. 'I am wounded that you felt you could not confide in me.'

A very pregnant silence followed the casual dropping of the explosive remark. Katherine studied her hands a moment before darting a glance at Cousin Sophia. Then she gave Mely a meaningful look that Katherine hoped conveyed her barely leashed anger.

She could cheerfully have slapped that silly Amelia Bonner clear into next Tuesday. 'Perhaps that is because I felt that the fewer who know of the plan, the better it would be. You had no right, Mely,' she gently scolded her old friend, congratulating herself on her heroic forbearance.

'It was not well done, Amelia,' Cousin Sophia added in a stern voice.

'Well,' Mely answered in a challenging

tone, 'I thought your very own cousin would surely be informed.' A malicious smile hovered about her dainty lips, her eyes sparkling with what Katherine would have sworn was spite. What she had done to deserve such treatment from a girl who had heretofore pretty much ignored any attention paid her was beyond Katherine.

'However, Mr Exton is to stroll through the various colleges with me tomorrow,' Mely continued. 'Or at least King's College and perhaps others if we get that far.' She giggled in a delightful way, tilting her head to gaze flirtatiously at Sidney.

Katherine exchanged resigned looks with Cousin Sophia. Tea was consumed in silence for a few moments.

What would Sidney Exton make of the plan to put on Katherine's play? She had no doubt that Mely had withheld not one word that she knew about the project. Katherine placed her teacup on the small Sheraton table at her side, then clasped her hands tightly lest she give vent to her desire to action. She would have to appease Sidney, but how?

While seated on the sofa, Sidney studied his cousin with astute eyes. He had flirted, hinted, in short, done everything short of offering for the chit since he arrived, and to no avail. While Miss Bonner might be charming in small doses, she was not his target during this stay in Cambridge. He wanted to marry his cousin, dear Katherine. He could, too, with a bit of guile. Either he achieved his purpose one way or another, but get her he would. He had observed a decidedly predatory look in Lord Ramsey's eyes. His attitude was that of one who guards what he considers to be his own as well. Sidney felt he dare not take chances, but he intended Katherine as his.

It was a relief for Katherine to realize the difficult hour was over. Mely would surely depart soon. Of course Katherine would have to deal with Sidney once she left, but perhaps that would not be too bad?

'I suppose Mr Exton will be sworn to secrecy as well,' Mely said as she gathered her skirts to rise from the sofa where she had cast sheep's eyes at Sidney at every opportunity.

'If he would be so kind, yes.' Katherine turned a beseeching gaze on her newly acquired cousin. For someone who had been in the house such a short time, he had become an integral part of the household. Yet she felt reluctant to include him in the venture. Yet what else might she do?

'I am honored that I am to be included in what I gather is a somewhat daring escapade.' Sidney inclined his head toward Katherine, leaving her to wonder if that meant he would hold his tongue between his teeth or not.

'You do understand? Repeating this story could have dire consequences for us all, not just for me.' Katherine fixed a firm look on Mely as she uttered these carefully chosen words. If only she could convince that widgeon to keep her mouth shut. So far, Mely's record had not been impressive. Apparently she had not told her mother, or the tale would be heard from one end of Cambridge to the other. But for reasons Katherine could not explain, she had rather that Cousin Sidney had not been told. Nervous and apprehensive, Katherine watched the two on the sofa.

'I hold myself a member of the family and would never breach your trust in me,' Sidney said before Mely could say a word of reassurance.

'You see, Katherine? Mr Exton is your family.' Mely rose from the sofa, then after many words of parting and reminders to Mr Exton as to when he might fetch her the following day, she finally departed.

Katherine could not refrain from the merest sigh of relief.

Cousin Sophia had left the room to walk with Mely to the door, rightly guessing that Katherine little felt like performing the courtesy. Katherine faced Sidney with a sense of wary expectation.

'I am sorry we excluded you from our secret. What I told Miss Bonner was the truth, however. I thought the fewer who know of the scheme, the better.'

'You actually wrote this play?' At Katherine's answering nod he strode about the room, one hand stroking his chin until Katherine wondered if he had seen this done upon the stage. It seemed excessively affected.

'I shall endeavor to assist you. I trust you need to keep Miss Bonner silenced?' He fixed Katherine with a penetrating stare.

'Mercy, yes,' Katherine replied with heart-felt fervor.

'I shall do this for you . . . on one condition.'

Katherine braced herself. Why she had the feeling she might not like his terms, she couldn't say.

'I am quite smitten with you, my dear,' said Sidney, bowing most properly in Katherine's direction. 'Permit me to pay my addresses to you? Allow me to speak to your father? You are such an enchanting, not to mention talented, young woman. I meant it when I said you are the ideal I have been seeking. To think I have looked in vain in London when my very own cousin is the answer to my wants and needs right here in Cambridge.'

Thinking this had to be the most curious

proposal in the world, Katherine could only sit in stunned silence for a few moments.

Sidney studied his cousin. Had he been precipitate? If Lord Ramsey had not been giving all the signs of a protective lover, Sidney would have bided his time, waiting to woo the lovely Katherine with proper deference. He held his breath, hoping she would at least promise to give his proposal some consideration.

Searching through her extensive vocabulary, Katherine tried to find the right words to express her thoughts. None came to mind. 'No,' she blurted out with the most disgusting honesty in her life. Surely she might have found a gentler way to depress his attentions?

'I cannot believe you have had time to consider my offer. Surely you do not have a *tendre* for his lordship?'

Since that was precisely what afflicted Katherine, she said nothing, merely looking as bland as she was able.

'For you must know,' Sidney continued, 'he is quite above your touch.'

'I scarcely know you,' replied Katherine, all too well aware of the awful truth of his argument. It was difficult to consider that Sidney was serious in his interest. They had met but days before. Katherine looked past him to where Cousin Sophia entered the room. Breathing a small sigh of relief, she beckoned to her dear cousin and friend. 'Cousin Sophia, do join us.'

Since Cousin Sophia had every intention of such, she merely gave Katherine an odd look, then settled herself in her favorite chair next to a large branch of candles. The light had grown dim with the fading daylight and even if Sophia could probably knit in the dark, she preferred to have some light on the matter.

'I have just declared my intentions to seek Katherine's hand,' Sidney declared to his other cousin, one he privately thought a bit odd.

'Why?' Cousin Sophia as usual got straight to the point.

Undaunted, Sidney replied, 'Because she is enchanting, the very ideal of a wife.'

'Have you been writing lines for him, Katherine?' Cousin Sophia inquired, looking strangely at Cousin Sidney first, then at her niece.

Coughing into her hand, Katherine shook her head. 'Not at all. I am persuaded that Cousin Sidney is carried away with the notion of marriage. He cannot be serious, I vow.' To Sidney, she added, 'Sleep on it, cousin. I am certain that, come morning and a day spent with the lovely Amelia Bonner, you will forget this nonsense. For I refuse to believe you are serious.' Katherine smiled gently, as one might to someone who is all about in the attic.

Frustrated in his efforts, Sidney muttered something to Katherine about going for a walk.

Understanding that any gentleman might wish to console himself after having a proposal rejected, even if it was one that was deucedly strange, Katherine waved him off. 'By all means.'

Sidney left the house feeling as if he was further from his goal than ever before. He strolled down to the White Swan and ordered a pint of their best. Glancing about him, he was delighted to see a crony from London. Sidney wended his way to his side, then sat down for a bit of conversation. By the time a considerable number of pints had disappeared down Sidney's gullet, an agreement had been reached and both men were well satisfied with the night's work. Staggering back to his cousin's house, Sidney leered at a light-skirt who beckoned from a dimly lit doorway.

'Not tonight, dolly. I have better things to come.'

10

Katherine crossed to the center of the newly constructed stage and stopped. Turning to gaze at a distant point, she began to speak.

' . . . I guess I loved him best of all, for he
Gave of his love most sparingly to me.
We women have, if I am not to lie,
In this love matter, a quaint fantasy;
Look out a thing we may not lightly have,
And after that we'll cry all day and crave.
For but a thing, and that thing covet we;
Press hard upon us, then we turn and flee.
Sparingly offer we our goods, when fair,
Great crowds at market make for dearer ware,
And what's too common brings but little price;
All this knows every woman who is wise . . .'

She broke off abruptly, seeing a shadowy figure appear in the rear of the theater booth. 'Who goes there?'

'You feel a kinship with the Widow of Bath?' lightly queried the figure remaining in the shadows.

'Well,' Katherine replied in a considering voice as she drifted to the edge of the stage, 'I doubt I've a wish to be common.' She looked about her, then gestured with a wide sweep of an arm. ''Tis a grand sight, is it not? At least it is for a show booth. You have done yourself proud, sir.'

'The Widow of Bath is an intriguing character.' Lord Ramsey emerged from the shadows to stroll to the foot of the stage, looking up at Katherine with speculative eyes.

'It was her third husband of whom she spoke in those lines, you know. I expect she had learned a thing or two by that time.' Katherine moved a few steps, then paused as something in his manner caught her.

'And what did you learn, pray tell?' Even in the dim light Katherine could make out the sparkle in his eyes. His jaunty stance didn't delude her. What purpose his line of questioning might have, she didn't know, but it would be well to use caution in her reply, for once.

'A woman must beware how she bestows her attentions, sir, lest she be deemed common and thus lose what value she might have. For I understand well that no man desires a woman who has nothing to offer him.'

She thought of Michael Weekes and his indifferent attitude. She had no great amount of money to appeal to his needs. Were she an heiress, it would be a different matter entirely. Somehow, standing on the stage with the smell of new lumber around her and the gaze of the tremendously appealing man fastened upon her, Mr Weekes faded into the dim obscurity of a suitor who had failed to meet romantic longings.

Lord Ramsey vaulted up to the stage to confront Katherine. She backed away from him a few steps, feeling intimidated by his virility and handsome charm. Those biscuit pantaloons fit superbly and that blue coat had not a wrinkle to mar it. If only Teddy might match Ramsey's talent with a cravat, so careless did it appear, although she guessed it must have taken great skill to produce.

'Do you think you have nothing to offer a man?' Philip watched her closely. Did her quote from Chaucer actually reveal an inner longing for that stuffed shirt Weekes? Did she fancy that someone as imaginative and lively as herself might possibly be content with the circumscribed life of a cleric's wife? Perhaps she needed to be taught a lesson in reality?

Incensed he would tread on so delicate a subject, Katherine flashed him a look of censure. 'My dowry is not great, my looks only passing, and I fear that if word of this involvement in the theater seeps out, I will truly be past praying for.'

'And yet you risk all to do this?' Here was proof of her unsuitability as Weekes's mate. She possessed too much spunk and vitality to be married to that unassertive fellow.

Katherine laughed, a silvery, musical trill that fell pleasantly upon the air, causing the man who stood in the shadows of the wings to sharpen his gaze at the couple who bantered so casually on center stage.

'I find I must, or I shall have no peace. Can you possibly understand? No, I doubt it, for a man has no such restrictions hampering him as does a woman. I ought to be dutifully practicing the pianoforte, improving my watercolors, and learning the art of gentle seduction via conversation. I ought to emulate Amelia Bonner; she does it so well.'

Katherine sighed slightly, then made to move away from Lord Ramsey. Casting a wry smile at that gentleman, she added, 'If I am not to sink beyond hope, I must find Cousin Sophia. She came along to lend a semblance of respectability.' Again a lighthearted chuckle rang out as Katherine hurried across the stage, disappearing in the wings opposite where the second shadowy figure stood, arrested by what he had seen and heard.

Katherine strolled about the rear of the theater, checking the construction until she caught sight of her new cousin coming toward her. Cousin Sophia had still not appeared. Katherine frowned, not wishing to have Sidney around, fearing what, she knew not.

'It looks well,' Sidney commented, running a hand along the smooth timber as if admiring the handiwork of the carpenters from Fairfax Hall. He continued to study his cousin.

'Teddy says it has features the actors find most agreeable. There are even proper dressing rooms for the cast. They are small, I fear, but not to be despised, considering what some of the inns have to offer them.' Katherine studied his face, then added, 'What brings you to this spot so early in the day?'

'Can you have forgotten? The oysters? You said you would go with me.' Sidney gave Katherine a narrow look, as though daring her to deny him the pleasure of her company.

Her hand fluttered to her throat. Indeed, she had quite forgotten the invitation to join Sidney in eating the oysters when they arrived at the fair. It was a great treat, but with all that had to be arranged, she felt it was one she must forgo.

'I am sorry,' she said with genuine contrition. 'We are arranging the costumes, and the scenery is due to arrive sometime this afternoon. I dare not leave here for the moment. 'Tis only a matter of days until the fair officially opens, you know. And, I must find Cousin Sophia, as I seem to be without a chaperone.'

Sidney knew a cold anger creeping over him. The chit was turning him away. Did she see him merely as a cousin? Or perhaps she thought she stood a chance with his carefree lordship? Ha! That man could look much higher for a wife than the daughter of a divinity professor, even if he did have high connections. Being appointed by the crown had little value in Sidney's eyes.

'If you will excuse me, I had best sort out the costumes.' She turned to walk toward the trunk from Fairfax Hall that sat in a corner of the carpenter's room.

Katherine found her arm grabbed and she stared down at Sidney's hand before looking up into his face. Had she seen a flash of anger? No, how silly. Surely he could see she was the logical one to perform this task.

'There is much to observe if you stroll about the rows of the fair. A rope-walker is setting up her booth just down the way and a puppet show is in the process of going up.'

She gave him a patient stare. 'Mayhap later. For the time being, I must stay here.' She turned from him to head off in the direction of the trunk that held the assortment of costumes. Some had come from the attic of Fairfax Hall. Others had been sewn up by a seamstress who knew only that they were for the fair, no more.

Sidney muttered, 'I was told that Cambridge is nothing but hazard and burgundy, hunting, mathematics, Newmarket, riot, and racing. Nothing was said about the impossibility of the resident females. Perhaps it was better when Byron lived here. That bear he took for walks must have livened things up considerably.' There was nothing for Sidney to do but take himself off.

At the White Swan he found his friend, one Lewis Rankin, and the two set out for a pleasant day. Thwarted in his intentions for Katherine Penn, Sidney put his mind to an alternative course. His good friend, when fully appraised of the situation, made a number of suggestions. One took Sidney's fancy. While they strolled about the fair site again, a plan was hatched that Sidney hoped would bear abundant fruit.

★   ★   ★

'What did your cousin want?' Lord Ramsey leaned against the wall while watching Katherine shake out the various costumes.

'Nothing much.' After hanging up the

208

maid's skirt on a peg, Katherine then held up a pair of leather stays of the kind worn by country maids. 'These look uncomfortable,' she murmured to herself before remembering that his lordship stood close by, watching her efforts. Why was it her tongue seemed to forget itself when he was present? There was nothing she might do to halt the warmth to her cheeks. How improper of her to comment on a garment obviously for intimate wear. Fortunately he refrained from teasing her, something Katherine almost expected, given his lighthearted view of life.

'He did not seem best pleased when he stalked out of here,' Ramsey persisted, a frown lingering on his brow.

'Well, and so he might be understandably annoyed. He had invited me to join him for oysters and I completely forgot. To tell the truth, I am not that fond of oysters.' She sought to conceal the stays from him, tucking them next to a crisp white apron and print shawl that was part of the maid's attire.

'It is an acquired taste.' He reached for the pair of leather stays and held them up, checking the lacing in the back for signs of wear. He glanced at Katherine's flaming cheeks and chuckled. 'I am not so blind that I am not aware of feminine apparel.'

Katherine could not meet that gray gaze,

suspecting that his knowing eyes would be full of mirth at her expense.

'These seem in good repair. Where did you get them?'

'I paid three shillings for them. The actress who is to play the maid had them fitted to her. Do you know,' added Katherine, forgetting she ought not speak of such things, 'there is an iron rod down the front? It surely would remind one not to slump.'

Katherine plucked the stays from his hand, then tucked them in the pile with the apron and shawl. She turned to pull the next costume from the trunk, the harem-style garment to be worn by Miss O'Neill in the final scene.

Katherine glanced at him, her eyes defiant. 'I think the less said about this, the better. I only hope that Miss O'Neill's father will permit her to wear this garment without a quarrel.'

'You know what I think? I think we will leave here for a time to give you a change.' he draped the somewhat scandalous garment over a crude chair, then took Katherine by the hand to walk toward the exit. From a wooden bench he scooped up a billowy pile of fabric, holding it out to Katherine. 'Here, you had best conceal yourself in this since you seek anonymity.'

She accepted what proved to be a fashionable cloak of silk and wool merino in dull black. She quickly whipped it about her form. Flipping the hood over her honey-blond hair, she allowed Philip to lead her from the building. How amazing that he should recall of her need for protection from view.

'When the men come with the scenery, I don't want you in the way. You might be hurt.'

Katherine gave him an oblique glance, wishing that what happened to her truly made a difference where he was concerned. But hers was an absurd wish, a kind of dream indulged in by silly little twits with more hair than wit, not practical girls who knew the way of the world.

'Look, there is a menagerie setting up its booth.'

Entering into the spirit, Katherine gestured to their left, where other booths were in the process of being constructed. 'See there?'

For the most part the booths were flimsy, subject to winds and rain. Open-fronted and made of wood and canvas, with pitched roofs covered with haircloth, they were frequently damaged by bad weather. Usually some, if not all, of the booth-holders created a rough sleeping apparatus from two or three boards nailed about a foot from the ground to four sturdy posts. Four boards were fixed cotlike around the side to keep them from tumbling out.

Ramsey glanced down at Katherine, bestowing his endearing grin on her with devastating effect, if he but knew it. 'Looks right uncomfortable. I'll wager you'd not welcome a night in something like that.'

'No, I like my creature comforts.'

Katherine had turned to watch an old woman setting about stacking her rush for mending chairs, so she missed the wicked gleam that now danced in Ramsey's eyes. 'I suspected as much,' he murmured.

Fortunately for Katherine's peace of mind, she could not hear him.

The final days of preparation for the opening of the fair brought people from far and wide to the site. The sound of hammers rang out, while horses neighed in dismay at the noise. Katherine watched a pair of Gypsies lead their horses toward the north end of the large field where the horse fair was to be held on the first two days.

'It is exciting, is it not?'

When they reached Garlic Row, they encountered Cousin Sophia marching toward the theater booth. 'I have searched every-where for you. What is going on?' Sophia said with disconcerting bluntness, especially when combined with a hard stare at Lord Ramsey. Sophia took her task seriously — most of the time, at any rate.

Distressed to consider that the gentleman who was doing so much for them would be placed in an awkward position by her plain-speaking relative, Katherine reached through the slit in the cloak to put a staying hand on Sophia's arm.

'Lord Ramsey sought me out at the theater and brought me this cloak to help preserve my identity. I am most grateful to him.' She glanced about her at the throng of people intent on their various tasks. 'Not that anyone might pay me the least attention. 'Tis monstrously busy here. I doubt I'd be noticed.'

Only slightly mollified, Cousin Sophia nodded politely to Lord Ramsey. 'Much obliged to you, sir. Since Katherine has become involved in this venture, it seems all sense of propriety has fled her mind.'

'Surely not all,' denied Katherine with a twinkle in her eyes. 'I was looking for you earlier and did not find you. For I knew I needed a chaperone, and so I told Cousin Sidney.'

'He was here?' Cousin Sophia demanded.

'Wanted Kate to eat oysters with him.'

Before Katherine could remonstrate with him regarding his calling her Kate, a landau rumbled to a halt close by. Katherine turned to discover Gisela Cheney and Mr Penn seated inside.

'So this is where you are,' Julian Penn declared in a carrying voice.

Gisela placed a hand on his arm. 'Katherine is like me, she finds the fair irresistible. Come join us,' she pleaded with Katherine and Cousin Sophia, evidently assuming her brother would automatically accept her invitation.

After a wary, questioning glance at Lord Ramsey, Katherine, Cousin Sophia, and Philip entered the spacious landau to slowly jounce along the dirt lane.

Activity bustled on every side. Katherine took note of the leather seller and glover, for his goods were of the highest quality. Next to his booth was a laceman busy constructing shelves for his wares. Furniture-makers, silver-smiths, dealers in everything from fans and toys to pattens and millinery were unloading merchandise and arranging their stock. All would sleep in the back rooms of their respective booths. Great wheels of cheese were stacked at the far end of the long row, while at the other were the pottery-makers and the coal-dealers.

About a mile or so down the lane, they came to where the oyster fair was set out. Already business was in swing, selling to the dealers before the official opening took place. Katherine glanced in that direction, glad she had not gone with Cousin Sidney.

'Look, everyone. The horses!' Gisela placed an excited hand on Mr Penn's arm, then gestured to where a number of racers and hunters from Yorkshire were being led into a pen. Beyond them could be seen Suffolk draft horses, indeed, horses from all over England gathered for the great horse fair.

Mr Penn studied the animals. 'In my youth this fair was far greater, you know. I can recall that the finest horses in the country were brought here for sale. There were more booths as well. Now, with London an easy drive, the things sold here are trivial matters, and people seem bent more on having a fine time rather than stocking up for the coming year.'

'Then why have you not sent Katherine to her Great-aunt Harriette? Katherine said she had been invited to London to make her come-out,' Gisela quizzed Mr Penn. The logical connection between a visit to London and the change in the character of the fair escaped Katherine, but she listened intently for her father's reply. She had wondered too often why he repeatedly refused her great-aunt's invitations to miss an explanation now.

Mr Penn gave his daughter a thoughtful look. 'It did not occur to me that Katherine would wish to go. Was I wrong, my child? Mrs Cheney has on several occasions made me aware of my negligence.'

Totally engrossed in the turn of the conversation, she did not notice the appearance of her cousin at the edge of the oyster fair.

Sidney had consumed a selection of the large Lynn oysters, all as big as a horse's hoof, as well as some of the more delicate oysters from Colchester and Whitstable. He felt satisfied until he caught sight of his pretty cousin with Lord Ramsey. Sidney totally ignored the others in the carriage, for there were really only two who mattered.

Katherine had declined to keep her promised excursion with him not because she had a task, but because she thought she stood a chance with Lord Ramsey, who most assuredly had no need of her. Sidney did. The scene firmed his resolve. The smile that curved his lips was not pleasant in the least.

Katherine wondered how to best answer her father's question. ''Tis not that I wished to leave you, you understand, but I should have liked to enjoy the balls and parties. It can be dreadfully dull in Cambridge, Papa.'

He looked affronted, then sighed. 'I fear this has been a season of facing unpalatable truths.' His glance at Mrs Cheney revealed what other facts had intruded in his pleasant and introspective life.

'By the way, sir,' Lord Ramsey said in a casual yet respectful manner, 'there is a likelihood that a living in my keeping will become vacant shortly. Do you have anyone you might suggest for that position?' Philip dared not glance at Katherine, yet he felt her stiffen at his side in the carriage.

Mr Penn gazed at Katherine, a pensive expression settling on his face. She wondered if he intended to compensate for her lack of a London Season by putting forth the name she would offer.

'Well, that might remedy a thing or two,' Cousin Sophia declared in her forthright way.

'Sophia,' Katherine pleaded in a quiet voice.

'Mr Weekes is eminently worthy of a living. He is a fine scholar and I believe he would like to have a family. Is that not right, Katherine?' Mr Penn replied.

She could feel the heat in her cheeks. 'I cannot vouch for what Mr Weekes might have to say regarding that, Papa. He usually comes to see you.' That had bothered Katherine a great deal. It seemed the only time she got to see the man she respected and wished to marry was when he came to see her father or to dinner. And dinner invitations were thin on the ground, for one could not be too obvious.

'Hm.' Mr Penn narrowed his gaze, looking first at Lord Ramsey, then at his daughter. 'I should think it a very good thing were you to offer him that living. He's a good man, a fine fellow at the college, and I believe he'd do well with a parish of his own. Likes to preach, as I recall.'

'I shall do precisely that.' Lord Ramsey settled against the squabs of the carriage, but anyone bothering to really look at him could see he was as tense as a rope-dancer about to set out across a high, taut cable.

Katherine was in a quandary. While she had hoped for a living to become available for Michael Weekes for what seemed like ages, now that the day had about arrived, her emotions grew mixed. It was difficult to plan for a future with Michael while so strongly attracted to Philip. The elegant and infuriating — not to mention kind and teasing — Lord Ramsey was a cut above her on the social scale. Katherine was far too practical to waste time daydreaming about a fine marriage to him, however she might adore such. Yet, could she muster enthusiasm for what she had desired for so long? She expelled a long breath.

'You sigh, Miss Penn?' Philip leaned closer to where she sat, ostensibly to inquire after her state of mind.

She was acutely aware of him. His proximity to where she primly sat on the cushion barely allowed her back to touch the squabs.

'I suspect we had better return . . . to town,' Katherine said after hastily changing her original direction of thought. She had intended to go to the theater, but with her father in the carriage, there was no way she might give voice to those words. She darted a warning glance to Gisela, then nudged Cousin Sophia lest that good woman inadvertently reveal her plans.

'Market today,' Sophia said blandly. 'Why the university insists on preventing the farmers from opening their stalls in the town center until after twelve of the clock is more than I can see. Downright foolish, I call it. If you wish fresh vegetables and poultry, one must wait. Most annoying.'

She glared at her cousin as though holding him personally responsible for what she considered a stupid ordinance. That the university had the right to fix the price of bread had further irritated Sophia. The friction that existed between the town and gown stemmed from many sources, not merely the frequent excesses of students. Smashing lamp posts and drunken brawls, however, didn't help the matter, as Sophia frequently pointed out.

A distressing silence hung over the carriage on the way back to the Penn house. Katherine gratefully stepped down, then offered her hand to Cousin Sophia when she joined her. Katherine studied Lord Ramsey with thoughtful eyes before the signal was given for the landau to move away from the house. He revealed nothing of his feelings. Katherine flounced into the house in a rare temper.

With her customary bland expression Cousin Sophia watched her charge disappear behind the front door. Turning to Mr Penn, who seemed about to stroll off to his college, she said, 'You will do well to keep your nose out of this affair, Julian. You have done quite enough for one day, I believe.'

'Woman, if I knew what was going on in my own home, I'd not have to make a fool of myself,' he growled back.

'Perhaps were you to be around more often, you'd not have to be told,' she snapped back at him. Then she whirled about and stomped up the steps and into the house, leaving a puzzled Mr Penn to head for his favorite spot, the common room, and a glass of port.

Finding that Teddy had gone off to the theater, Katherine decided that she would join him. It was best to keep busy. Before she might depart, she found Mely marching up the front walk.

'Blast and tarnation,' Katherine fumed.

'That is rather a drastic and unladylike thing to say, Kate, dear,' Sophia declared.

'I am not Kate,' Katherine said between gritted teeth as she moved forward to greet Mely.

'One might be forgiven for thinking so,' Cousin Sophia answered in a soft and exceedingly smooth voice.

'Oh, good, you are still here. I made sure you might be off to the fair site. Have you heard? One of the old clerics has gone aloft. That means there will be a living available. I wonder if Mr Weekes will make the final list of candidates for the position?' Mely smiled while studying Katherine with an assessing gaze. 'It is a very prosperous parish, you know. Most desirable.' Finding that Katherine either knew nothing or refused to add to Mely's fount of knowledge, the pretty girl took herself off in a huff.

'Widgeon,' muttered Cousin Sophia.

221

'I'm going back to the theater. I want to see all is in readiness for the dress rehearsal tomorrow.'

'I shan't go with you. If your brother is there, you won't need me. All this traipsing about has kept me from my shopping.'

Bestowing a forgiving and most understanding smile on Sophia, Katherine pulled the soft cloak about her, then set off toward the fair. It was a walk of some two miles, but the day was pleasant, although the cloak offered welcome warmth in the coolish air. She smoothed the soft fabric about her. It seemed Lord Ramsey frequently saw to her welfare.

Once she reached the theater, Katherine carefully glanced about before sneaking to the side entrance. She was certain she had not been observed in her oblique approach to the large theater booth.

The cries of the walnut man as he roamed the lane reached her ears as she pulled open the door.

'Twenty a penny, walnuts! Walnuts, twenty a penny! Crack 'um away, crack 'um away here.'

The door swung shut and a different sort of sound reached her: the muted noise of sets being shifted and soft discussions about the probable profit to come. In moments she was deeply involved in sorting out costumes and soothing Eliza O'Neill over her harem outfit, or more precisely, her father.

Her patience already much tried this day, Katherine struggled to maintain the sort of bland calm Cousin Sophia so successfully dispersed.

'Looks tolerable, wouldn't you say?' Teddy said in a masterful understatement as they moved apart to look over the sets.

'Indeed,' Katherine replied, smiling warmly on her brother. 'I believe I shall stand in the center to get the feel of the final set. Oh, Teddy, is this not exciting?'

Teddy grinned, then wandered away to sigh over Miss O'Neill, her father notwithstanding.

Thinking how far the scene was from her current reality, Katherine strolled to stand beneath the fanciful set portraying the upper room of the castle where Belinda was held captive awaiting her evil count. It really was well done. Katherine could almost sense an impending doom, feel the threat of evil in the air. If the audience got the same foreboding of danger, she would be well pleased.

The door at the lane entrance slammed shut and Katherine whirled about just as the thud of a weight fell so close to her that it tore the flounce of her dress. She stared down at the weight, one used to help move the sets, and her hand slid up to touch her throat. Had it not been for that sudden sound, she would have been a few inches over and now likely crushed. Rather, she shook like a leaf while she noted the scrap of muslin protruding from underneath the weight.

Teddy rushed to her side. 'What happened?' He seemed stunned when he caught sight of the weight so close to his sister. Turning to the man who ran to join them, he said, 'Ramsey, look here. Must have been a poor length of rope. The weight landed just short of Kitty.'

'You little fool,' shouted Lord Ramsey to the pale-as-death woman who trembled before his rage. 'If you had remained at home, as you ought, you'd not have been in this danger. No, you but must come and poke your nose in every corner.' The cast had gathered in the shadows just off-stage. Even Cousin Sidney witnessed her humiliation.

'Why,' Ramsey thundered, 'could you not trust another to see that all is as it should be? It is a retribution for your impropriety, Miss Penn.' He turned to order Teddy to see his sister home before anything worse happened.

Eyes blinded with tears and shaking so badly she could barely walk, Katherine stumbled from the theater. She allowed Teddy to summon a cart to take her home.

Whatever had made her think she was attracted to Lord Ramsey? The man was an odious beast, a complete wretch. She burst into a flood of tears that continued all the way home, much to the consternation of the driver.

11

By the following day Katherine had ceased to tremble at the close call she had suffered while at the theater. Cousin Sophia had alternated between cosseting her and predicting dire consequences for Katherine's foolhardy behavior until she was quite prepared to scream.

' 'Tis the dress rehearsal today. I intend to be present, Lord Ramsey notwithstanding,' Katherine declared after another spate of words from Sophia. 'I am fully aware of the debt we owe him. I shan't know a moment's peace until we have paid him off. Completely.' The final word was uttered with a loathing that revealed the depth of Katherine's anger. Never had she felt so betrayed. The man she thought so teasing and lighthearted, even concerned for her welfare, had turned into a monster.

'There might be another reason, you know,' suggested Cousin Sophia from her chair by the window of the sitting room.

'And what might that be?' Katherine paused in her pacing about the room to stare at Cousin Sophia. 'No, do not answer that. I do not wish to know what your explanation might be.'

'Closed mind, just like your father.'

'Do not speak of men just now, please. Any men!'

A stir in the hall heralded the arrival of her brother.

'I say, Kitty, are you bound for the theater today? I warrant you'll want to see the dress rehearsal.' Teddy hovered in the doorway uncertain what mood he would find when he addressed his sister.

'Naturally I intend to go. I might,' Katherine added in a rather heavy attempt at humor, 'need you to fend off his lordship. He may not be best pleased to see me there. I could be banished.'

'Rubbish,' Teddy replied with a deal more optimism than he inwardly felt.

'I shall fetch my cloak and be with you in a trice.' Katherine slid past her brother, giving him a reassuring pat on his arm before walking down the hall to climb the stairs to her room. Just as she placed her foot on the first step she heard a knock at the front door. Not wishing to bother the housekeeper and feeling very democratic today, she answered it herself. It was Lord Ramsey.

Katherine fell back a step or two, placing her hands carefully behind her as she went. She tilted her head, her heart-shaped face assuming a bland expression worthy of

Cousin Sophia. 'Good day, sir.'

He resembled nothing so much as a small boy who faces a very distasteful task. 'Katherine, I must talk with you.'

She gestured to the small room off the entry, judging he wished privacy for his speech.

He stood by the door, watching as she gracefully walked across the room to stand by the window. 'About yesterday . . . ' he began.

'Have you thought of another way in which to tell me I am a silly fool, perhaps?' She spun around to pin him in place with an accusing glare.

'You aren't making this any easier for me,' he muttered.

Since she had no intention of doing any such thing, she merely inclined her head in what she hoped was a regal manner.

'I was upset, you might have been . . . ' he began.

Katherine sputtered, interrupting what apparently was an explanation of his behavior to declare, 'You were upset? Why, I was as calm as a dead duck.'

'Kate,' he warned to no avail.

'That horrid weight came crashing down, tearing off a part of the skirt of a favorite gown and nearly killing me in the process, and *you* got upset. My, my,' she finished in a soft but effective voice.

'That tears it,' he muttered, striding across the room to clasp her arms. Staring down into her face, he continued, 'I was frightened out of my mind when I realized what might have happened to you, you foolish girl.' With those words he bent his head and kissed her with none of his previous tender regard.

Katherine wilted under the onslaught. This was no mere kiss; it constituted an entire pronouncement, although of what, she had not the faintest idea.

Bewildered, she drew back once he had released her to gaze at his face with troubled eyes.

'It was an accident,' she said, seeking his reassurance. 'It will never happen again. Will it?' Her hands had lifted of their own accord to clasp his arms and now she exerted a slight pressure on them in emphasis.

'I have had everything checked and rechecked. I believe you will be as safe there as any place.'

'Splendid,' she replied in a subdued voice. She dropped her hands when she realized that she had been shamelessly clutching him, backing farther away from his far-too-appealing self.

'I say, Kitty, are you never coming?' Teddy queried from the doorway before catching sight of Ramsey. He stopped, warily eyeing the other man and trying to assess the atmosphere in the small room.

'I take it you were about to depart?' Ramsey looked from one to the other, his brows raised in query.

She nodded. 'I was just going up the stairs for my cloak when you knocked on the door.'

'I am pleased I did something right, at any rate. I am glad you have the sense to wear it.' He backed away from her, allowing Katherine free access to the door.

Ashamed of her harsh words, Katherine threw up her hands in a gesture of surrender. 'You have, for the most part, been a kind and generous partner in this undertaking. I am most grateful to you.' Head bent, she walked to the door. 'I shall be but a moment, Teddy. We shan't presume upon his lordship's time.' Glancing back at Ramsey, she added, 'I am going to the theater, I hope in time for the rehearsal.'

The two men watched the quiet young woman march up the stairs, her back as stiff as an iron rod. 'Offhand, I'd say she is still a bit annoyed,' ventured Teddy with the sort of knowledge that comes of long-standing proximity.

'I hope she gets over her pique.'

'It was an accident, sir,' Teddy reminded in

a respectful manner.

'I suppose so,' mused his lordship, reluctant to inform the brother that the new rope had been cut, not frayed.

'Well, once the rehearsal is over with, perhaps we can get her away from the place.'

'Away? Her? What do you suggest?' The wry expression on Lord Ramsey's face amused Teddy, for he chuckled.

'Take her for a boat ride on the Cam. She'd be trapped, if you get my meaning.' Teddy winked.

'I do, I do. Perhaps we can even slip the chaperone?' Ramsey wore a suspiciously pleased smile when Katherine returned, her cloak around her and reticule in hand.

She wished to ignore the hand offered by Lord Ramsey and far preferred to walk the two miles from town.

'Don't be a clunch,' Teddy said as he nudged her up into the carriage. 'If you want to get there promptly, best accept the transport offered. And say thank you,' he reminded quietly.

Katherine shot his lordship a resigned look and repeated after her brother, 'Thank you, kind sir.'

On the way to the field where the fair was located each year, Katherine espied Amelia Bonner. She stood, on Trumpington Street chatting with a man, a circumstance scarcely unusual, as that was Mely's chief occupation when she wasn't emulating her mother at gossiping. What shocked Katherine was the identity of the gentleman. It was Mr Michael Weekes! A flutter of fear crept up into her heart. Mely chasing after Mr Weekes? The prettiest girl in all of Cambridge seeking the attention of the man most likely to get the prosperous living from Lord Ramsey?

Abruptly she turned from the sight that actually didn't upset her nearly as much as it ought. She attributed that odd reaction to her nearly being killed the day before. A shock like that was enough to put a girl's emotions all out of order. Yet she was curious enough to inquire of his lordship. 'Have you decided quite definitely on who is to fill the vacancy? Or am I out of turn in asking?'

'Not at all,' replied Lord Ramsey, watching carefully to observe her reaction to his words. 'I believe your father is correct. Mr Weekes seems quite suitable.'

'Oh, I say, jolly good, Ramsey. Weekes is a dashed good teacher and I'll wager he does well at the preaching end as well.' Teddy beamed an approving smile.

'Katherine, are you pleased?'

'I know how many of the fellows anxiously hope for a living to become available. I'm sure that Mr Weekes is an admirable choice.' But she wondered. He had been so unattainable before. Now, quite suddenly, since he would be able to marry, he seemed to have lost some of his romantic appeal. Perhaps not to Mely. But as far as Katherine was concerned, she was not in raptures as she fully expected to be. How odd. Was she a fickle creature, after all?

They sped along the Newmarket Road to where the theater sat across from the cheese stalls. Lord Ramsey jumped down, then assisted Katherine. Teddy rushed off ahead of them.

Katherine looked after her brother, then gave Lord Ramsey a rueful smile. 'I beg your indulgence. I rather imagine he is going to see how Miss O'Neill does today.'

When Katherine and Lord Ramsey entered the theater, it was to find total chaos.

'What is going on?' Katherine said, with no fear of being overheard in the din.

Lord Ramsey strode across the stage to consult with Miss O'Neill and Ninian Denham. The remainder of the crew subsided, but still Katherine could not overhear what was being discussed.

In a short while Lord Ramsey returned to Katherine's side to report. 'They refuse to do the rehearsal. Miss O'Neill is superstitious about your being here. At least for today. We still have a few days before the fair opens, come this Wednesday. Perhaps it will be best to go off for the day and come back tomorrow?'

Looking about her with an even more subdued air, Katherine could see the hostile looks being sent her direction. 'I expect you have the right of it. It seems the outside of enough that I should suffer again for that stupid accident.' She glanced up at the ceiling where fresh ropes hung in loops.

Lord Ramsey exchanged a warning look with the stage worker who stood nearby when the man was about to speak. 'I believe things will be better tomorrow.' Lord Ramsey looked to Teddy, who frowned, but nodded back his agreement of the suggestion from Ramsey.

In short order Katherine found herself bustled from the theater and back in the carriage again.

'I suppose I had best head for home,' she said with no enthusiasm at all. Her disappointment was all too clear, she feared. Michael Weekes didn't enter her mind at all, which would have been peculiar had she thought about it. Her only concern was for the production. Pray that the cast's superstition ended before Wednesday. The alternative was for her to remain outside, a thing she found insupportable.

The driver followed his instructions to the letter and soon Katherine found that rather than heading back to Cambridge, they made their way along Garlic Row toward the place on the Cam where the ferry docked. There were other boats to be found there as well, especially now during fair time. She glanced wistfully at a shallow boat, the sort the young lovers used to take an afternoon's ride down the river. They were large enough for three, the couple and the required chaperone.

'I think a change of scenery is in order, Katherine. Your brother suggested you might enjoy a pleasant, relaxing trip down the river.' He assisted her from the carriage, then led her past the pottery booths to the edge of the river.

A slow smile crept over her face. Would she? The grin she bestowed upon Lord Ramsey was the sort given by little girls about to be given a treat. 'I should like that very much, I believe,' she said primly, her sparkling eyes revealing just how much she would enjoy such a treat. Then her smile dimmed. 'However, Cousin Sophia is not present.' A mischievous look crossed her face. 'We need not tell, I suppose.'

Before long Lord Ramsey had arranged to

take one of the boats, a pretty little thing painted a soft green, for the rest of the day. 'That way we do not have to be worried about returning it precisely on time, you know.'

Katherine did not know what he meant, but she was too intent upon settling herself in the back of the boat to worry overmuch about it. Pillows appeared from the carriage, a fancy white parasol was handed down to her.

'We're off,' Lord Ramsey announced as they were pushed from the shore by eager hands. He managed the oars with surprising skill as the little craft shot out into the center of the river, then settled into a gentle drift in the current.

Katherine discovered when she unfurled it that the white silk parasol had ruffles around the edges that made her feel positively decadent. 'How deliciously wicked,' she said, chuckling as she gave the parasol an experimental twirl. What a pity Mely couldn't see Katherine at this moment. But, then, knowing Mely, she might well manage to do that. Katherine leaned against the cushions and twirled the parasol again.

There were several swans farther along the bank and an enormous old willow cascaded its branches into the water, trailing leaves in pretty patterns of green and bronze.

'How very lovely, to spend an autumnal day on the river. I love the water. Sometimes I lie on my bed and watch the ripple of passing boats reflected on the ceiling of my room.' She trailed a finger in the slow green river as they more or less drifted along. Lord Ramsey made the motions of rowing, but actually seemed to exert little power and no direction at all.

'Katherine, about what happened . . .' Lord Ramsey seemed at a loss for words.

'Which happening do you mean?' She gave the parasol another twirl, decided she adored it, and settled back to study her escort, a very pleasurable occupation.

'Well, the kiss,' he replied in a low voice. 'I meant no disrespect, but you did anger me and at the time it seemed an excellent way to stop you.'

She managed a thoughtful nod of her head. 'It certainly silenced me.' It also had made her feel like a wilted daisy. Except a dead daisy didn't experience the sort of thrilling sensations she had.

'That it did.' Seeing that Katherine didn't seem to be the least angry, Philip was encouraged. 'You noticed your friend Miss Bonner as we drove through town?'

'She was flirting with Mr Weekes, I

noticed.' Again Katherine marveled that it didn't trouble her in the least that Mely was setting her cap at Michael. For a long time Katherine had daydreamed about Michael and how it would be when the magic day came and he would get a living. Now the day had arrived and she was far more interested in floating down the river with Lord Ramsey. If only, she considered wistfully, he might be ordinary Philip Fairfax rather than the lofty, aristocratic Lord Ramsey.

She might as well wish for the moon, silly, foolish girl that she was.

'You come here to sketch at times?' Philip offered, wondering what was going on in her mind.

'When I can evade the cows, not to mention the small boys that love to pester a person. Why they persist in playing their games right beneath one's nose, I shall never know.'

'But, then, it is a delightful nose.'

Why, thought Katherine with amazement, he is flirting with me. She giggled, something she never did. 'What a tarradiddle.' Placing one experimental finger on her nose, she grinned at him. 'Very ordinary, sir.'

'I used to be Philip. Can't I be Philip again?'

Katherine sobered at those words. It was all

very well to fantasize, but reality was reality. 'You know it would be most improper.' Not to mention hopeless, she longed to add. One didn't do that sort of thing, however.

'Who is to know, when we are alone?'

A duck paddled along the boat, giving them an inquisitive look before turning aside. 'Alone?' Her lips curved into a half-smile. 'I doubt that we are unseen, even if we may feel ourselves to be alone.' She gestured ahead to where the town began.

They drifted, for the most part. Katherine was totally unconcerned as to who might see her casually sprawled against a pile of pillows in the little green boat. Students strolled along the grass by the river. At the Bridge of Sighs, Katherine could make out several figures she recognized even through the grillwork of the Gothic windows.

'I believe that is your friend we just passed. Miss Bonner.' Philip glanced up to study the couple standing on the center of the bridge. He was glad they saw him with Katherine, for he hoped it would draw a final response one way or another.

'Yes, it was. She was with Michael, too.' Curious, it didn't even hurt to say the words.

'You can say Michael and not Philip? I protest.'

'I did not mean for it to slip out, but I shall

oblige you. It seems the least I can do for the one who is giving me this treat.' She fluttered her eyelashes in the coy manner she had seen Mely use. Philip laughed.

'I do not think that was amusing.'

'What shall you do if the actors refuse to permit you to join them? They are a superstitious lot.'

'Yes, I could see that today. Assure them that nothing else will happen, I fancy. You said you had the men check everything and that all appeared safe.' She watched his face, taking care to observe a possible change of expression in his eyes. If only they were not shaded, what with his having his back to the sun.

'I personally went over all the apparatus. I want to take no chances.'

Katherine sobered at the inflection she caught in his voice. Was she imagining things? Or was Lord Ramsey overly concerned?

Then she caught sight of her house. 'Look, over there. Poor Gabriel, he looks utterly wretched.'

'I fail to see a wounded expression on its beak. Isn't that your Cousin Sophia coming down to the bank of the river?'

'I believe it is. Come, let us give poor Gabriel a ride with us,' she commanded, although very nicely.

Lord Ramsey had done well enough while all that was required to maintain their progress took an occasional guiding stroke of an oar. But to cross the current, albeit a lazy one, required a bit of maneuvering. He plunged both oars into the water, pushing, pulling, turning about until Katherine feared they were going to overset the boat. She sat up in alarm, determined to protect her new parasol with the pretty ruffles. 'Look out,' she cautioned as he headed straight for the bank, dead-on.

'It was your idea,' he muttered as he attempted to draw the boat alongside the bank without throwing Katherine as well as himself into the Cam.

'Well,' Cousin Sophia said, 'that was a silly bit of work. What do you propose? If you think for a moment I'll join you in that flimsy craft, think again. Better off taking that stupid goose.'

'Sophia,' cried Katherine, very affronted at these unkind words.

'We came for Gabriel,' Lord Ramsey said through clenched teeth. Whether he was a bit angry or merely trying not to laugh, Katherine didn't know. She had no desire to know, either.

'Come, Gabriel.'

The goose waddled down to the water,

looked over the boat with what Philip thought was a malicious leer, then hopped down into the river. The goose swam close to his mistress, the one human in the world he genuinely seemed to regard with what might be termed affection.

'Come on, then,' Katherine said with patience.

Philip thought it a great pity she didn't have a clutch of children to fuss over, what with the forbearance she exhibited. He watched while she scooped up the bird, depositing it gingerly on the bottom of the boat. The white parasol had been carefully placed as far away from the dripping bird as might be.

Philip shook his head. 'This has to be the most ridiculous thing I've ever seen, taking a goose for a ride in the boat.' He had wanted Katherine to himself. The bird intruded, for it took her attention away from him, where he wished it.

'He's been feeling very blue-deviled lately, poor thing.' Katherine gently stroked Gabriel, and the bird responded to her as he would to no other; he placed his head on her lap. If he'd have been a cat, he'd have purred.

'I don't believe what I am seeing,' Philip muttered as he kept a wary eye on the bird in the boat.

Suddenly Gabriel perked up at the sight of a gaggle of geese along the far shore, which actually was not all that far away, given the narrowness of the river in this area.

'I suspect your pet wants to find a friend.'

'A lady friend, perhaps? Wrong time of year, is it not?' Katherine paid no heed to the man at the oars, which was just as well, for he was trying hard not to laugh at her as they drifted beneath the Silver Street Bridge.

'Oh, dear,' she murmured as the boat went around a bend in the river. There beyond the trees that gracefully leaned over the water was Sheep's Green on one side while on the other was Coe Fen. And the warm autumn afternoon had brought out the boys from the university. They were jumping off the river-bank of Coe Fen into the water, and they were quite, quite without clothes of any sort.

Before she could put up her parasol to protect her eyes from such a shocking sight, Katherine was aware of the band of pink bodies splashing about, mostly diving beneath — thank the good Lord — the water. She buried her head, holding her parasol at an angle and keeping it directly in line with the shouts and laughter. Never in her life had she been in quite such an embarrassing position.

'You needn't laugh, you know,' she snapped. 'And you might row a bit faster, if you please.'

'It is vastly amusing, Kate,' he said with a chuckle.

Annoyed at his calling her by that dratted name, she raised her parasol to shoot him a narrow look. 'I am not Kate.'

'Sometimes you are.'

Another pink body jumped into the river within sight, and Katherine shifted the white silk barrier again. Curious to know why he persisted in calling her by a name she had always fought to avoid, she said, 'Why?'

'You like to argue, and do it adorably, if I may be so bold to say so.' His eyes held that warm glow she had observed on several other occasions.

Katherine forgot all about the pink bodies on the riverbank to lose herself in that gaze. She decided that anyone who wished to pay her a fulsome compliment could be as bold as he wished . . . within reason, of course. She had not forgotten that improper kiss. And then she wondered what a proper kiss might be like. What a pity she couldn't ask.

'And what is it that has your brow so wrinkled in puzzlement, my sweet Kate?' he teased.

As he so often was able to do, he caught her by surprise and she replied before thinking. 'I merely wondered what a proper kiss might be like.' Then she realized what she had said and blushed a deep rose while the parasol dipped lower than before.

'Kate, dear Kate. Tempt not a desperate man. What did I do before I met you?' He chuckled in a manner Katherine found rather endearing, in spite of her being so flustered.

Her salvation came in the form of Gabriel. He had decided he wished to join his feathered friends and waddled in his most ungainly manner to the side of the boat. Taking one awkward step on Katherine's leg, he managed to leverage himself to the point when he could drop over the side of the boat.

'Heavens!'

'It will be just fine. Perhaps I ought to find Gabriel a friend in safer waters,' he mused.

Katherine hadn't the foggiest notion of what he meant by that odd remark, and decided to let it slip past her. She turned to search for Gabriel, espied the pink-skinned boys in the distance, and promptly gave up her hunt as the boat slipped past the small island in the river. The boys and the geese were left behind.

The town now far behind them, Katherine wondered how Philip would manage the return journey, given his questionable ability at the oars.

She twirled her pretty parasol while she studied Philip. The afternoon sun picked out glints of copper in his hair and outlined his broad shoulders admirably. He was more than handsome, she decided. He had a special aura about him, a quality that made him stand head and shoulders above any others. Ninian Denham might be able to play the hero. Philip actually was one.

That was precisely when it struck her, the truth of the matter. The reason why she didn't care a fig about Mely flirting her head off with Michael Weekes was because she, stupid, foolish Katherine Penn, had tumbled disastrously into love with Philip, Lord Ramsey, the son and heir of the Earl of Fairfax. The viscount was enormously wealthy and undoubtedly sought by every eligible girl in London when he went up for the Season.

How very, very amusing. Katherine swallowed with care, noting she had an obstruction in her throat and that her vision blurred. What was she to do? To allow him to know she had succumbed to his abundant charm was unthinkable. What had a provincial girl, the daughter of a mere professor to offer the likes of Lord Ramsey?

'Katherine? Are you all right? The boat is becoming damp, I expect. I'll put in here and hope that my man can find us.' Philip quickly brought the boat to shore. He helped Katherine out of the little boat with great courtesy.

She stood holding the frivolous parasol in

her hand, looking at the boat as though it would take all her dreams with it when it went up river once again. Absurd girl, she chided herself. All she was required to do was be herself. He would never suspect her of harboring such flights of fancy in his regard. Ludicrous. Mad. Quite, quite silly.

'I believe I see him now,' she said with a calm she certainly didn't feel.

Philip touched her arm, then tilted up her chin, looking deeply into her troubled eyes. He wished he knew what thoughts were spinning about in her head.

'Had a fine ride, I'll be bound,' said the driver when he reached them. He caught his breath after his run, glancing with distaste at the craft pulled ashore. 'I'll be on my way, then.'

Katherine paused, watching the little green boat as it disappeared up the river and around the bend. Then she turned and joined Lord Ramsey as they walked to the lane where his carriage awaited them.

'It's over,' she said, supposedly referring to the boat ride, or possibly their day on the river.

Philip had an odd feeling that she meant more, but what?

12

Cousin Sophia did not say a word about Katherine sailing down the Cam with Lord Ramsey without a chaperone. She did inquire about the trip, however.

'It was pleasant,' said Katherine in the most bland voice she could summon.

'That was a charming parasol he gave you. Odd, I would have expected you to be in raptures after such a treat.' Sophia studied her niece, then picked up a piece of needlework. It was a design of acanthus leaves, and very artistic. One could almost tell what the thing was.

'It is certainly a lovely parasol,' Katherine dutifully replied. She turned with relief at the sound of steps in the hall. The dinner hour neared. Surely someone would come to her rescue. The last thing on earth that Katherine wished for was a dissection of her outing on the Cam.

'Good evening, Katherine. And you as well, Cousin Sophia. It has been a splendid day, has it not?' Sidney entered the room with a cautious step. Katherine's face seemed to contain a supply of thunderclouds dropped from the heavens.

'Hello, Sidney. I am glad to hear you spent a good day.' Katherine began to pace somewhat restlessly about the room.

'After you left, I joined several of the actors for a turn about the town. We saw you floating down the Cam.' His eyes narrowed. 'I also saw Miss Bonner. Tell me, is she always such a shocking flirt? Her behavior with Mr Weekes is little short of scandalous!'

Katherine turned from where she had contemplated the view out the window to stare at Sidney Exton. 'I somehow doubt that Mely would behave that much out of line. For all her coquettish ways, she would not exceed what is proper, especially with Mr Weekes.' Katherine looked at Sophia, then added, 'We observed Mely with him in town. I confess she was flirting with him, but he seemed to take it in good heart.'

'Tossing her cap for him, is she?' replied Cousin Sophia with her customary directness.

'That doesn't bother you, Katherine?' Sidney strolled across the room, his boots making tiny clicks on the wooden floor.

Katherine wished they might have an Oriental carpet such as she had seen at Fairfax Hall. In fact, there were a good many things she wished.

'Why should it bother her? Mr Weekes has

come here chiefly for Mr Penn's advice and counsel.' Cousin Sophia quickly interposed her remark, for which Katherine was grateful. It galled her to acknowledge that Sophia was utterly right.

'I do hope that Mely succeeds,' Katherine added evenly. 'She has had the pick of the university for ever so long. And she does not have the opportunity to travel to London for a Season.'

'And you do?' There was an odd note in Sidney's voice, more than curiosity. Katherine couldn't tell what it was, and so ignored it.

Katherine picked up a pillow from the sofa, playing with its tassels as she thought. Why not? Her father had admitted he believed she had no desire for such. 'Yes,' she replied in a considering voice. 'I rather think I shall. Great-aunt Harriette has begged me to come ever so many times. I had no idea that Father didn't care a pin as to whether I went or not. It ought to be splendid.' She hoped that she didn't sound as though she was contemplating a trip to the tooth-drawer:

'It will not be until spring, I gather?' Cousin Sophia inserted dryly.

'Oh, yes, the spring,' Katherine agreed, wondering if she might be more inclined to seek a husband by then. Would her heartbreak heal that quickly? One didn't die of a broken heart. One merely felt like it.

'You should remember that Great-aunt Harriette is hardly likely to be in any condition to show you about, much less be able to sponsor you to Almack's. And if you are in the husband mart, that is the finest place to be.'

'How excessively vulgar that sounds,' Katherine exclaimed. 'Besides, I suspect that our great-aunt is far more active than you lead us to believe. Her letters are full of her activities and all the delicious bits of scandal she gathers. Does it bother you that I might avail myself of her chaperonage? I cannot see what possible difference it could make to you,' Katherine observed in conclusion.

Cousin Sophia laughed, rather rudely, Katherine thought.

'On the contrary,' Sidney denied, a rather unctuous smile crossing his face. 'I admit my thinking is selfish.' He gave Cousin Sophia an impatient glance, as though wishing her a mile away. 'You see, I nurture modest hopes of my own in your direction.'

'Why, Sidney,' Katherine exclaimed. 'I beg you — '

Her words were cut off by the arrival of Mr Penn and Teddy.

'Sidney, you here?' Teddy blurted with all the finesse of a young cub. 'I mean,' he amended, 'I saw you with your friend and I thought you might be spending the evening with him.'

'Rankin? And so I shall later on. I've to see to a bit of business first.'

'Business at this hour of the day?' Cousin Sophia said, her inflection reflecting her doubt of the matter.

'Nothing much, but of interest to me.' Sidney studied Katherine with speculative eyes.

'Did you spend your day at the hall, Papa?'

'I was not floating down the Cam, my dear.'

'Dear me, did everyone in Cambridge see me today?' she cried in vexation.

'I happened across the bridge at Silver Street as you floated by. You were wielding a white parasol to good effect, as I recall.'

Recollecting the gathering of pink bodies that had dotted the landscape, Katherine willed herself not to blush. 'It was kind of him to think of the sun.'

'To be sure,' murmured Mr Penn before turning to Sophia. 'I trust Mrs Moore has our dinner ready? I find myself rather sharpset this evening.'

'Is it books or beauties, I wonder? How goes the discussion on Jonah, Julian?' Sophia rose to give the bellpull a tug, signaling the housekeeper that the family had at last assembled for the evening meal.

'Jonah? We are past that. The Beatitudes was the topic of discussion today.' He rubbed his hands together, evidence of how he had relished the conversation.

'Interesting?' Cousin Sophia took Julian's arm to lead him to the dining room.

'She has a fine mind,' Julian mused.

'And that shocks you?' Katherine said with a hint of sharpness in her voice.

'There are few women who could hold their own on the subject.' He said this reflectively, as though surprised.

'And as long as the university refuses to permit women to get an education, it will undoubtedly remain that way.' Katherine gave her father an annoyed look while decorously seating herself at the table.

'I am aware you do more than dust my books when in the library, Katherine. I doubt you will come to a bad end as a result, in spite of your learning.'

'Really, Papa!'

Teddy guffawed as he slid on to his chair. 'Small chance of that. She is too busy planning for her future. Now that Mr Weekes has a living, I'll wager we shall see more of him around here.' He grinned at Katherine, oblivious to her discomfort.

Katherine exchanged a pained look with Cousin Sophia. 'Actually, I rather doubt that. I expect Amelia Bonner will see more of him than we shall.'

'Amelia Bonner, is it?' Mr Penn said with surprise. 'She's an ambitious little minx, as I recall. You can do better, Katherine, if you put your mind to it. At least, that is what Mrs Cheney says.'

'She does?' Katherine said, incredulous that she had been discussed between her father and Gisela.

'Katherine says she intends to visit her Great-aunt Harriette, come spring. Does that meet with your approval, Julian?' Cousin Sophia looked up from her plate, fork in mid-air as she waited for his reply.

'There is the possibility Katherine may not have to go to London for a husband,' Sidney inserted in what Katherine considered a disgustingly coy tone.

Katherine flashed him a withering look. If he thought she would succumb to his rather obvious attempts to fix her attentions, he was all out. 'There is also a possibility that it will not rain between now and then, but I would never count on it, Cousin Sidney,' she said with false sweetness.

Mr Penn bestowed puzzled looks on both young people, then applied himself to his meal. When he concluded, he rose from the table, waving the rest to remain in their chairs. 'Excuse me, I want to hunt up a passage in my favorite commentary on the Beatitudes.' He strolled from the dining room, humming an amazingly cheerful tune.

'Wonders — ' began Sophia.

'Never cease,' concluded Katherine as they exchanged amused looks.

Sidney finished his dinner, trying to catch Katherine's interest with tidbits of gossip he had gathered during his stroll about the town. As well, he went into lavish detail on the wonders to be found at the fair.

'You missed a goodly amount of action today by sailing off with his lordship. Ah, the aroma of gingerbread, the cries of the sellers. It is a treat, I tell you.'

'He has the right of it there, Kitty,' Teddy added with enthusiasm. 'I got a glimpse of that rope-walker who has a booth down the road from ours, and she is a real dasher.'

'And did you notice the selection of lace, perhaps?' Katherine gently twitted. 'Or if there is any improvement in the design of pattens this year? I vow, if they do not improve the city streets, we shall need a boat just to get to the baker's shop, come the next rains.'

'I broke one of my pattens,' commented

Cousin Sophia. 'I must remember to get a new pair. They have an excellent selection, better than the shop in town.'

'Have the Norwich players arrived?' asked Katherine, concerned for her play.

'Indeed,' Sidney answered. 'They quickly set up their booth. One can see they are accustomed to the task. I wonder if Miss O'Neill will have trouble from that quarter?'

'The parting was inevitable, Exton,' Teddy said in a hurry lest his sister get upset. He jumped up from the table, gave his Cousin Sophia a hurried salute, then excused himself from the room as though a devil had tapped him.

'I trust that does not mean what I fear it does. I intend to go to the fair tomorrow. There will be a dress rehearsal or I'll know the reason why,' declared Katherine, her resolution clear.

Sidney left the house a short time after. He was in an angry mood, the good meal notwithstanding. Katherine had made it quite plain he was as nothing to her. Not even a spark of interest or a desire to flirt was revealed. Certainly not the tender smiles such as she gave his lordship. Sidney couldn't believe she had flouted convention to sail alone with Ramsey. That just showed that the peerage could get by with most anything they desired. Well, Sidney thought with a calculating sneer, he would fix that, he would.

Down at the inn, he met his friend. Mr Rankin had been busy in Sidney's behalf, and the two spent the evening secreted in a corner, drinking ale and making plans.

★   ★   ★

The next morning Katherine dressed with haste, yet a desire to look her best. She pulled a gown of mulberry kerseymere trimmed with delicate blond lace from her wardrobe. Her bonnet was trimmed with matching ribands. She thought the effect was rather fetching, and hoped it wouldn't rain so as to ruin her bonnet. One never knew about September — or any other month, for that matter.

She studied the white parasol for several minutes before succumbing to the feminine wish to look all the crack with such a fancy accessory.

'Ready, Cousin Sophia?' Mr Penn had already left for the fair, as he would participate in the opening, then return to the college. The fair had once begun with all due pomp and ceremony. All that had ended many years ago, being deemed too expensive by the city fathers of the day.

'Just imagine,' Katherine said as the two

women drove along Trumpington Street on their way through town. 'The fair must have been a sight for the eyes to behold. Fancy the town crier leading a parade of constables, kettle drums, the grand marshal. There were two trumpeters and the town band, Papa told me, including two French horns.'

'I have seen the mace once carried by the head sergeant. And we still see the town clerk and the mayor in their robes from time to time. But it must have been a glorious sight, as you say,' Cousin Sophia agreed. 'Do not look now, but is that not Amelia Bonner across the street?'

Katherine immediately glanced to the side and said, 'To be sure. She has seen us and waves for us to stop. Say nothing,' Katherine pleaded. She tugged the reins of the donkey, and he drew to a halt with a toss of his head, the ribbons Katherine had tied on him earlier fluttering about quite gaily.

'Cousin Sophia, Katherine,' Amelia cooed, her voice sugary sweet. 'You are off to the fair, I'll wager. And wearing your best bonnet, Katherine?' Mely glanced to the sky, then laughed. 'We can only hope it does not rain.'

'Mely, you look ravishingly, as usual. How that shade of yellow becomes you,' Katherine declared, determined to be more than charitable to her once-good friend.

'Why, thank you, Katherine.' For a moment Amelia actually looked a bit uncomfortable. 'You know, of course, that Mr Weekes did get the living from Lord Ramsey?'

'So Lord Ramsey told us.'

Cousin Sophia spoke up then. 'He has been all that is amiable and civil to Katherine. So kind of him to shower her with his attentions, don't you think? But, then, I know you are too busy to have noticed. Show Amelia the attractive parasol he gave you, Katherine,' Sophia prompted.

Wishing she had left the pretty thing at home, Katherine reluctantly opened the item to reveal the ruffles.

Looking quite chagrined, Amelia nodded. 'Yes, I noticed it when you sailed past in that boat. Without a chaperone, Katherine?' she chided even as she smiled.

'One hardly expects the daughter of the regius professor to be other than correct when in the company of one of the officials of the university,' snapped Cousin Sophia, tugging at Katherine's sleeve. 'We best be on our way. It would be a shame to miss a thing.'

'Oh, I agree,' murmured Katherine, hoping to be on her way before she yielded to a desire to fall into a round of whoops.

'What a shocking tease you are become, Cousin,' Katherine said, laughter in her voice.

'Humph,' muttered Cousin Sophia, and urged Katherine to a faster pace.

Katherine obliged, commenting only, 'Would you say she was chagrined or crestfallen?'

'Neither. It was a curious admixture of vexation with sullen peevishness. I suspect Miss Bonner is not accustomed to being bested by anyone, let alone one who has always kept out of the limelight.' Cousin Sophia smiled, a small, satisfied sort of expression. 'I trust you will admit his lordship had been attentive of late?'

'That is due to the theater, nothing more,' Katherine replied in an even tone, hoping she did not reveal her inner emotions on the subject.

The drive along the Newmarket road was busy with carriages, nearly all of which were headed for the fair. Sturbridge Fair had once been the greatest fair in all of England, and while it might now be more of an amusement fair than one where people stocked up goods for the coming year, it was nonetheless welcome to the town and surrounding area.

Katherine guided the donkey along Cheapside to where the linen drapers and silk men were set up. They were to see about fabric for new curtains for the sitting room. Katherine wished to get the ordinary things out of the way before she went to the theater booth to, it was to be hoped, watch the dress rehearsal. From there, once Cousin Sophia was satisfied with a subdued print of classical design and sturdy weave, she went along Garlic Row.

'Look, there is a milliner I've not seen before, and a perfumer, too. I should like a bottle of pretty scent.'

'And so you shall have it, too,' Cousin Sophia declared.

Again they paused while Katherine selected a compound of floral scents that reminded her of a garden in midsummer. Roses and lilacs with a hint of spice teased her nose, and she hoped the scent would entice a gentleman. Not that she'd confess to any particular gentleman, mind you.

'After we put this cart behind the theater, I believe I shall stroll along Booksellers' Row,' Cousin Sophia declared. 'I think it would be nice to find some way to pass the time besides my embroidery. That can become tedious. Especially acanthus leaves,' she concluded in an undertone. 'I've not read *Cecilia* and perhaps Miss Edgeworth's latest.'

'Do not forget Miss Austen. Find me a book of plays. I should like a good copy of Garrick's *Bon Ton*. A farce is what I need at the moment, I believe. Not Reynolds. I found Lady Melmouth a trifle wearing in her preaching in *Folly as It Flies*, for all it's touted as a comedy. I certainly don't need another melodrama, as amusing as I find them. Mrs Radcliffe may keep them to herself.'

'She has done well, however. At least ten of her books have been dramatized,' reminded Cousin Sophia as Katherine turned over the reins of the donkey to the man from Lord Ramsey's estate who was around to serve as a jack-of-all-trades for them.

Katherine watched her aunt wend her way through the spaces between the booths on her way to Booksellers' Row, then turned to enter the theater by the side door. As Katherine crossed the cornfield, stepping daintily over the remains of the harvest, she noticed that the Norwich Company had indeed arrived. Their establishment looked plush at first glance. Only a closer inspection revealed the paint was thin and the construction hasty. The town workers had done a poor job of it, it seemed. She was fortunate that Lord Ramsey had his own carpenters.

How proud she was of the Ramsey theater. Tomorrow the play opened and already broadsides of the playbill were being distributed among the fair-goers. In addition to the play she had written, there was to be a short, rather witty farce called *Raising the Wind*. Katherine enjoyed the silly thing, although having a hero outwit his rival *and* the heroine's father seemed a bit farfetched to her. But the audiences loved it, and that is what mattered.

Inside the theater all was a-bustle. She soon learned what had been going on.

'The dress rehearsal for the farce went extremely well, Katherine,' Teddy proclaimed. 'Everyone knew the parts perfectly, and the costumes from Fairfax Hall were good. Really good.' He rubbed his hands together, gave her a satisfied smile that reminded Katherine of Cousin Sophia's, then he was off. Over his shoulder he added, 'After we take a break, we shall begin your play.'

Katherine wondered if all playwrights felt as useless as she did right now at this point. She had written, cast, and costumed the production. Teddy had overseen the final rehearsals, although Katherine had worked with Mr Denham.

'Cousin Sidney,' she cried with less than pleasure. 'I am that surprised to see you here at this hour of the day. Do not tell me you are forsaking the pleasures of the fair to watch the dreary business of a rehearsal.'

'Anything you do could never be termed dreary, cousin,' he replied with a faint bow in her direction while darting a glance at the comely young girl who acted the maid in Katherine's play.

A lift of her brow revealed what Katherine thought of this heavy-handed gallantry. 'I see.' And she thought she did. He was on the lookout for a dalliance. He'd not have it with one of the town girls. 'Do not look that direction, Sidney,' she warned. 'Her father is a local fighter, famed for the clever use of his fists. Best try for one of the Norwich group, if you are in line for a bit of fun.'

'Why, Katherine,' he teased, returning his attention fully to her, 'what a remark for a professor's daughter to make.'

'But, then,' she returned quickly, 'I am not just any daughter.' She sought to quell the unease she felt when he was about. The knowledge he wanted to wed her did not please. Perhaps it was because she would far rather have it another who sought her hand. A slight difference of opinion between two of the players caught her ear. She nodded at Sidney, dismissing him abruptly from her mind as she marched across the room to confront the problem.

Sidney gave her a resentful stare, then left the theater booth to find Lewis Rankin.

After settling the dispute, she turned, to find Ramsey approaching her. She clasped her hands to stop a sudden tendency to tremble.

'Good news, Kate. Nearly all the boxes

are booked for the first performance. Since the Norwich Company allows for booking the same day, I thought we'd extend it to the day before. It seems to be a successful idea.' He showed her the fistful of receipts with a happy glow on his handsome face.

So delighted was she that she neglected to admonish him for the use of that dratted name. 'What would we do without you?' she blurted out impulsively. 'It was a good thing when Teddy convinced me that we ought to seek your assistance. You are far more practical than either of us.' That had astonished her, that he should prove to be so efficient and businesslike in the planning of the production. But, then, she reflected, he undoubtedly had found out quite a bit if he'd frequented the green rooms while in London. Perhaps that had contributed to his frivolity as well.

As a compliment, it lacked a certain something, Philip decided ruefully. Would he ever understand Katherine? He felt sure she had no interest in her Cousin Sidney; he'd seen the way she looked at the smarmy fellow. And as for Mr Weekes, well, she might have entertained notions about him once, but Philip doubted she did any longer. Witness how she had shrugged off Miss Bonner's determined flirting. He was grateful to Miss

Bonner. She had proved most helpful.

By the time the rehearsal reached midpoint Katherine was a frazzled bundle of nerves. Someone brought her a sandwich and she simply could not eat it. Glancing down, she saw a stray cat had entered the building. She stooped down to offer the animal the food her stomach refused.

'Katherine, what about this costume for the final act? Miss O'Neill wants some changes,' Teddy called from the front.

Wondering if dear Miss O'Neill was pampered at every turn when with the Norwich Company, Katherine hurried off to work out some compromise. After listening to the objection, then to the intelligent suggestion the actress offered, Katherine was of the opinion that Miss O'Neill earned every penny of her high fee.

'She is right, you know,' Katherine said to Lord Ramsey when he strolled up to her side. 'The costume will be more effective this way. The brocade shawl will reveal, then conceal, thus teasing the audience.'

'You seem to understand teasing well, Kate.'

'I would that you not call me that.'

'But it fits you so well,' he responded, his voice that meltingly warm tone again. Katherine shivered and turned from his side with reluctance.

She shrugged, aware that he would do as he pleased regardless of what she said in the matter. And, in a way, she was inwardly pleased that he wished to bestow a personal, familiar name on her that only he dare use. And what did he mean about her teasing him? She was anything but a tease. She left that sort of thing to girls like Mely.

From that point the rehearsal proceeded perfectly. When they were done, some of the actors dispersed to their lodgings while others went strolling about the fair, trying out the treats offered.

Once the door finally closed after the last of them, Katherine sagged down upon a crude chair, relief that the final hurdle was over.

'Kate, there's trouble afoot.'

Alarmed, Katherine struggled to sit up properly, turning to face Lord Ramsey. She hoped that the deep affection she felt for him wasn't revealed on her face, for him, or anyone else about, to read. She thought it must be, for she felt it so keenly.

Lord Ramsey wasn't looking at Kate. Rather, he had a cat cradled on a piece of newspaper before him. A very still cat.

'What happened?' Katherine asked, glad the cast had gone, for they were such a superstitious lot.

'It is dead. And from all appearances, poisoned.'

'Poisoned! Are you sure? It might have been hit by a carriage or something.'

'Did I not see you feeding it a sandwich earlier?' He walked over to the door to place the dead cat outside, intending to study the animal later before burying it in the field.

'Well, yes,' she confessed. 'My nerves were in such a state, I could not think of putting anything in my stomach. You do not think . . . No, you cannot believe it was intended for me. It must have merely been a bad bit of chicken. You know how it can be if it is not handled carefully. I would not be the first to get a stomach ache from spoiled fowl.'

Philip stayed in the shadows, unwilling for Katherine to see the worry he felt. Unless he missed his guess, someone was trying to kill Katherine. First there had been the weight that ought not have fallen. Now a dead cat that ought to still be alive, had it not consumed Katherine's chicken sandwich. But who could it be? Who wanted her dead?

A sick feeling spread through him as he tried to think. Someone connected to the Norwich Company, perhaps? Maybe their advance man? It was a thought that would bear consideration. He would rack his brain tonight to see if there might be another who could want her dead.

'I would like you to come out to the hall for dinner this evening. There are a few things we need to discuss.'

'And what might they be? Not that I do not appreciate your invitation.'

The door opened and Cousin Sophia entered in great agitation. 'Katherine, Lord Ramsey, there is a dead cat just outside the door. It seems most carefully placed there. How curious.'

'Lord Ramsey believes someone wishes me dead, for it ate the sandwich intended for me,' Katherine replied with what she hoped was composure.

'I see.'

'I want Katherine at the hall this evening.'

'Of course. I should think it would be best if she went there directly from here, with no one seeing her or the wiser.' Cousin Sophia studied her calm-faced niece. 'I can arrange for a change of clothing to be sent out.'

Katherine looked at them, then rose and walked to the door. 'We may as well go now.'

Philip followed the two women out of the theater, casting shrewd looks about him to discover if there was someone lurking about waiting to see if a hue and cry was raised. Aside from the people he had observed the past days, there was no face that ought not be there.

Katherine was not going to die if he could help it. He would do anything necessary. Anything.

13

Katherine remained silent on the drive to Fairfax Hall. She thought all the fuss utterly ridiculous. Lord Ramsey had well and truly gone beyond the acceptable as far as she was concerned. Never mind that she was past praying for when it came to her heart. *He* ought to be more sensible. But she had perceived him as a frivolous man from the very beginning when he had laughed at her while she dripped pond water. Yet those laughing eyes entranced her.

'How are you going to keep this from my father?' she wondered aloud. They had been successful to this point. She suspected Papa would be angry. Whether he would put a halt to the production of the play was another matter.

'Gisela will think of something. I am convinced, you know. I rather think you believe the threat against you is all a hum.' He glanced at her stoic face, then returned his attention to the road ahead. They were approaching the town and there were numerous carriages abroad, mostly strangers here for the fair.

'Well, and it seems nonsense to me,' she

retorted, albeit with good temper.

The carriage clipped along at a goodly pace. They quickly passed through the town, fortunately seeing no one they knew, for Lord Ramsey took a less-frequented back road. Once over the Silver Street Bridge, Katherine relaxed.

She brushed off her gown, dusty from her time in the theater. An army of maids would have their hands full keeping that place tidy. 'I hope Cousin Sophia does not forget to send out my change of clothes. Why can I not go home? I do not understand the haste of all this.'

Philip really couldn't tell her, for he wasn't sure himself. He only knew that he felt Katherine to be in danger, and he wanted her close to him so he might protect her. But he couldn't reveal the particulars regarding that at the moment. He first wished to make sure that Mr Weekes and Cousin Sidney were definitely past history where Katherine was concerned.

'When we get to the house, you will go up with Mrs Moore and take a lovely bath. Then you can rest before dinner. I shall endeavor to see that your path does not cross your father's. He usually goes home of an evening. I'll see to it that Gisela knows that he is not to remain tonight.'

'This is nonsense,' sputtered Katherine. Actually, it was anything but. Why, when she had determined that she would keep aloof from his lordship as much as possible, was he bent upon taking her under his wing?

'Not to worry. I shall see to everything.'

Katherine turned her head to study him for a moment, peeking at him from beneath the brim of her neat chip-straw bonnet. He was daft. She also tried to tell herself that he was an odious, masterful, aristocratic gentleman beyond her touch, much too frivolous in his view of life, but that did not stop her heart from fluttering with hope.

They were met by Hector at the house, the dog gamboling about his master with unrestrained joy. Katherine found herself inspected and approved, apparently, for he gave her a doggie grin of bared teeth and a polite woof.

Mrs Moore spirited Katherine up the stairs to one of the bedrooms while Lord Ramsey strode off in the direction of the library, Hector at his heels.

Trusting that Katherine was enjoying her bath and trying not to dwell on the vision of her floating about in the water, Philip sought Julian Penn. The image of Katherine draped about from calf to neck with an enormous towel had haunted him since he had glimpsed her by the fireside in the little room off the plunge bath. A shapely ankle below the curve of an equally appealing calf lingered long in his memory. His recollection of her form as revealed following her fall in the pond was little short of spectacular. Ah, she was a lovely lass, had a fine mind, and possessed a bit of a temper. Her eyes flashed with fire when she was provoked. He could see how she longed to give vent to it, just barely curbing her passion. Philip wondered how that wonderful passion would be when channeled to another, more intimate scene.

'Good day, Lord Ramsey,' Mr Penn said, his voice respectful to the younger man.

Philip repressed a grin, for he was the one who ought to be overwhelmed. Mr Penn was a fine scholar, a man of even temperament and inquiring disposition. Kate must take after her mother.

'How does your study progress?' Philip joined the older man at the far end of the library, wondering what he had found to fascinate him today.

'Dipping into law and the Church,' replied Mr Penn genially. 'I fear I am making a bother of myself, but I do enjoy the search.'

'Not at all. I believe my sister has occupied much of your time while here. The Beatitudes, now?'

Mr Penn actually colored slightly, then nodded. 'True. Your sister has a remarkable mind.'

'For a woman,' came a voice from the archway where Gisela Cheney stood listening. She was dressed in a particularly pretty lavender gown trimmed in white ribands and lace. There was a panel of delicate embroidery down the front of the dress. Philip recognized the gown as something new, and he silently applauded Mr Penn for the change wrought in his sister.

'I expect you must be off to your common room. How congenial that must be for you. I trust we shall see you here whenever you can manage the time.' She drew him along with her, smiling persuasively at him.

Mr Penn gave her a puzzled look, then nodded. 'I am truly grateful for the happy hours spent with these wonderful books, dear ma'am.' He allowed himself to be led from the room after a polite farewell to Philip.

Alone, Philip turned his thoughts to the danger he suspected faced Katherine. Who might be the one who had tried to kill her? Even if Katherine thought it a lot of nonsense, Philip did not. Perhaps he ought to have told her about the rope? She would likely blame it on the Norwich Company. Philip decided they had best explore every avenue.

'Philip, why did you insist upon all this secrecy? Why was Mr Penn not to know of her presence?' Gisela glided into the library and up to confront her brother.

'She does not wish him to know of her involvement in the theater, at least until the play has begun and is a success.'

'You are so certain it will be?'

'It is a good plot and Eliza O'Neill is a gifted actress. She makes that insipid heroine believable.'

'I suspect there is more than merely the desire to keep Julian in the dark.' There was a hint of speculation in Gisela's voice, not to mention a teasing desire to know what was going on that had been kept from her.

'You are too clever by half, Gisela,' Katherine said from the doorway. She had bathed, dressed in the fresh gown sent out by Cousin Sophia, and felt able to face the brother and sister with equanimity. Attired in a sea-green gown of soft mull that she knew became her, she watched Lord Ramsy in particular as she stepped forward.

Faced by two determined women, Philip did what any sensible man in that position would do. 'Let us discuss this over dinner. I imagine Katherine must be starved by now.'

Momentarily diverted, Katherine smiled. 'A lady does not admit to being hungry, sirrah.'

Once seated at the table, Gisela returned to the topic that had drawn her earlier. 'Philip, you must explain about this business with the fair and Katherine.' She met Katherine's gaze to smile in apology. 'Not but what I do not adore your company, my dear, but this havey-cavey sneaking up the back stairs and hiding away does prompt questions.'

Her brother sighed. He pushed away his nearly empty plate to study the two women, so alike in determination, so different in appearance. 'You know that a weight fell, just barely missing Katherine. The rope was new, and cut as well as frayed. It was no accident. Then with the matter of the dead cat — '

'Dead cat,' Gisela exclaimed, clearly horrified.

Patiently Philip continued, 'Someone let a stray cat into the theater and Katherine fed it her chicken sandwich. Some time later it was found dead outside the door.'

'I still say the meat could have gone off,' insisted Katherine. Appealing to Gisela, she added, 'You well know how it can be with any poultry. One must forever be careful. I ought to have chosen cheese.' She had tucked away the information about the cut rope for later contemplation and possible scolding of Lord Ramsey. How dare the man withhold the information from her?

'I suspect that had you selected cheese, that would have also been the instrument of death, and there would have been no mouse handy to eat it for you.'

'At any rate, I was too nervous to eat.' Katherine eyed the food on her plate. All this talk of poison quite put her off her appetite.

'But you might have nibbled,' Philip objected.

'Is not arsenic called inheritance powder? What are you due to gain, Katherine?' Gisela inquired, only half joking.

'There are no fortunes in our family that I know about. What Father has will fall to Teddy. Cousin Sophia owns a small cottage by the sea, hardly worth killing for, I'd say.' Katherine frowned. Poison? Murder? 'This is utterly farfetched. There is no reason in the world for anyone to wish me dead.'

With that statement, Katherine eased back in her chair, willing the discussion to be over.

'Nevertheless you will oblige me by taking extra care the coming days. I'd not want your death on my conscience.' Philip opened his mouth to say more, then glanced at his sister. What else he wanted to say could be left for the moment.

'I intend to go out to the fair quite early tomorrow. If you wish to come along, you may,' Katherine said with a saucy tilt of her head. 'I am not about to request a guard.'

Philip groaned as the door opened. A footman entered bearing a tray of sweets. Katherine eyed them with longing. Cook provided excellent fare, but no pastries such as these.

The three sat drinking tea and nibbling fruit tarts while lost in thought. Katherine wondered how much of all this foolishness was solely in Lord Ramsey's mind and what might be reality. Personally, she thought it all a great hum.

When it came time for Katherine to go home, for she absolutely insisted upon sleeping in her own bed tonight, Lord Ramsey took her there while it was still light out. And they traveled in an enclosed carriage, a piece of stuff and nonsense if Katherine ever saw one.

'You truly believe in this threat?' she gently queried as one might of someone who is slightly deranged.

'I can only hope that all my instincts are playing me false in this instance.' Philip hoped that the nervous plucking of the sea-green mull meant that Katherine was beginning to listen to him.

She allowed him to escort her into the house, then slipped up to her room as quietly as possible. Her father, as usual, was out.

Where Teddy and Cousin Sidney might be, she didn't know. Cousin Sophia was in her room, for Katherine saw faint light coming from beneath the door as she tiptoed past.

A creak of the old wooden floor betrayed her as she entered her room. She wasn't surprised when Cousin Sophia rapped on her door a few minutes later.

'All is well? What did Lord Ramsey have to say?'

'I think it all a humbug. He is of the opinion that someone is out to murder me. I shan't believe it on the flimsy evidence he offered.' Katherine extracted her dainty muslin night rail from the chest, tossing it on the bed while she began to undo the tapes of her gown.

'I wonder, my dear. Lord Ramsey does not seem the sort of person to see things where they do not exist.'

The older woman stayed a short time, helping Katherine while offering a running commentary on Lord Ramsey's theory. When she had left the room, Katherine plumped herself down beneath the covers to think a bit.

Fatigue overcame her, and the next thing she knew, the soft light of morning crept over her still, slipping across her covers with fingers of sunshine.

Cousin Sophia met her in the breakfast room, her concern quickly concealed behind a hastily bland face. 'What do you plan today?'

Katherine gave her an affronted look. 'I shall go out to the fair, of course. I very much like that bottle of scent and intend to buy another.' She thought Lord Ramsey had noticed it, for he had bent over her shoulder to open the door for her when they had come up to the house. He had not wanted to disturb anyone, he'd claimed.

'See if they have a bottle of Tea Rose, I rather think I'd like that. I shan't come out today until time for the evening performance.' Cousin Sophia watched as Katherine picked at her food, the nervous nibbles, anxious glances darted out the window at the sky beyond. 'It does not look to rain. That will be good for the crowd tonight.'

'I know it can make all the difference between success and failure. Can you imagine the Newmarket road after a bad rainstorm?'

'Do not even think it, dear girl.'

Gisela was with Lord Ramsey when the carriage arrived at the Penn house to pick up Katherine.

'Lovely day, is it not?' Katherine said gaily. She had not seen either her brother or Cousin Sidney this morning. She didn't know if that was good or bad.

Philip watched Katherine come gaily tripping down the walk to where he awaited her by the carriage. She was wearing that pretty yellow muslin, the one that she'd worn the day they met. He hoped the dark-blue spencer would keep her comfortable, for the morning was cool. Katherine's honey-blond curls were nicely tucked beneath her favorite bonnet, one she wore frequently. He was pleased she'd been waiting for them and had not kept them standing. For all that she was obstinate, she was also very considerate.

The noise from the fair could be heard at a goodly distance. When the carriage drew close to the booths, they found a merry scene, colorfully garbed tradesmen plying their wares while visitors to the fair picked and chose with care and not a little pleasure.

'I see Mayor Mortlock is here,' Katherine commented sourly as the pompous man who had held control over the town for ages passed not far from where they stood.

At Lord Ramsey's questioning look, Katherine flushed. ''Tis said he loves power for its own sake. Goodness knows the city is corrupt enough. Witness the problems with the water. Of course, he calls it naught but 'influence,'' she scoffed. 'If you have a large-enough purse, you can do as you jolly well please around here.'

''Tis the way of the world, my dear,' Gisela whispered. 'Tell me, what is the Spinning House? I heard a man inform a woman she ought to be there, wherever it is.'

Katherine looked askance, then decided plain speech the best reply. ''Tis the place for lewd women. That is another disgrace. There is no fire, nothing to help sustain them but what they can earn by spinning or beating hemp. No sewer, so you may imagine what the place is like. They need something to keep them warm, and beds, rather than pallets of straw on that cold floor. The dab of money spent there years ago did little to alleviate the situation.'

'Pity for lewd women, Katherine? From the doctor of divinity's daughter?' Philip glanced down at her with twinkling eyes.

'Let him who is without sin cast the first stone,' she said quietly, wondering what manner of life his lordship had lived while in London. 'I've found the people who live rather dashingly are the ones who profess great piety in public.'

Philip turned away, feeling slightly uncomfortable with that direct gaze fixed upon him. For one who had such a wicked sense of humor, Katherine was a surprisingly decorous girl. Compassionate, as well, he reflected as he watched her stroll down Garlic Row.

He could hear the sounds from Adam's Circus, where animals restlessly prowled while customers gawked. All along the booths people bargained for everything from fine leather gloves to figures in painted porcelain and wood. Gisela paused to inspect a tea caddy in fine rosewood.

Katherine located the booth where she had bought her vial of scent, purchased another, plus a bottle of Tea Rose scent for Cousin Sophia. She felt more at ease once here at the grounds of the fair. There was absolutely no reason to listen to the warnings from Lord Ramsey. He was naught but an alarmist.

He was also at her side more often than not.

'Finding all you wish?' he inquired from over her shoulder after he had watched her pay for her bottle of scent. So that was what produced the lovely flowery fragrance that clung to Katherine. He made mental note of the essence.

Having little money for frivolities, since her father seldom saw fit to remember to leave her much, Katherine politely nodded. 'Yes. I do enjoy looking, however.'

Philip had no knowledge of Mr Penn's attitude toward money and Katherine, but he knew how absentminded the man was. Philip smiled, then took Katherine's arm to stroll along Garlic Row, inspecting the contents of every booth they passed. He was happily unaware that Katherine fully intended to offer her pressed-flower pictures for sale in the following days to obtain a bit of extra money.

Gisela complained, 'You go too fast, brother dear. I wish to look over these fans. See, Katherine, are they not charming?' She held up one of fine lace with sandalwood sticks.

Philip picked up a fan that had hand-painted roses on the silk and beautifully carved ivory sticks. The fan would look delightful when held by Katherine, so he bought it. Presenting it to her was more difficult.

'For a charming lady,' he said with a deal of gallantry.

'You ought not,' Katherine began, trying to conceal how she longed to possess such a lovely item.

'Fiddle,' interrupted Gisela. 'It does him good to buy a pretty now and again.'

Taking the hint, Philip proceeded to pay for the delicate lace fan that Gisela had chosen. It seemed to set Katherine at ease, and for that he was thankful he had his sister along, even though she was a costly baggage, what with wanting everything in sight.

'You are no better than a child,' he chided. 'What will you take a fancy to next, I wonder?'

'Look, Philip! Some enterprising man has set up an archery range.' Gisela tugged his arm, leading him toward the end of the side row near the open field. From this spot Philip could see the rear of the theater.

'Small wonder,' added Katherine, crossing to watch a young gentleman from the university take aim at a butt. 'It seems one of the favorite pastimes here for the students, along with billiards, hunting, driving tandems, and cockfights, all of which are banned, although they pay little heed to that.'

'And bathing?' Philip inquired with an innocent air.

Her cheeks flamed. 'Also banned. They give as much attention to the prohibition of that as to any of the other pleasures they enjoy.'

Gisela watched the archery competition with a critical eye while Katherine turned away to look at the theater. 'I believe I shall go over to check on things, sir.'

'I'll come along.' Philip was feeling a bit foolish with his insistence upon Katherine never being alone, but once he had begun, there was no leaving off until the fair was concluded and she was still safe.

'Very well,' she replied with good grace. After all, she reasoned, if she was given the treat of Lord Ramsey's company, ought she not enjoy it?

They began to traverse the cornfield, Katherine carefully picking her way through the stubble. Suddenly she stumbled, grabbing hold of Lord Ramsey's arm as she nearly fell.

At the same moment an arrow whished past Philip, directly over Katherine's head, and about where her heart would have been had she not half-fallen.

She straightened up, turning her head to apologize for clutching at him, then stopped in her tracks. 'What is it?' Lord Ramsey looked grim, not to mention exceedingly pale.

'Look ahead of us and tell me what you see.'

'An arrow. The man back there has a great pile of them; I doubt if he will miss it overmuch.'

'Katherine, that arrow was deliberately sent your way with intent to do great harm, if not kill.' They moved forward to stand near the missile. 'Look at it. 'Tis not an ordinary arrow. 'Tis a hunting arrow, the sharp metal point of which could pierce a body with ease. Had you not stumbled and nearly fallen, I have no doubt I would now be holding you in my arms, and you would either be dead or near enough so as not to make a difference.'

She swallowed with care, then swayed as she considered his words. This was not imagination. Philip had seen this with his own eyes. 'I cannot believe it. Why?' She turned trusting eyes up to him, her fear clearly visible.

He put a protective arm about her while searching the throng of young men about the archery booth. Drawing her closer, he murmured into her hair, 'There is no telling who it might have been. Far too many are clustered over there to know which one sent the arrow 'astray.' Best stay by my side, for what little good it does you.' He felt bitterly inadequate as a protector. She would have been hit but for that stumble on a bit of stubble.

Gisela bustled up to them, her eyes wide with inquiry at the sight of Katherine trembling in Philip's arms.

'Come,' he ordered. 'We had best get somewhere safer.'

'Safer?' Gisela echoed in alarm.

He kicked the arrow with the toe of his Hessian. 'This deadly little missile was intended for Katherine.' Bending down, he picked up the arrow, studying it for a clue to ownership. Nothing was visible.

'Good grief,' whispered Gisela, glancing about while following Philip and Katherine into the theater with cautious haste.

Once safe within the building, Katherine settled on to a chair, her legs being quite unequal to the task of supporting her any longer. 'Now what do we do?'

'Go home,' suggested Gisela. 'I shall stay with you every hour.'

'Not leave your company, for certain,' Philip added.

Katherine shook her head. 'That is not practical, you know. You are very kind to desire to protect me, but have you given thought to how long this may continue? I could grow old while waiting for this would-be killer to strike once again.' She propped her chin on her fist, staring off to the rear of the theater. 'I think I had best go on as usual. Whoever it is will be bound to reveal himself . . . or herself, ere long.'

Philip and Gisela exchanged uncomfortable looks. They had discovered how stubborn Katherine could be, given a position she firmly believed correct.

'I would not keep you from watching the opening of your play this evening,' Philip said slowly.

Katherine popped up from the chair, her anger prompting her energy. 'I should hope not. I do appreciate all you have done and are doing. But this, this madness cannot control my life.'

Gisela nodded thoughtfully. 'I can see what you mean. But how can we keep this from happening again?'

'It is never the same. I must say, whoever it may be is an inventive person,' Philip mused, escorting Katherine and Gisela to the door of the theater. 'Let us get some tea, or something of the sort.' They bustled off in the direction of the coffee house on Hatters' Row. On the way they encountered a familiar trio.

'Katherine, Lord Ramsey, and Mrs Cheney! How charming to see you here,' Amelia Bonner cooed while clinging to Mr Weekes. She had several parcels and a happy face that told Katherine all was going well with Amelia's plan. What that was could be easily guessed. Sidney Exton stood close by, his eyes watchful.

'Cousin Katherine, have you seen your brother this morning?' Sidney stepped up to the group, his brow furrowed with obvious concern.

Katherine darted a worried glance at Gisela, then to Lord Ramsey. 'I fear I have not. When did you last see him?'

'Yesterday evening, I believe.' He glanced

about, then continued. 'I suspect he'll show up later in time to assist with the play.'

'Play?' Mr Weekes said, looking confused but sharply alert. His thin nose tilted upward at the mere notion of the theater.

Katherine rushed in to explain. 'You know how Teddy adores doing odd things. He is helping with the play this evening. Indeed, we paused to see if he might be here.'

Amelia looked smugly skeptical while Mr Weekes gave Katherine a puzzled glance.

Katherine studied the two, then quietly suggested, 'We are on our way for a cup of tea. I vow, shopping is a tiresome, although delightful pastime. Would you join us?'

'Lovely,' breathed Amelia while tugging on her escort's arm. 'What a pity you have not had my luck in shopping,' she continued, tossing Katherine a superior smile.

'I had no idea he was such a stuffed shirt,' whispered Gisela as they trailed after the couple. 'Fancy her wanting him.'

'Indeed,' echoed Katherine, wondering how she had thought him a worthy husband not too many weeks ago.

Philip leaned over to say quietly, 'If we stick close to friends, there will be less chance for the villain to get at Kate. Agreed?'

Katherine nodded reluctantly. It bothered her a little to see Amelia Bonner clinging to

Mr Weekes. That might have been herself, had she not permitted delusions to lure her mind and eyes elsewhere. She wound her way past the gingerbread sellers who had set up in front of the theater to stroll with the others down Garlic Row. At Hatters' Row they turned off to find the very respectable coffee house. Katherine allowed herself to be guided to a table neatly covered in green baize.

Amelia gave Mrs Cheney a considering smile, then graciously explained, 'This place is kept by the proprietor of the finest coffee house in Cambridge. You need have no fear of paltry refreshments here.'

Katherine exchanged a guarded look with Gisela. What else might she have to fear? Sidney spoke to the young woman tending the tables and shortly they were served with a variety of beverages, tasty pastries, and fruit pies.

'These ought to be fine,' Philip said close to her ear. 'Not to worry.'

Nevertheless, she picked at her fruit pie, although it tasted ever so good. The knowledge that someone was out to harm her, fatally if possible, was rather off-putting.

'I suggest we all stay together,' Philip said, keeping a close watch on Amelia. While he doubted the young woman responsible, poison was considered a woman's choice, and she seemed to delight in sniping at Katherine. He had missed none of the sly little digs sent in that direction. Were they alone, what might happen?

'I trust you will join me now in a sampling of the oysters, Cousin Katherine?' Sidney said as they ambled from the coffee house after a leisurely repast.

'Silly,' replied his cousin, a grin touching one corner of her attractive mouth. 'I am much too full now. Perhaps later?'

'I shall hold you to that,' Sidney replied, all amiability.

Amelia seemed not to be content with snaring the eligible Mr Weekes, for she sidled close to Sidney, tucking her arm in his when she stumbled on a little stone. She presented a pretty picture, arm in arm with the two men.

Katherine was amused and shared a warm look with Lord Ramsey. 'What would she do on the stubble?' Katherine wondered aloud, secure that Amelia couldn't possibly hear what she said with all the din about them.

'True,' Philip replied thoughtfully. Amelia Bonner could scarcely draw the bow sufficiently to send the arrow a foot, much less a distance. His gaze shifted to the ubiquitous Cousin Sidney. What did anyone actually know about him? He was always around, agreeable, and seemed fond of Katherine. But a close watch of her face revealed she treated him much as she did her brother.

Had he ambitions in her direction? Philip suspected that Katherine was unaware of them, or at least did not encourage them. The knowledge comforted.

'Ho there.' Teddy bounded up to the group, his face eager and happy. 'Splendid day. Jolly good merchandise this year. Did you purchase the Tea Rose scent for Cousin Sophia? When I stopped at home, she said to remind you.'

'Done,' Katherine replied with a relieved look at her brother. The thought had occurred to her that if someone wanted her out of the way, they might well want Teddy disposed of as well. 'Do stay with us, Teddy. 'Tis much nicer with a Party.'

He seemed taken by the suggestion and strolled along, urging his sister to buy this and that with little success.

Philip, seeing the wistful looks and the frequent negative shake of Katherine's head, began to understand better why she had bought so little at the fair. Evidently her father was generous with his son, but felt his daughter ought to be satisfied with little or nothing. It was not an uncommon attitude, but it gave Philip the desire to shower

Katherine with lovely gifts. That pair of soft York tan gloves she admired, for one, and the green-and-blue paisley shawl that would look well with her honey-blond hair for another. There were many things he longed to do.

The rub was, would he get to do them?

14

They left the fair in good time so that they could have a light luncheon, for that was all Katherine might have managed under even the best of circumstances.

'I feel quite safe here,' Katherine said as she strolled about the grounds of Fairfax Hall with Philip, Gisela, and Cousin Sophia. Hector trotted along near his master while keeping a quizzical eye on Katherine. Sidney and Teddy were due to arrive shortly — Teddy with a surprise, so he claimed.

'Good, good.' Philip could not have been more pleased. He wanted her to feel safe and comfortable at his home. It made the trip to the theater no less hazardous, however. When one had no notion as to when the villain might strike, it filled each hour with tension.

Gisela undertook to show Cousin Sophia a particularly lovely bed of China asters in full bloom. They discussed the problems of needlework as well in amiable concern. Gisela quite understood the vexations of matching wools.

Katherine and Philip strolled toward the Gothic Tower. The grass had been well-clipped, the pond was clear and free of weeds now. Katherine recalled her plunge into the cold water, with the subsequent sodden dress and green spots that dotted her person when she emerged. 'You laughed at me.'

'What? When? I would never do anything so unkind.' His eyes twinkled down at her with those interesting lights deep within them.

'The day we met by this pond. I believe you said I had a terminal case of the green measles, whatever that might be.' She flashed him an indignant look.

'Imaginary, my dear. Forgive me for my abysmal sense of humor. But I wasn't laughing at you. I was delighted at this lovely creature who reacted so calmly to a situation that would have had most women in spasms, or at least mild hysterics. You have not failed to charm me from that moment on.' His voice seemed to caress her.

Katherine gave him a disbelieving glance. She thought his tribute mere flummery. Did she appeal to him? It was a lovely notion to warm one's heart. He was practiced in the art of dalliance; she was not. That placed her at a great disadvantage, yet she took comfort that he sought her out and wished to protect her.

In companionable silence they climbed to the top of the knoll upon which the tower was built, Hector running circles about them. Constructed of brick and rubble and faced with clunch, it rose up for three ragged stories. The walls were pierced with two-light windows and cross-shaped embrasures. Katherine decided it appeared to better advantage from a distance. Hector flopped down, energy flagging.

She turned to look back at the house. It was an impressive sight, with the gardens and the ponds, which had a pretty Chinese bridge spanning them, the expanse of green lawn up to the magnificent house itself. What a silly fool she was to entertain for even a moment the idea that she might wed this man and share this lovely home with him. He could have most anyone in the country if he so chose.

'What makes you look so sad, Katherine?'

'What? Oh, I was thinking . . . ' She espied her brother and cousin making their way cross the lawns to where Cousin Sophia stood with Gisela. 'Am I seeing things?'

Hector looked up, alert to possible fun.

Philip gave the two an impatient glance, then looked again. 'It seems they have brought Gabriel.'

'Sidney is carrying a goose as well. Oh, do let's go down to see what is going on.' Katherine extended her hand to Philip, who instantly accepted it.

He had wanted some time alone with Katherine, to help him understand these peculiar feelings that assailed him whenever he was close to her. When she had nestled in his arms after the near hit this morning, something had stirred deep within him, an emotion he'd not felt before and wanted to explore further. That she had gazed into his eyes with a look of complete trust had nearly undone him. If he'd had the chance at that moment, he'd have wrung the neck of whoever tried to murder her. He remained militantly at her side on the walk back to the garden.

'Theodore,' Cousin Sophia demanded, 'what do you think you are doing?'

Katherine joined the group, with Philip close behind her. He chuckled at the sight of the elegant Sidney carrying a large white goose and looking vastly uncomfortable.

Teddy dropped Gabriel to the ground and a relieved Sidney did the same, brushing off his once-fastidious oyster-gray inexpressibles with a distressed hand.

'I say, Katherine, I do hope you appreciate what we are doing for your blasted pet,' grumbled Sidney.

'Gabriel was getting lonesome so I found him a friend,' Teddy cried, his boyish face alight with glee.

Katherine could hear Lord Ramsey chuckling softly behind her, and she succumbed to the same urge. 'Oh, Teddy,' she sputtered, 'I hope you are prepared for a flock of goslings, come spring. That is not a gander, you know.'

'I am well aware of that, widgeon. I felt sorry for old Gabriel. He needs something to blow his horn about, if you know what I mean.' Teddy's eyes danced with mischievous delight.

Hector chased the geese to the pond with great enthusiasm, running in circles and barking loudly.

At that sight Lord Ramsey could no longer contain his amusement, joining in the general laughter.

'You are a dear,' Katherine said fondly, ruffling her brother's blond curls before walking over to inspect the newcomer. 'But I fear we can't keep them at home. Perhaps,' she said with a deal of daring, 'we can leave the young lady to tend Lord Ramsey's ponds and bring Gabriel out for a visit now and again?' It would give Katherine a chance to see him, maybe. She didn't know if that might be too painful or not, particularly if he married, as she supposed he must to get him an heir.

'Not to worry, Katherine,' Philip urged. 'Allow Gabriel to enjoy his expanded horizons for a time. The lady has a name?' he added in Teddy's direction. The female aimed for the center of the pond and proved to be an excellent swimmer.

Gabriel joined his lady fair and swam about in search of the tidbits he seemed to recall from a previous visit.

'Belle, of course,' Teddy announced with modest pride.

Which proclamation brought on a fresh round of laughter. Philip congratulated Teddy for finding a charming companion for Gabriel, especially such an intelligent-looking bird. Hector kept a vigilant watch from the grass.

They slowly ambled toward the house, Philip taking care to tuck Katherine's arm in his. He was concerned that she not tumble, he convinced himself. And then, he added in all honesty, he truly enjoyed her closeness. Her delightful scent floated across on the late-afternoon air to tease his nose. He inhaled with gratitude, thankful she did not lean toward the heavy perfumes favored by so many ladies in the city.

'How fortunate your father was not due here for dinner, Katherine,' Gisela said as they entered the saloon. 'We would have had a time explaining why we all wanted to go to town so early in the evening.'

'Nonsense. Julian knows I always go to the theater when it comes with the fair,' Cousin Sophia declared stoutly. 'He would wonder if I failed to go, or for that matter, if Katherine did not pester me to go with her,' Cousin Sophia turned to Sidney. 'Young man, you are to join us this evening.'

Clearly amused, he replied he would be honored to go with the ladies. Whereupon Philip said that if they expected to leave him behind, they were sadly mistaken.

Gisela chuckled, adding she had no intention of remaining at home either.

Philip was well-pleased with his sister as of late. She was in first looks, her eyes shining with contentment, an aura of happiness settling over her shoulders like a cape of sunshine. For this he thanked Julian Penn. After Gisela's husband left, leaving her alone to face the loss of her baby, then the later news of his death, she had faded to a mere shadow of herself. Now she was more the young woman he remembered as a boy. Mr Penn seemed to have given her a special interest in living, one badly needed.

Dinner was a gay event, with much laughing and teasing, mostly from Teddy. He was in high spirits, eager to head for the fair, anxious for the outcome of their production.

'Your scenery is of first-rate design, Ramsey,'

Teddy avowed. 'The spy that Norwich is sure to send over will be green with envy. Just see if we don't get a visit from their scenery men once the word gets back.'

Katherine had become oddly silent as the talk turned to the play and the evening to come. She looked about the table at the familiar and dear faces. Well, almost dear, she amended as her gaze reached Sidney. He had fitted into the household with ease. Few claims, little fuss, after his first display of moods. Yet she felt she knew him no better than that day he had arrived at the door.

At first sight she had thought he would make a good wicked count. That remembrance brought a reluctant smile to curve her lips. Instead, he had indicated he wanted to marry her. She had not encouraged him in the least, and he seemed to have given up that particular notion. She did not hold with the business of marrying cousins. Her father had once commented that it seemed to bring about bad blood.

If Lord Ramsey or anyone else observed her abstraction, nothing was said. They left the table promptly the meal was done and in short order were settled in the carriages. Teddy and Sidney went ahead in the donkey cart. Philip, Gisela, Cousin Sophia, and Katherine followed in the closed carriage.

Katherine suspected Lord Ramsey was still concerned over the villain, as he called the would-be killer. A melodrama come to life? Hardly. She thought she might write one better than this sad plot, using a hero much like Lord Ramsey, herself as the heroine, naturally. But the villain had to be someone logical, with a reason for the murder. That was the rub. She could think of no earthly motive for someone to do away with her.

Katherine was a quivering mass of nerves by the time they arrived at the theater. Her play — that silly spoof on the melodramas most people found utterly delightful — came once the comedy concluded.

'Sidney, help me to find a seat,' Cousin Sophia ordered, much to Katherine's surprise. At the inquiry in her eyes, Sophia added, 'With you and Theodore traipsing off, Gisela and I will require company.'

Since that made great sense, Katherine nodded, then hurried off to check to see that all was well with the costumes and the players.

The comedy was well-received. Katherine watched from the side of the theater, Lord Ramsey standing close behind her. She had laughed and applauded, but all the while there was a strain within her. Her play. Would it also be well-received? Would the audience understand her perspective?

There was an interval between plays, and Katherine hurried behind the curtains to see if she might be of help.

The theater was soon darkened as much as was possible, considering that the lamps must remain lit. The bracketed oil ring lamps left much to be desired. They smoked and sputtered. Katherine gave the nearest one an impatient glance, then shook out the pretty gown that Eliza O'Neill wore in the first act. Now the verdict was to come on Katherine's play.

The twelve lamps that made up the footlights shone brightly as Eliza entered from the wings to say her first lines. The woodland set that Lord Ramsey designed looked incredibly real. Katherine almost expected a fawn to timidly peek from behind a tree.

She felt fluttery and vulnerable and leaned weakly against the strong figure that came up behind her.

'This is the least of your fears, sweet Kate.' Philip slipped an arm about her to shield her from the actors who brushed past them to enter and leave the stage.

Before she knew it, Ninian Denham had swept the fair Eliza into his arms and dramatically exited the evil count's castle in the final scene. The curtains were drawn to thunderous applause.

'It went well, I think,' Katherine said cautiously, reluctant to leave the security of Lord Ramsey's protecting arm for the more sensible independence of her own two feet.

'More than well, I believe. It truly shimmered with wit and charm.' Philip allowed her a measure of liberty, yet stood close enough to keep her from harm.

The cast was jubilant, predicting a profitable run for the length of Sturbridge Fair. Eliza O'Neill and Ninian Denham held an animated discussion on the final scene, each bent on improving it. Miss O'Neill's father stood by, ever the watchful guardian.

Katherine and Philip were shortly surrounded by their families. She wished her father might have joined them, but she had little doubt as to what his reaction might have been. She contented herself with praise from Cousin Sophia and Gisela, not to mention Teddy's elated words.

They strolled from the theater, leaving instructions for the following day. Philip had hired two rugged men as guards. Not knowing what the villain had in mind, he felt it best to play everything safe.

Katherine and Cousin Sophia entreated the others to join them for a cup of tea. Philip swept everyone into the house; then, with a wink, he ordered Mrs Moore to bring on the refreshments.

Astounded, Katherine could only sit with her mouth ajar as the housekeeper and a maid brought trays of biscuits and meringues, dainty sandwiches, bottles of fine wine and champagne. Mrs Moore placed the display on a low table with a proud flourish, then paused to fuss with a sprig of parsley while offering a word of congratulations to Katherine from the staff.

'I say, Ramsey,' bubbled Teddy as the champagne worked its magic on him, 'this is capital stuff. Simply capital!'

Katherine sat in quiet joy, feasting her eyes on the faces so dear to her. Cousin Sophia was actually jolly, her biting remarks tempered. Gisela glowed with inner happiness. Teddy was jubilant. Philip? Well, he was hard to understand. At last her gaze strayed to Cousin Sidney. He sipped his fine wine with a connoisseur's pleasure. He seemed agreeable. Once the excitement of the play was behind her, she fully intended to write Great-aunt Harriette to find out what his story might be.

On the far side of the room, Philip watched his Katherine. She sat quietly in her chair, modest, unassuming, her wide smile encompassing all. Her beautiful eyes shimmered with pleasure, while her slender hands toyed with a glass of champagne. She seemed to glow, radiate a sensual joy.

With a jolt he realized what that peculiar feeling he had experienced when he was around her must be: he had fallen in love with his little maid of the pond. This certainly was an unexpected development to his country visit. Yet it was welcome. His parents would be pleased he had found a proper young lady. If they but knew the inner, more provocative side to her. It would be a distinct pleasure to marry her, have a family with her, travel, live a lifetime with her at his side.

He wanted to be her hero, not only to defend her from that Bedlamite who wished to murder her, but also to keep her to himself for the rest of their lives. There was so much to learn about her, so much they might explore together.

Visions of trips to Paris and Italy to study the theater sprang to mind. London, of course. She hadn't been that far as yet. He fully intended to rectify that.

But first he must take care of the villain.

Reluctance to break up the party was best expressed when Cousin Sophia hiccupped softly and said, 'This is ever so lovely, but tomorrow is upon us. We all need our sleep.'

Philip knew no desire for sleep, but could

hardly remain. With good grace, he helped his sister with her pelisse, his gaze lingering on Katherine.

'Good night all,' Katherine caroled as the last of the guests left the house. She bid Sidney and Teddy good night, then went up the stairs with Cousin Sophia.

'It was delightful, my dear. I knew it would be. So like you, you know,' Cousin Sophia said with her odd sort of logic.

It wasn't easy to fall asleep. Katherine kept her candle burning a long time. At one point she thought she heard a noise outside her door, but when she softly called to see who it might be, only silence followed. Then she heard her father coming up the stairs and she relaxed. Surely she could sleep in peace now that he was home. Without examining her reasonings, she closed her eyes to snuggle beneath the covers.

The next day Katherine slept in. When his lordship stopped by the house, Cousin Sophia informed him that she doubted if the girl would get up very early.

Philip set off for the fair, almost glad that Katherine would be safe in her bed instead of prowling about the grounds with him. He intended to do a bit of detection work, to see what he might uncover.

The archery butts and arrows were gone

today; no trace remained that they had ever been at the end of the row. Philip stood, amazed that such could happen so quickly. He strolled along the lane, peering at the contents of the various booths while keeping his ears sharply attuned to what was said about him. He learned nothing of interest.

The price of workman's shirts was up. Turnips were down. A new, improved plow was being touted as the best yet. There was a horse that fair promised to beat them all coming on the block today, the final day of the horse sale.

He paused to quench his thirst at the coffee house the group had patronized yesterday. Coffee helped him keep alert, and he badly needed that. He settled on a chair in a corner so he might watch and listen, tilting his hat over his eyes and slouching down so as to better disguise his identity. He'd chosen to dress simply, as a rural visitor might. He didn't resemble his usual sartorial elegance in the least.

He had called for a second cup of coffee when he saw Sidney. The young dandy entered with that friend of his, Rankin. The two gave a furtive glance about, then settled down at the only vacant table, not far from Philip. He blessed the poor light that helped conceal him, and shifted slightly so he might overhear what was said. It might be innocent conversation. On the other hand, he had learned nothing of interest this morning; perhaps their chitchat might prove of benefit.

The scrape of chairs was followed by a call for coffee. Once they'd been served, Sidney cleared his throat.

'You think 'tis safe in here? To talk, I mean?'

Rankin looked about, nodded. 'Who would listen to what we have to say? You worry overmuch.'

'I confess I am fearful. I have no liking for what I do. But I have no alternative, either. The chit shows no inclination in my direction and I cannot chance more time. We have failed three times so far. We cannot miss again. This time it must work. Old Harriette might pop off any moment. Does she, and it puts paid to any hope I have to gain the inheritance. As it stands, every penny of her lovely estate goes to my dear little cousin Katherine, the sweet and good.'

'Yet you'd have wed her,' Rankin reminded.

'What's to that? A ceremony, then freedom in London. I'd not have taken her along,' Sidney exclaimed in horror before he remembered to keep his voice down. He glanced about him, then returned to the subject to hand. 'Tonight, no longer.'

'Agreed. The business with the falling weight proved too cumbersome. There must be another way of doing her in,' Rankin said callously.

'The poison . . . Who'd have thought she would give that little sandwich to a stray cat? It would have done the trick.' Sidney sipped his cooling coffee, then shifted in his chair. 'But what next?'

'The river? You could take her for a ride, then dump her over the side. A tap on the head would assure she don't paddle to shore.' Rankin spoke with the assurance of one who has done away with unwanted kittens and puppies by the score.

'No, there are always people along the bank and the like. Just the other night some poor maid threw herself in the river. One of the fellows jumped in to save her, almost died in the rescue. She was nigh dead, but survived. Katherine seems strong. She'd live.' He shook his head in disgust of healthy females.

'I really thought that arrow would hit her,' Rankin mused while Sidney stared into the depths of his cup for an answer to his dilemma. 'It would have done the deed, you know. Efficient things, arrows. Had she not stumbled just then, you'd be in clover by now, my friend.'

'Wouldn't I just,' agreed Sidney sourly.

'No ideas?' Rankin probed.

'None. I'm not accustomed to this sort of thing.'

'And you think I am?'

'Well, I always wondered how it came that your uncle died just when you needed the blunt to pay off the duns or face Tangier.' Sidney's reference to the room in Newgate where debtors were confined brought an angry flush to Rankin's face.

'See here, Exton!'

'Sorry.' Sidney waved a placating hand in the air, then turned back to contemplating his cup.

'You might have to be bolder,' Rankin offered.

'I thought I had been bold,' Sidney snapped, his patience clearly tested. 'Why she could not cooperate is beyond me.'

'Right,' Rankin agreed, then sipped his dark brew. 'No poison in her tea?'

'Too easy to detect. I thought of that already.'

'Pity you couldn't merely stab her in the back and be done with it.' Rankin traced a pattern on the table with the tip of his spoon.

Sidney sat up straight, snapped his fingers, nodded. 'That is it, the very thing. There are any number of knives to be had in the booths at the fair. It will be a simple matter to purchase one and do the deed.'

Rankin looked at his friend with a grim smile. 'Simple,' he agreed. 'I can get my valet to buy the knife.'

Sidney turned a speculative gaze on Rankin, but said nothing. Valets were useful fellows and could turn a hand to almost anything, even assisting at a murder.

'I shall linger about this evening. When the cast is rushing about and dear little Katherine retires to the wings to watch, I can slip the knife silently into her back, and who will be the wiser?'

'Wear gloves; you can throw them away and not worry about blood on your hands,' Rankin advised.

'Excellent suggestion. Best to buy some ordinary sort, the kind worn by locals. No point in using my own.' Sidney shuddered at the thought of losing even one pair of the expensive gloves he had bespoke at a fashionable London glover's.

''Tis set, then?' Rankin pushed back his chair and rose. 'I'll tell my man to find the, er, item?' He chose to be discreet, aware of others nearby who might hear them.

'Set,' Sidney agreed. 'I'm off to find a pair of those gloves. Perhaps my man can do that deed for me as well. Shall we meet for oysters later?'

The two paid their shot, then walked purposefully from the little coffee house.

Philip dared to take a breath, then shifted so he could see out of one of the spotlessly clean sashed windows. Rankin headed off toward town, Sidney in the direction of Garlic Row.

A wave of anger swept over Philip. It was his Katherine they spoke of callously murdering. His hands clenched as he fought back a desire to tear after Exton and choke the life from his worthless body. Then he forced himself to remain seated. He could not kill the man, not unless it came to actually defending Katherine's life on the spot. There had to be another way around it.

He dropped some coins on the table, then sauntered from the coffee house deep in thought. The booths along the row had little interest for him until he caught sight of a Punch and Judy. She battered poor Punch over the head while children and adults alike chuckled at his plight.

A puppet, he thought. The idea took root. Philip hurried along Garlic Row, taking care to avoid being seen by Exton. Once at the theater, he approached one of the cast who happened to be there, running through his lines. Philip pretended he planned a joke, something played in good nature on a friend.

315

The fellow grinned and allowed as how it would be a simple matter to manage. Philip begged he come along to help plan the prank. They settled down to chat over a pint of home-brewed at the nearest tavern in town, Philip feeling the farther from the fair they got, the better. He kept a wary eye out for Rankin. He also kept the talk as careful as possible. No one who might listen in to the conversation would get an inkling of the import of it.

Once the discussion concluded, Philip paid the shot, then offered a piece of gold to the actor. It was not a coin often seen by the man, and he took it with a raise of an eyebrow. When they parted outside the tavern, he said, 'Aye, some joke this will be. And I'll take good care to keep my tongue between my teeth, my lord.'

Philip watched him head back toward the fair, then he turned toward the Penn house. Somehow he had to obtain a gown that belonged to Kate. And where might he find a wig? There was nothing to do but take his sister into his confidence. He'd have need of her wise head. When she learned Exton was the source of Katherine's threat, she'd be wanting to do all she could to bring the man to justice.

'Katherine has gone with Amelia to run a

few errands, my lord,' Cousin Sophia announced when he begged a word with her.

'That is just as well. I have need of your help on Katherine's behalf. I wish to borrow a gown of hers. Just a prank,' he added, recalling the words of the actor from the fair.

'Which one?' Sophia was not stupid. She well knew that his lordship would not request something so outrageous if he had not a sound reason.

He almost said the yellow one, then hated to see it torn. 'One people might recognize as hers. A familiar one.'

'Well, there is little problem with that. Her father forgets she needs new gowns and she is never one to fuss about such. Had I my way of things, her lot would be different. When one is on the fringe of the family, it is not always best to speak up, you see.' She rose from her chair in the morning room, dropping the acanthus needlework on a bench as she walked past. 'I shall be but a few minutes; there is little to choose from.'

Philip paced impatiently up and down the room during the ensuing silence. He turned with gratitude when Cousin Sophia returned, a soft-rose gown draped over her arms. 'Ah, good.'

'This is not one of her favorites. I gather she might not see it again?'

'You are as shrewd as she has said. I promise that my Kate shall have a pretty gown to replace this. Will that please you?' He hurried from the house and sped off toward Fairfax Hall.

Cousin Sophie smiled. Perhaps she might be spared another winter in Cambridge, after all. Her thoughts turned to sunshine and flowers and the mist from the sea. It would have been nice, she considered, to know what that young man intended to do with Katherine's gown.

15

Philip bounded up the front steps of his home, then threw open the door, an astounded Kendall hastening to meet him. Kendall's reproving frown was quickly concealed.

'Where is my sister? There is no time to lose.'

The unruffled butler bowed his head, then gestured toward the saloon. 'I believe Lady Gisela is in the saloon.'

Philip checked a moment to note the change of address. He marched into the saloon, where he found his sister staring out at the Gothic Tower, a bemused expression on her face.

'*Lady* Gisela? Since when have you allowed yourself to be styled thus? Our parents will be pleased,' he said with what had to be the understatement of the year.

'Oh,' she replied with an embarrassed dip of her head, 'I thought it time to change my ways. Mr Cheney is long gone and there is no reason I may not indulge myself, especially if it makes everyone happy.' She peeped up to see his reaction, then caught sight of the rose muslin gown draped over his arm. 'But what is this?'

'I have need of your help. I know who is trying to kill Katherine.'

Gisela jumped up from her chair, rushing to his side. 'Who? I shall shoot him myself.' She ignored the interesting fact that she did not know how to load a gun, much less fire one.

'Peagoose.' He eyed her with fondness. 'Cousin Sidney, our elegant dandy, is the culprit. Seems our modest little Kate is a great heiress. I did a bit of investigation on Lady Winstanley. She married some nabob baronet who'd amassed a fortune in India, then popped off once he returned to England. Upon her death all her money goes to Katherine. Sidney expects he'll be the one to inherit if Kate is out of his way. He intends to plant a knife in our Kate's back tonight.'

'Murder for money!' Gisela inhaled sharply. 'I fear it is done all too often,' she said, horrified at the thought. 'But our Kate?'

'Sidney seems to have found himself an expert on the subject.' Philip recalled the conversation when Rankin almost admitted he'd done away with his uncle, and shuddered.

'What do you intend to do? You plan to trap him and hand him over to the authorities?' Gisela tilted her head in perplexity.

'Perhaps. But I wonder if our justice is adequate for him?'

'What else is there?' scoffed Gisela.

'There is another choice, for I have no wish to commit murder. Could you see Sidney arrayed in all his splendor in the wilds of Australia?'

'How cruel, and to such a dandy as he,' she declared with a touch of irony coloring her voice.

'There is little we can do to prove that Sidney has been behind all the near attacks on Katherine's life. He might well get free and arrange a more deadly revenge on her, not to mention my own person.'

'Oh, Philip, you must see to it he cannot harm either of you ever again.' Gisela placed an anxious hand on her brother's arm.

'I might be able to arrange transportation for Sidney Exton, provided I can keep Kate safe until then. That is where you come in, my sweet.'

'Anything! Just tell me what to do.'

'First, help me create a puppet, using Kate's gown.' He thrust the rose muslin at his sister, then rang for Kendall. He issued several orders in succession, then turned to his sister again. 'Where can we get a blond wig?'

'In the attics. I saw one in a trunk up there

321

when we were hunting for costumes. What is your scheme?' She shook out the gown, then turned to him, a frown marring her forehead. 'I do not see how you intend to make a puppet.'

The housekeeper entered the room. Philip consulted with her, joined by Gisela, who grew more enthusiastic as they spoke.

'Oh, famous,' she crowed. 'All you have to do is convince Katherine to hide out while you capture Sidney, knife-handed, so to speak.'

'There's the rub. Can you imagine her sitting tamely at home while the rest of us are at the theater snabbling Sidney? I fear if she is there, she might get hurt.'

'And she means a great deal to you, does she not?' Gisela inquired gently.

'Aye,' he replied, then turned with relief as the housekeeper bustled into the saloon with some old sheets. Behind her a footman carried a bundle of straw, his nose twitching with curiosity.

'The idea,' Philip explained to an intrigued Mrs Stedman, 'is to create a somewhat plausible body. It must seem to be the figure of a woman, at least in half-light.'

Gisela danced from the room, relieved to be actually doing something. Her humming could be heard all the way up the stairwell as she rushed to the attics to fetch the blond wig and a likely bonnet.

It took about two hours for the three of them to assemble a lifesized puppet. Once Gisela plopped the blond wig on the head, they all sat back to study the figure. Philip placed the puppet on a chair across the room. He tied on the bonnet as a finishing touch.

'Well, what do you think?' he asked of Kendall, who had entered the room with a tray of tea and biscuits.

The butler glanced at the housekeeper. He set the tray down, then stood back, studying the results while judiciously rubbing his jaw. 'Very good, my lord. If you will permit me?' He crossed the hall, then returned with a large shawl. This he draped over the puppet's shoulders. It was the final touch needed.

Gisela clapped her hands with approval. 'Well done, Kendall. This is truly a family project. We must save Miss Penn, you see.'

While neither Kendall nor Mrs Stedman knew precisely what was going on, they had a fair idea which way the wind blew. They approved. Anything to help the sweet Miss Penn had their instant support.

Kendall poured two cups of tea. Gisela took hers, then watched as her brother sipped at his, deep in thought. She picked up a biscuit, then said, 'What a pity you cannot do like those heroes in the Minerva Press novels.'

He glanced her way, then looked at Kendall. Both men shrugged. 'And what do they do, pray tell?' Philip asked.

Gisela took a nibble from her biscuit before replying to his query. 'Abscond with her.'

'What?'

'Kidnap her.'

'I do not have evil intentions, my sweet. I am all nobility of conduct.' His grin was wry, for there were moments when he had harbored distinctly uncivilized desires toward his lovely Kate.

'Stupid. Kidnap her for her own good, do you not see?'

'Katherine? Do you think it would work?' He turned to Kendall, thus annoying his sister, whose idea it had been in the first place.

'I am told it can be most effective, my lord,' Kendall replied with austere simplicity. The how and where of it was best left to those involved. 'If there is anything we can do . . . '

'Get that puppet to the carriage. I must dash out to the fair and stow it safely away before the cast returns for the evening performance. Do not be surprised if I have Miss Penn with me when I return.'

Philip hurried from the room, leaving Gisela deep in thought. While she sympathized with her brother in regard to Katherine's safety, she wondered if the venturesome Katherine might not have a thing or two to say about the matter.

Philip clattered away down the drive and out of the park in the phaeton, his 'passenger' bouncing about in the most reckless manner imaginable. That the puppet remained on the seat at all was due to Kendall's forethought. He had the presence of mind to tie the thing down.

By managing to whisk along the back streets that ran along the river, Philip drove down the Newmarket road before long. He drew up next to the theater booth and untied his passenger from the phaeton. Few gave him but a passing look, for it was not unlikely that a strange-looking prop would be carried into the theatrical area. Puppets were not unusual and warranted little notice.

As soon as he stowed the straw-stuffed figure neatly behind a set where it would likely be safe until he needed it, Philip rushed back to the carriage and feverishly drove back to town. He glanced at the timepiece he pulled from his pocket while he waited at the front door of the Penn house. The hours were ticking by all too quickly. There was yet much to be done.

'Mrs Moore, is Miss Penn at home?'

'Aye, I will fetch her at once.' The matronly figure turned to leave, then glanced back. His lordship was in a rare taking. She hurried.

Within minutes Katherine came hastily down the stairs, her simple gown of sea-green cotton floating about her, trailing slightly on the steps. 'Lord Ramsey? Mrs Moore told me you were here and a bit impatient. Is there a problem?'

'Forgive me for causing you a moment's worry. I wanted to take you for a drive. Will you come?' He extended his hand and smiled at her with those beautiful eyes.

Katherine met his gaze. It really wasn't fair in the least for a man to have such dark curling lashes and intriguing lights in the depths of his eyes. She took note of his splendid figure and, wonder of it all, a wisp of straw on his pantaloons. What had his lordship been doing this morning?

'Will I?' she echoed, then sharply reminded herself not to be a ninny. Take what comes your way and be glad of it, she sternly rebuked that mind of hers that wanted so much more. 'It sounds lovely.'

She tied her bonnet over her curls, then gathered up her favorite shawl. He seemed unusually impatient today, she observed and wondered. 'Do you have something special to show me today?'

'In a manner of speaking,' he admitted, giving thanks that Kate chose to be agreeable. He ushered her from the house just as Cousin Sophia came up the walk. He nodded and winked at the older lady, who had the good sense not to demand an explanation.

Katherine greeted Sophia with affection. 'We are off on some sort of surprise. 'Tis a mystery, for he will not reveal a word to me.'

'Enjoy yourselves and do not forget to be respectable in your jaunting about.' She caught the expression on Lord Ramsey's face. She'd give a great deal to know what was going on. However, she knew better than to impede whatever scheme he had in his mind. She trusted him to take care of Katherine, and that was all that mattered to her.

''Tis a lovely afternoon,' Katherine ventured to say as the carriage set out to the east. She was surprised they drove the opposite direction from the fair, yet perhaps if he had a surprise, it might be at the hall.

Her heart fluttered a bit. He looked so dashing in his rig, wisp of straw notwithstanding. She daringly reached over to pluck it from his leg, then tossed it aside. 'Are we in a hurry?' The carriage rocked with alarming motion as they racketed over the Silver Street Bridge and picked up speed. She couldn't hazard a guess at their velocity, but she knew she had never traveled so fast in her entire life. The scenery whizzed past at a shocking rate. She clutched at the sides of the phaeton for dear life.

'We are,' came his reply as he feathered a turn on the road.

Katherine prayed they'd not meet a slow-moving stage wagon or farmer's cart. Somehow, she suspected that Lord Ramsey would keep the phaeton on the road, leaving the others to cope as best they might. She shrank against the squabs, wondering what would come next on this wild outing.

Recalling the last novel she had managed to borrow from Amelia Bonner, who, in spite of her mother's strictures against such, read them frequently, Katherine said, 'I should say you are kidnapping me, my lord, did I not know there is not in the least reason for such behavior.' The chuckle in her throat died as she caught sight of his expression.

'Quite so,' came his terse reply, a far from satisfactory one where Katherine was concerned.

'And what does that mean, pray tell?'

They rushed through the gates to Fairfax Hall, narrowly missing the stone entrance.

Katherine breathed a sigh of relief as Kendall hurried down the steps to assist her from the carriage. She placed a trembling hand in his, then stood a moment to regain her composure. Philip jumped down, murmured a few words to the groom who stood at the ready, then ushered Katherine into the house. Kendall followed, managing to open the front door, then show them to the saloon with unruffled ease.

'That was a bit of a dash, I suspect. It seems you left the house but a short time ago.' Gisela rose from her chair to cross the room and place a comforting arm about Katherine.

Philip pulled his timepiece from its pocket and nodded. 'You might say that it was done in jig time. Now, if everything is fine, I shall be off again. I trust you to do the right thing, Gisela.' Philip slapped his gloves against his hand while studying his sister's face.

'Shall I bring tea, Lady Gisela?' Kendall inquired with his customary serenity.

'Would someone kindly tell me what this is all about?' Katherine demanded.

Lady Gisela gave her younger brother a defiant look, then took Katherine's hands in hers. 'Philip has learned who it is that plans to kill you. He feels it would be safer for you to remain here.' She again tossed him a look. 'He is going to trick the would-be killer into revealing his identity and then capture him. I suspect that before the night is up, you will have to worry no longer.'

Katherine gave them a numb stare, then sank down in a chair that was blessedly close to her. Had she been required to search for one, she'd have been in dire trouble. So astounded was she that she neglected to inquire who the villain might be.

'I see.' She turned up her face to meet Lord Ramsey's shuttered gaze. 'I want to go with you.' She rose and took a step toward him. 'You might be hurt.'

He gave her an impatient look, a worried one, if she had really trained her eyes on him. 'And you might be killed. Trust me to know what is best for you, my dear. I do not wish a hair on your head to be harmed.'

'You can say that after the wild drive from town? Hah!' She crossed the room to where he edged toward the door, her hands held in a gesture of appeal. 'Please?' It was not an easy matter for one as independent as she to beg.

'It is for your own good.' With those words, he was gone, whirling out the front door in a swirl of black cape that Kendall managed to throw over his shoulders before Philip disappeared.

'How convenient,' Katherine muttered bitterly. 'I know I ought to be grateful, and a lady ought not even think of such a dangerous, risky business, but how I'd like to be there. For my own good,' she echoed, mimicking his tone perfectly.

She began to pace the floor, pausing from time to time to glance out the window. 'The utter gall of the man,' she declared with asperity. 'That he should decide whether or not I ought to be present.'

'It is ever thus,' Gisela said in an attempt to soothe. 'Your cousin intends to use a knife, and they can be nasty items.'

'Sidney?' Katherine screeched. 'Sidney, the dandy, our guest, the Sidney who sleeps in our home? I cannot credit it. Why? Why would he wish to murder me? Not long ago he asked me to wed him.' Katherine stood stock-still in her shock, unable to find a chair in which to sink.

'I was not supposed to tell you that, I fancy,' Gisela said in a contrite voice. 'But you would learn of it eventually.'

Katherine fixed her friend with a steely gaze, then sweetly inquired, 'Now tell me why.'

Gisela rubbed the tip of her nose, then began to parade up and down the room, taking dainty steps befitting her station. 'Your Great-aunt Winstanley married well, I take it. When her nabob husband died, Lady Winstanley possessed a fortune. She still does. And you are her principal heir, or so

Philip informed me.' Gisela paused not far from Katherine. 'We fear Sidney will stop at nothing to get what he wants, and I suspect he wants the money more than he wants you. He plans to thrust a knife in your back, then slip your body where it will not be easily found until after he is far away from Cambridge, I imagine.'

Katherine found a chair, managed to sit down, a faint 'Oh' slipping between her lips. Then more firmly, she added, 'But he cannot do that.'

'Which is why Philip wants you safely here.'

Katherine jumped up from her chair, pacing about much as Gisela had done, only using longer strides. 'You do realize Philip might be the one who is stabbed if I am missing. If one is in the stabbing mood, I daresay one is not precisely too particular who one stabs, if you follow me?'

Gisela shook her head, mute with confusion.

'You must see that I cannot allow Lord Ramsey to sacrifice himself for me,' Katherine declared in ringing accents. 'I am going.' She scooped up her things, then marched toward the front door.

Gisela barred her way. 'I promised Philip you would remain safely here with me.'

Katherine gave her a frustrated look,

debating whether she might push Gisela aside and rush from the house. It was unthinkable to be so crude. But Katherine was determined to go, nonetheless. She bided her time, waiting, pretending to be reluctantly agreeable.

Gisela avoided all talk of the evening to come, apparently believing that if Katherine might have her mind on something else, she could be diverted. They discussed, in a crazily abstracted way, bonnets and slippers, gowns and shawls, until Katherine wanted to scream.

At last Gisela found it necessary to leave the room. She had shared innumerable cups of tea with a worried Katherine, and they had taken their inevitable toll. Since Katherine appeared to accept her fate, Gisela believed it unnecessary to place a guard on her friend.

She was wrong.

No sooner had Gisela walked up the stairs than Katherine had again gathered up her things, plunking her bonnet on her head any old way, and slipped from the side door to the saloon. She ran to the stables, where she made her demands known.

'I need a horse, or a carriage, or something.' Her imperious tone was such the groom had obeyed all his working life. He was not about to challenge it now. 'Yes, miss.'

Twenty minutes or so later Katherine was tooling a neat little gig down the drive. Every moment of Katherine's wait had been filled with dire worries of what might happen. If only Gisela believed that Katherine had gone on a similar errand, all would be well. Hector watched her with wary eyes, curious what she might be doing here.

Just as she passed the house, Gisela ran out, waving frantically at Katherine to stop. She ignored the summons and kept going toward town at top speed.

A troubled Gisela stood at the top of the stairs, arms wrapped about her against the chill until Katherine had disappeared from sight. She entered the house in a thoughtful mood, then went to the library desk, where she scratched out a note. This was promptly folded, sealed, and dispatched on its way with a footman.

Her deed accomplished, Gisela returned to the saloon to sit by the window, waiting.

★ ★ ★

Meanwhile, Katherine careened through Cambridge in much the same manner that Lord Ramsey had done shortly before. She also took the road along the Backs, that lovely spot of green between the River Cam and many of the colleges.

The Newmarket road was thronged with vehicles. Katherine curbed her impatience with great difficulty. A glance at the sky revealed the hour grew late. When would Sidney strike? During the bustle before the play began? Or when the lights were lowered and it was hard to distinguish one person from another? The area backstage was not particularly well-lit in the best of moments. One could trip and fall if not careful. If Sidney were clever — and she suspected he was extremely so — he would choose a time when he might sneak up behind . . . 'Good grief,' she murmured. 'Who will he kill if I am not there?' No one had thought to pass that little detail along to her. She ought to have inquired as to the identity of the killer straightaway. Instead, Katherine had sat like a lump on a log, stunned and stupid.

It was a simple matter to maneuver the gig behind the theater booth. Looping the reins over a post, Katherine dashed to the side door, then cautiously slipped inside.

There was the usual bustle of the actors getting ready for the comedy. Muted laughter mingled with the voices of those who repeated their opening lines. The smell of paint and sweat was strong, mixed with the perfume Eliza O'Neill wore at all times. It floated about her like a cloak to ward off less desirable odors.

Katherine waited to grow accustomed to the dim light. Sidney seemed to be nowhere within sight. She glanced about her, then sidled over along the wall toward the rear of the theater. She was quite certain she was undetected, when a hand reached around her from behind, covering her mouth.

Katherine was hastily dragged to the shadows, then thrust against the rear wall. She accidentally bumped her head, hard. She sagged to the floor, quite unconscious.

★　★　★

'Lady Gisela? I received your note and came as quickly as I might.' Julian Penn joined the lovely lady in the saloon, his bewilderment at the wording of the summons clear on his handsome, though mature, face.

'I hoped you might come promptly, sir.'

'Julian, I think.' He smiled kindly down at her, leading the way to the sofa near the fireplace. The warmth of a fire was welcome on this chilly day.

'Julian,' she repeated obediently, 'if you will call me Gisela. We are good friends, I believe.'

'Nay, more than friends, my lady. I have foolish aspirations that someday I shall share

with you. Now, what is all the to-do about?'
He sat after seeing her arranged nicely on the
sofa.

Gisela ignored the flutterings within, took a
deep breath, then plunged ahead with what
she suspected was to be a vastly difficult
explanation.

'It is Katherine. Did you know she writes?'

'Aye, she scribbles a good deal, judging by
the number of quills she consumes, not to
mention paper.'

'Julian, she has written a play, a prodigiously delightful spoof on the current
melodramas. And,' Gisela said, reaching out
to touch his arm, 'it is being produced in a
theater out at Sturbridge Fair. My brother
built the theater, hired the actors, and even
designed the sets. His carpenter constructed
them here. Philip has a great deal invested in
this production, more than you can possibly
guess.' Gisela had, but she felt it not right to
reveal her speculation.

'I cannot take this in. Katherine wrote a
play that is being produced?'

'And your son Theodore produced it,'
Gisela added. That Mr Penn was flummoxed
was comically clear to Gisela. He was also
angry. 'I cannot accept they have not
confided in me.'

'That is not the worst.'

'What is it?'

'Did you know your aunt is an exceedingly wealthy woman? She intends to leave her entire estate to Katherine. Your nephew plans to capture that fortune for himself, for he thinks if he removes Katherine from the scene, he will stand to inherit. Sidney means to kill her this evening. Stab her, if my brother is correct, and he usually is.'

'But this is terrible!' Julian rose to his feet in agitation. 'I must find her. Do you know where she is?'

'She was here earlier,' Gisela admitted. 'She escaped from my guardianship, I suspect in a harebrained attempt to help my brother. Philip is determined he shall catch the fiend and punish him.'

'She is in danger. I must go to her.' Julian took one of Lady Gisela's hands to his lips. 'Adieu, dear lady.'

'If you think to leave me alone to wonder what is going on, please think again,' announced a resolute Gisela. 'I am tired of being alone.'

He paused, arrested by a nuance in her voice. 'Are you, my dear?'

'Definitely,' she stated in no uncertain terms. What he made of that, she could only hope.

Kendall entered with Gisela's warmest

hooded cloak and Mr Penn's things. As usual, the butler had timed matters to a nicety. 'The carriage awaits, my lady. And I have taken the liberty of including a simple repast for you to consume while on the way.'

'Well?' she challenged Julian.

'Best we get started without further delay.' Julian held out his arm to Lady Gisela, and the two walked to the carriage arm and arm.

'I trust we shall find things in a bit of a muddle once we get there. Pray we are not too late,' murmured Gisela as she entered the carriage.

Julian gave an order to the coachman to spring 'em, then entered the carriage behind Gisela. Neither of them was able to nibble very much of the light meal Kendall had the foresight to have waiting for them.

'Later,' murmured Gisela. 'We shall feel more the thing once we know Katherine is safe.'

* * *

In the theater shadows concealed the crumpled body of a woman. She lay on the floor, shoved into a corner, with a drapery tossed lightly over her form. She did not move.

16

The stage was set. The stuffed figure dressed in the soft-rose muslin sat in a chair close to the wall, but not against it. The shawl concealed any wisps of straw that might have otherwise peeped out. The head bent just slightly toward the figure's lap, as though in deep reflection or perhaps catching a moment's nap. How provident that the bonnet Gisela brought from the attic was one of those enormous things that women fancied a few years back. It had belonged to his mother, if he was not mistaken. Now it served to conceal the absence of a face quite well.

Philip studied the tableau from a safe distance. He lingered in the shadows after carefully revealing to the cast members that he arranged a surprise for Sidney Exton. The actors had looked hostile, for it seemed Sidney was not well-liked among them. Philip learned that Exton has been overly forward with one of the girls, the daughter of a fighter from Cambridge, and used this information to his advantage.

'Rude and insulting, he was,' one of the cast said.

The curtains parted and the comedy now was well along, the audience laughing and applauding the excellent acting of the cast. In the back room, Philip hoped that the ensuing noise that was bound to be made didn't disturb the actors.

The light from the bracketed wall lamp neared the door flickered, almost going out as the door opened. A man slipped inside the theater, staying close to the wall. He stood very still, looking about him with an intent gaze.

After seeing that none about paid him any heed, he quietly strolled along toward the rear of the theater. There he stopped, seeing precisely what he wanted, the figure in the familiar rose muslin gown.

Off to one side of the area someone groaned. Sidney paused, searching the shadows. Hesitant to proceed, he took a step forward, then stopped once again as the sound was repeated.

Philip slipped silently to where Katherine lay, swiftly clapping his hand over her mouth. He placed his lips close to her ear, then whispered, 'My love, whatever you do, make no noise. 'Tis most important. Believe me.'

When he felt her nod ever so slightly, he slowly removed his hand, watching Sidney as he did. Apparently the other man had not pinpointed the source of the sound he had heard, for he had resumed his calculated advance upon the figure in the chair.

Katherine eased herself up, wondering why her head ached, and why she was huddled on the floor with Lord Ramsey. She trembled as he drew close to her again, placing his lips against her ear. 'Not a sound. Promise?'

She nodded again in response to his whispered command, then observed him inch along the wall, always watching to see what Sidney was doing.

Sidney! Katherine opened her mouth, then snapped it shut. She remembered now precisely what was going on and why she was where she was. The only thing she didn't know was how she'd been knocked out, and she suspected Lord Ramsey could tell her that. She placed a hand against the dull throb on her head, but never took her eyes off the two men.

Something in Sidney's hand glittered. Katherine realized it had to be the knife Gisela had told her about. Katherine had found it difficult to credit that Sidney intended to kill her. Now she believed.

How badly Sidney must need that money to consider murdering to get it. Perhaps it had not occurred to him that Great-aunt Harriette might well leave her money to another in the event of Katherine's demise.

A member of the cast left the stage, hurrying to the dressing room to change his costume. Sidney stepped into the shadows, then, when the man had disappeared, hastily returned to the side of the figure in rose. He'd not be interrupted again very soon.

The glitter was seen for a moment, then the knife disappeared . . . right into the back of the figure just at the moment of loud applause from the front of the theater. The deed done, Sidney hurried to the door and his escape.

Katherine felt ill, nearly faint. That might have been her! She fought to remain alert, watching as Lord Ramsey quickly strode to Sidney's side.

'Exton, a moment?'

A startled Sidney halted in his steps, turning to snarl at Lord Ramsey. 'What do you want?'

'You are looking for someone?' Philip grasped Exton's arm, drawing him inexorably along with him toward the figure in rose.

'I must leave,' said Sidney Exton, a hint of desperation in his tone, tugging to pull himself free of that firm grasp.

From where she huddled, Katherine spotted a glimmer of perspiration on her cousin's brow. He looked anxious and not a little worried, as well he might, she thought with indignation.

'Problems, Cousin Sidney? You must say good night to Katherine before you leave,' continued the smooth voice of Viscount Ramsey.

'No,' cried Sidney, his face pale with panic.

'Why, what could possibly prevent you from wishing your dear cousin a good evening? She looks lovely in rose, does she not?' They drew closer to the figure on the chair.

Sidney glanced at the figure, then whirled about, only to come face to face with the burly person of that champion fighter from Cambridge. He had been only too pleased to come along with Lord Ramsey, not liking his only daughter being insulted by that slime, Exton.

'You wouldna be thinkin' of leaving just now, would you?' The fighter's whisper was more menacing than his bulk or stance, and that said a great deal, thought Katherine from her vantage point.

'You don't understand,' Sidney whined, his face now devoid of all color, but for those two pale eyes. His beautiful curls flopped in disarray over that damp brow.

'I believe we understand all too well. What would Great-aunt Harriette say if she knew what you had done?' Lord Ramsey said, his tone harsh.

Sidney turned an unattractive shade of green at Ramsey's words and inched away from the chair.

'What do you think, Katherine?'

She remained where she hid, desiring to play a trick of her own on that fiend of a cousin. 'I feel sure she'd not be best pleased.'

The words produced a startling effect on Sidney. He turned white and looked near fainting. His mouth worked but produced no sounds.

Katherine rose from where she had been placed against the wall and stiffly walked to stand by Lord Ramsey.

Sidney pointed a shaky finger to the puppet, then Katherine. 'But you cannot be! You're a ghost!'

She took a step forward, stretched out her hand to touch him.

Sidney shrank away from her, whimpering, 'No.'

'Why ought I be a ghost, cousin?' Katherine tried to make herself sound like one, using a sort of crooning tone. Eerie. Sepulchral. She wanted to scare the very daylights out of this loathsome creature.

'Be-because . . . ' His voice failed as Katherine whirled and walked to stand behind Lord Ramsey before she lost her temper and slapped that stupid man silly.

'You may have noticed that the ghost is not wearing rose, Exton,' offered Philip, sliding in the observation much as Sidney had the knife into the straw puppet.

'But I am very much aware of what you tried to do,' Katherine snapped, her patience exhausted. The game was no longer any pleasure. Her head hurt and she wanted to go home. 'You may collect your things, then we never wish to see you again. Rest assured that I will tell our great-aunt that you tried to murder me for the inheritance. I can almost guarantee that you'll not receive a penny, regardless of whether I live or no.'

Unnoticed by the others, another figure had entered the theater. A reed-thin elderly woman supported by a stout cane moved out of the shadows to join Katherine. She looked at the woman, puzzled as to who this stranger might be.

'How vastly informative this all is.' The woman's voice fair bristled with anger.

Sidney backed into the wall as he faintly said, 'Great-aunt Harriette!' It was the final blow to the dandy. With a gasp of anguish, he slumped to the floor. The champion of Cambridge picked up the body with one hand and turned to his lordship with a grim smile. 'Where shall I put him, milord?'

'The pie powder court for the moment.

Explain there has been an attempt at murder, but that Mr Exton will be leaving for Australia on the first available boat.'

Sidney's limp body floated out the door over the champion's shoulder as Lady Gisela and Julian Penn rushed in.

'Gracious,' Gisela exclaimed as she watched Sidney disappear. Then she turned to rush to Katherine's side, enfolding her in a warm embrace. 'Oh, I am so happy you are all right, my dear,' she whispered, recalling there was a play in progress — nearing its conclusion, actually.

'Why do we not leave here so that we need not fear being heard?' Philip suggested.

All in agreement, they filed from the theater, walking to the carriages lined up behind the building.

Katherine could not contain her curiosity another minute. 'I am pleased to meet you, Great-aunt Harriette,' she said with a pretty curtsy.

'Enough. You make me feel like Methuselah. Or older,' the old lady barked, heading for her comfortable carriage.

'Would Lady Winstanley be acceptable?' Katherine suggested kindly. 'How did you know where we were? And how did you get here?'

'Have you forgotten that you wrote me you

were to put on this play?' Harriette replied with a twinkle in her faded blue eyes. 'I could not miss it for the world. Sophia told me you were apt to be out here. I am glad I arrived in time to observe that scene with Sidney.'

'He is not a nice person,' Katherine said, hoping her great-aunt would not be too disappointed.

'He is a toad of the worst order,' snapped her great-aunt in reply.

Julian Penn chose to enter the conversation at this point. 'It has been a long time, Aunt Harriette.'

'We shall discuss that matter when we reach your home. I trust that is where we are bound?' Lady Winstanley asked this of Lord Ramsey, rightly judging that he was the leader of the situation.

'Katherine and I shall have to make a few arrangements regarding Sidney, then we shall follow. Mr Penn, perhaps you and Gisela can take the phaeton? I can send the cart home later. Katherine and I shall use the gig.' He cast a dark look at the neat little vehicle, then at Kate. He wanted to have a few choice words with her before they joined the others.

'I shall follow you home,' Lady Winstanley announced, prodding Mr Penn with her cane. 'And it is deuced chilly standing about here, Julian.' She spoke to him as though he were no more than two-and-twenty, Katherine noted with amusement.

Katherine watched the others leave, then joined Lord Ramsey on the walk to the building where the pie powder court was held. Sidney would hear a thing or two from her.

★ ★ ★

In the phaeton, Julian Penn tucked a rug about the lovely Gisela, then proceeded toward home, not at a spanking pace, however.

'Before we join the others, there is something I wanted to discuss with you.' He nervously cleared his throat.

'Yes, Julian?' Lady Gisela leaned against the strong, dependable figure next to her, thinking that he would not be off to the mountains or across on the Continent. Rather, he would be safely here, always about.

'I had not planned it quite this way, but this evening has changed everything. I can see now that I badly need taking in hand. Had I been a better father, this evening would not have occurred. I never thought to wed again, regardless. Life seemed quietly dull, but comfortable nonetheless. That is, until a certain young lady ranted and raved at me over a particular sermon.'

'Julian, I? Young? How nice of you to think so,' cooed Lady Gisela.

'You must confess, dear lady, we have had some stimulating conversations. Dare I hope that you return my regard? I should like above all to be able to spend my days and evenings with you, provided you do not believe me too old?' The hesitancy in his voice endeared him to his love.

'Never old, Julian. Just right, I fancy. I should be pleased to be your wife, my dear. I am persuaded we shall suit each other to a tee.'

At which Julian urged the horse to greater speed, pulled up before the Penn house, and swept Lady Gisela into his arms. If there was any sign of advanced age in the ardor of his kiss, Lady Gisela could not notice it. She happily nestled in his arms until the sound of Harriette's carriage disturbed their romantic interlude.

'We shall continue this later, my dear,' promised Julian.

'I shall hold you to that, my dearest,' Lady Gisela whispered back as the tart voice of Lady Winstanley drifted to them on the evening air.

'I could do with a cup of hot tea, Julian,' she commanded.

stroll along Garlic Row.

The merchants were beginning to close up their booths. Here and there a curtain had been drawn. Katherine stifled a yawn, surreptitiously rubbed her sore head, then stumbled as Lord Ramsey led her through to where the gig stood waiting. Noise from the animals at Adam's Circus drifted across the field. Cries of the walnut-sellers mingled with the laughter of those enjoying the theater and the various shows. The little Italian rope-dancer was doing well, as was the Punch and Judy.

Here, in the near darkness behind the booths, Katherine stopped to stare up at her benefactor. It was a romantic setting. The stars shone brightly, a partial moon glowed in the sky, oil lamps flickered along the rows, all lending to the mood, stirring the senses. She searched his face, wondering what lurked in those beautiful eyes now shadowed.

'Have you nothing to say?' He sounded amused.

Katherine cleared her throat, then said, 'Was it necessary to stuff me in a corner?'

He threw back his head to laugh, then quickly hugged her.

'Bless you. I felt badly about that. I am not accustomed to this sort of thing, as you may guess. I am sorry, my dear.' He stroked her cheek with a tender, feather-light touch.

'You might have used greater care,' she observed, moving toward the gig at a slow pace, while speculating whether her heart could withstand its mad rhythm.

'I hope I never have to confront that sort of a situation again, dear Kate. Who would have suspected the dandy?' he mused.

'True,' she agreed. There was a pause, during which Katherine wondered if she would ever feel herself again. This trembling was bad enough, but the longing ache deep within her refused to go away. Perhaps it was merely heartburn? Cousin Sophia would have to bring Katherine one of those nasty but efficacious tisanes she made.

Somehow, Katherine doubted if that was really the problem. More than likely it had to do with the odious man standing at her side, handing her up into the gig as though he would be delighted to see the last of her. Indeed he might.

'You will undoubtedly get back your investment with a handsome profit, sir,' she said in a meek little voice.

'Blast it, Kate, I'm not worried about that. How is your poor head?' He walked around the gig, then climbed up to sit close beside her.

He did not pick up the reins; she wondered

when they would set off. 'Better.'

'You know,' he said in a sensual growl that set off warning bells in Katherine's head, 'the university claims the right to prosecute strays. I did not tell them about you, however.'

'I was never a stray, precisely,' she said, curious to know why he had brought up this old chestnut.

He tilted her chin, studying the pretty face revealed in the light of the stars and moon. 'No, I suppose I could merely say you were trespassing, although the sentence is harsher for that offense.'

Prompted by some imp, Katherine dared to inquire, 'And what is the sentence for strays, pray tell? I ought to know what I face.'

'You walked right into that so beautifully it is almost a shame to catch you on it, but I have waited so patiently, I deserve my reward.'

Totally at sea, Katherine gazed up at him with questioning eyes. 'Which is?' His self-satisfaction was so tangible a thing, she felt she could take it in her hands.

'Strays are awarded to the owner of the land. I thought you would know that.'

'Your father is to get me?' she was prompted to say, even more fascinated by the turn of their conversation.

'Goosecap. I own that land; it was deeded

to me some years ago. I suspect my parents thought to encourage me to marry and settle down to raise a nursery.'

'I see, I think.' Very daringly she inquired, 'And what, good sir, will you do with this stray? Prosecute?'

'First of all I decree you call me Philip. Perhaps darling and sweetheart later, but Philip for now.'

Katherine's head felt decidedly light. 'Philip, 'tis most improper.'

'Not for a wife, my dear Kate. Say you will marry me as soon as the banns can be posted?'

Awed by the prospect of a lifetime with Philip, Katherine sat tongue-tied for a few moments, leaving her suitor in anxious suspension.

'You would have the plunge bath,' he said by way of inducement. 'And our very own theater.'

'As if any of that mattered in the least,' she retorted. Then, surging ahead before she lost courage, she said, 'Because, you see, I love you very dearly, you impossible man. You have no need for prosecution or anything of the sort. It might help,' she added judiciously, 'were you to take me in your arms and bestow another of those delicious kisses, if you truly wish to persuade me to agree.'

In mere seconds she found herself clasped in strong arms against that wonderfully enticing body. 'Kate? You'll not say nay, for I'll not hear of it. As soon as can be, you'll be mine.' With that fervent declaration, he kissed her most soundly.

Somehow her bonnet got lost and her shawl greatly disarranged. Her head ceased to ache, and that peculiar feeling deep within melted to a puddle of warmth. Loving a man had a lot to recommend for itself.

When at last released, Katherine said, her voice oddly breathless, 'I expect we ought to go home. That is, my home.'

He sighed rather woefully, agreeing. 'I fear you are right.' He picked up the reins and in short order they were clip-clopping along the road, not hurrying in the least.

'I've never seen a gentleman drive with the reins in one hand while his arm was about a lady,' Katherine observed dreamily.

'If we were on our way out to Fairfax Hall, the horse would know his own way and I would not need to hold anything but you, my love.' He paused a moment, tightening his clasp of her before continuing. 'One thing I insist upon. No more productions at Sturbridge Fair, or any other commercial theater.'

'What?' Katherine sat up, most indignant. 'But I am a success. You said so yourself.'

'Easy, love,' Philip replied, wishing he'd had the brains to bring the subject up later on, when she was more settled as his future wife and the entire world had been appraised of the wedding.

'I enjoy my writing,' she warned.

'And so you shall, my sweet. We shall have our very own theater and productions.'

She gave a dubious nod. 'We will need a cast.'

'Ah, I have a notion or two about the best and most efficient manner of supplying that,' he answered in a low tone that sent shivers all through Katherine. 'I fully expect that along about the time that Belle and Gabriel sail out with their goslings, we will be close to having our first cast member, if you do not mind, that is?'

She swallowed with care, wondering if she ought to pinch herself, then decided the bump on her head was enough for the night. He was real, and the future never had looked rosier. 'I think that it sounds splendiferous.'

He brought the gig to a halt before the Penn house, then swept his love into his arms to carry her up to the house.

When Mrs Moore opened the door, having positioned herself for just such an event, he explained that Katherine was weak after the ordeal of the evening.

'Silly man,' Katherine whispered. 'I believe you are more intent on having me in your arms.'

'You are a fast learner, Kate.' He marched along the hall, then placed her on the sofa in the drawing room, where the others were gathered.

For a moment shocked silence reigned, all concerned at the slight figure reclining on the sofa. Cousin Sophia crossed to ascertain that Katherine was not suffering from a fever, for her cheeks were suspiciously pink.

Then Gisela spoke. 'Your father and I are to be married, Katherine. I hope you do not mind.'

Teddy had joined the group, and upon hearing this, he let out a whoop of joy. 'Oh, I say, jolly good.'

'I'm immensely pleased for you both.' Katherine's quiet words were nearly lost in the buzz of conversation following the announcement.

'But what about Katherine?' interrupted Cousin Sophia in her abrupt, practical way.

'Indeed. Why have you not allowed Katherine to visit me in London, Julian?' demanded Lady Winstanley. 'Or are you like that miserable wretch, Sidney, who expected me to drop any day? I always used to say that you had deep pockets and short arms, Julian.

The poor girl wants a good wardrobe and making over. Why, her gown looks years old and village-made, at that.'

'That was not the reason at all,' Julian replied, flustered and dismayed at the older woman's forthright words. 'I did not think she desired to go, for she seemed content here, and she was so young.'

Gisela placed a comforting hand over Julian's. 'He has been busy and alone. Sophia could do only so much, you know. It is difficult for a man to raise two children when he has an important position to take much of his time.'

Julian looked gratified, while Harriette snorted in disagreement. 'Then you ought to have sent her to me. Why, she is near to being on the shelf. A Season in London would cure that. I trust your son can look out for himself. Men have a tendency to do that.'

Katherine fought an urge to chuckle. 'It would be lovely to visit you.'

'Later,' interposed Lord Ramsey. 'For, you see, this coming Sunday the banns are to be read for us. We shall be wed in a month. I may bring her up to London for a new wardrobe in the next week or so, if she can leave the theater at the fair, that is. I trust you, Mr Penn, and soon to be father-in-law *and* brother-in-law, as well, will not protest?'

Julian chuckled and shook his head. 'What can I say, other than I wish her happy.'

Katherine reached for Philip's hand, content to hold it and dream a little about the days when Gabriel and Belle would sail along the pond with a flock of goslings trailing behind them.

Why had she thought Philip frivolous? There was nothing superficial about him. Nor was the emotion she felt a mere trifling. She sighed in contentment and considered the plunge bath. She had much to enjoy. As though reading her thoughts, Philip squeezed her hand and whispered, 'Later, my love.'

We do hope that you have enjoyed reading this large print book.

Did you know that all of our titles are available for purchase?

We publish a wide range of high quality large print books including:
Romances, Mysteries, Classics
General Fiction
Non Fiction and Westerns

Special interest titles available in large print are:
The Little Oxford Dictionary
Music Book
Song Book
Hymn Book
Service Book

Also available from us courtesy of Oxford University Press:
Young Readers' Dictionary
(large print edition)
Young Readers' Thesaurus
(large print edition)

For further information or a free brochure, please contact us at:
Ulverscroft Large Print Books Ltd.,
The Green, Bradgate Road, Anstey,
Leicester, LE7 7FU, England.
Tel: (00 44) 0116 236 4325
Fax: (00 44) 0116 234 0205